# SKIN DEEP
## and Other Stories

# SKIN DEEP
# and Other Stories

Edith Reveley

COLLINS
St James's Place, London
1980

William Collins Sons & Co Ltd
London · Glasgow · Sydney · Auckland
Toronto · Johannesburg

This collection first published 1980

ISBN 0 00 222397 X

Set in Linotype Plantin
Made and printed in Great Britain by
William Collins Sons & Co Ltd, Glasgow

*For Semund with love*

# Acknowledgements

'Skin Deep', 'Brent' and 'Mrs Wingate' were first published in *Woman's Journal*; 'Fast Train To Brighton' and 'Romance' in *The London Magazine*; 'The Village', 'Gifts' and 'Do not Forsake Me, Oh My Darling' in *Good Housekeeping*. 'Certain Standards' was first published in *Woman's Realm*; 'The Apparition' in *Woman*; and 'The Birthday' in *Woman's Own*.

# Contents

# Skin Deep

ഌ

George dreaded his return to London on home leave. To begin with, he would have to cope with his family's quite natural curiosity about his new fiancée. Then there was the fiancée's insistence that he try to find a better job – better, anyway, by her own rather austere definition. Finally, he was riding right into the tail-end of a bizarre family crisis. A year or so ago his mother had submitted to a lunatic whim for cosmetic surgery. The results were calamitous, but by the time she tried to sue for malpractice the quack who had performed the operation for her on the cheap had already vanished. The Harley Street plastic surgeons whom she then consulted told her frostily that the damage was irreparable.

George had been in West Africa during all that time, but his mother's decline from shock to despair to intermittent attacks of agora-, dysmor- and other varieties of phobia had been well documented in letters from his sister Henrietta. He shrank in anticipation of their first encounter. But when they did in fact meet at Heathrow airport it was clear that his mother had made a gallant effort to pull herself together. Her hair was freshly waved and blue-rinsed and she was fashionably dressed. She wore huge dark wrap-around glasses. He could see nothing whatsoever wrong with her face. It was not until they were assembled for dinner at her Putney flat and she tremulously removed the glasses that he saw and barely managed to suppress a shriek of horror. One faded blue eye glared at him piteously, permanently open under its skewed shred of lid as if propped up by a length of toothpick. 'Why, it's not so bad . . .' George quavered, and his mother burst into tears; that is to say, water leaked from the normal eye and gushed liberally from the mutilated one. He sat speechless with pity, fat and sweating, having been subject to alternate bouts of dysentery and over-indulgence while in West Africa. Henrietta and her husband sighed, both patently fed up with the tragedy with which they had been lumbered for so many months. His mother's sobs trailed off into sniffles and a grotesque attempt at a plucky grin. It was better when she replaced her sunglasses. The fool, the poor fool, George thought helplessly.

At dinner they all seized with relief on the topic of his forthcoming marriage with the Swedish doctor he had met in Accra. Vigdis would be joining him in London in a week's time, and as it was to be the second time around for both of them the wedding would be a quiet affair in a registry office. His brother-in-law, who fancied himself a bit of a lad, grinned at him salaciously. 'You lucky devil! I've heard about those Swedish birds!' George smiled back reservedly. Vigdis wasn't really like that. Well, in a way she was but . . . 'You'll be returning to West Africa then?' his sister enquired. He hesitated. That was all still a bit up in the air, he told them. Vigdis had a very good job with the University Hospital in Ghana which she was naturally reluctant to leave. His own company was well pleased with his achievements and he could probably go on marketing black pancake make-up and brilliantine down there for the rest of his working life. But he felt – he and Vigdis felt – that it might be time for him to switch to something a little more meaningful. His mother gave him a smile that was rendered inadvertently enigmatic by the sunglasses that covered half her face. 'She sounds like a quite lovely serious girl, Georgie.' They all delved into the coq au vin and passed over in delicate silence any reference to his first wife.

That night he slept badly on the camp bed his mother had set up for him, partly because it was too narrow for his girth and partly because certain problems which had seemed trivial in Africa were also suddenly and uncomfortably making their weight felt. What meaningful and dignified new job was he supposed to find, for instance? He was a salesman after all, and had never been anything else. Perhaps he could switch to the selling of medical equipment or drugs, but that required a certain technical savvy and the training of an entirely new crew of native agents. It seemed like rather a lot to take on in middle-age just so he could say he was peddling forceps or streptomycin instead of hair pomade. And starting with another firm he would undoubtedly take a financial loss which just now he could ill afford. His ex-wife had been abandoned by the lover for whom she abandoned him, so he was still burdened with her support, not to mention his son's increasingly horrendous school fees. It had been hard to explain this to Vigdis. She couldn't see that he owed Vanessa any support at all and her egalitarian Scandinavian principles were affronted by the idea of private education. When he tried to convey that Vanessa was entirely incompetent to keep herself let alone a child, Vigdis's straight coppery eyebrows had arched incredulously. Although very much the injured party in her own divorce, she had contemptuously forsworn all support and single-handedly raised her twin sons, one of whom was now a bio-chemist and the other an architect.

His mother woke him the next morning with a cup of tea. She wore a pretty flowered housecoat with ruffles at the neck and wrist, and her hair was still in its silvery-blue scallops and her shades were in place. It occurred to him that for one or another reason he had never told Vigdis about his mother's misadventure. Meeting her, Vigdis would be bound to wonder why she always wore dark glasses like a Tonton Macoute.

His mother sat down next to his bed, turning her head so that his view was of the undamaged side of her face. 'It's so good to have you back, Georgie.'

'I'm sorry I couldn't be here during your trouble,' he said awkwardly.

His mother laughed but the hand holding her own cup of tea shook slightly. 'Oh, I'm quite over it by now. I suppose I was a very silly girl. It's just that Althea Crawley had it done by the same man and the effect was quite miraculous. It was only supposed to be an eyelid lift anyway. You remember how dreadfully old and pouchy your Gran's eyes got when she came up in age . . . ? Well, anyway, the fellow was very cheap. Of course, that should have warned me. And it was idiotic to attempt anything like that at my age even under the best of

circumstances. The people on Harley Street told me that afterwards. But you know something, George?' She giggled sadly.
'I've never really felt my age. Perhaps it's because I had you
and Hen when I was so very young. I suppose I never properly
grew up.'

Again George felt a wave of pity for her. It was true that
she had always been rather childish, pretty, frivolous and vain.
But it seemed unduly harsh that she must spend the rest of her
life hiding behind black goggles; it seemed like too heavy-
handed a retribution for her guileless little shortcomings. And
when it came to vanity, he, just twenty years younger than
she, had recently caught himself musing over ads for hair
transplants.

'Tell me more about Vigdis,' his mother said. 'I can hardly
wait to meet her. She sounds like such a lovely girl.'

'Well, she's not exactly a girl – she's about the same age as
me,' George said. 'She's very mature and sensible and independent. Not that she's dull . . .' he added hastily. His mother
patted his knee. 'Why, I'm sure she is, darling. The things you
said first, I mean.' She seemed suddenly at a loss for words.
'I'll make you some breakfast.'

While waiting for his breakfast, George lay back and
indulged in a little reminiscent lust. Filial decency forbade
that he should tell his mother the way in which Vigdis was
most strikingly not dull. He remembered the night before last
and many nights before that. It was not, of course, that she was
the Swedish sex-pot of his brother-in-law's imaginings; on the
other hand, for a woman of her generation she had some
remarkably advanced ideas. But it also had to be added that
she was no less passionately egalitarian in the sexual sphere
than the social and political. Her ex-husband, she had told
George, had been a lazy and selfish lover. George had felt a
secret qualm because he suspected that Vanessa might, with
some justification, have said the same of him, although Vanessa
had always been quite easy-going on that score. 'Oh, one knows
about Englishwomen – they just lie back and think of England!'
Vigdis had said with her rich and hearty laugh. George had
started to demur a bit defensively but Vigdis suddenly turned
solemn. 'It is true that I also often think of Sweden when we

climax. The nature, I mean.' He had been forced to respectful silence, as her pantheistic reverence for nature was already known to him; but he had wondered how there was time for views of birch forests and blue lakes to flash through her mind what with the suggestions, instructions and sometimes outright commands that issued from her lips. But of course she was entitled to her own gratification, he reminded himself hastily, and having achieved it would become wonderfully loving and compliant and sometimes even murmur to him the moody mysterious gutturals he associated with Ingmar Bergman films. His welfare had improved no end since he no longer had to resort to African whores or brief perilous liaisons with wives from the diplomatic community; in fact since Vigdis also watched his health, disciplined his servants and vetted his friends, his welfare had improved altogether.

His mother called him in to breakfast. He looked down at the plate with mixed delight and dismay. Fat bacon, fried eggs and fried bread were not on the diet list Vigdis had lovingly commanded him to follow. But it was his favourite boyhood meal and the diet had rather gone to pot during the last fortnight anyway. 'I'm supposed to be slimming,' he said as he sat down. 'Rubbish!' his mother scolded. 'A bit of weight suits a man of your height. You look very distinguished.' George grinned sheepishly. It was quite untrue, he looked fat as a pig, but it was nice to hear just the same.

During the next week he was busy. For the short time that he and Vigdis would be in London before embarking on their Nordic honeymoon, he took a suite in a hotel that was modest but clean as her insistence on cleanliness verged on the obsessive. He discreetly scouted his old friends in the City as to other work openings but they stared at him in amazement: in these times of unemployment and redundancy did he seek a new job when the one he had offered security, an excellent income and manifold perks? Anyway, his heart was not really in it. Secretly he felt that Vigdis sometimes carried her idealism to rather impractical lengths. At the weekend he went to Charterhouse to visit his son. Toby was fourteen – a bright, handsome, mannerly lad. They took lunch together and then a walk and then tea. As the boy conversed easily and charmingly, George found himself stuffing his own mouth with food. Blanquette de veau, cream cakes, strawberry ice-cream sundaes, he crammed it all greedily into himself as if it were he, not his son, who was the famished adolescent. They parted on the most cordial of terms, but afterwards in the toilet of Godalming railway station George leaned his forehead against the distempered wall and wept. His only child was lost to him and there would be no others; he could hardly expect Vigdis at age forty-seven to start popping babies. A new thought, startlingly crude and defiant, suddenly struck him. He could marry again, yes, not a silly feckless bitch like Vanessa, not even Vigdis, but some placid young creature easily impressed by the life-style he could offer her in West Africa, someone who wouldn't give a damn whether he sold french letters or cured cancer, someone who liked him fat, someone who didn't mind being lazily and selfishly screwed or even just fobbed off with a kiss and a cuddle when he was tired, someone he could keep in a continual and blissful state of pregnancy like so many of the young wives down there.

The stationmaster's announcement shocked him out of his lamentably brutish fantasy. As he hurried out on to the platform he reflected that it was high time he saw Vigdis again.

When he did see Vigdis the next day at the airport he was slightly nonplussed. Perhaps it was her winter clothes. Back in Ghana she always cut a fine figure, high-coloured and statuesque whether in her hospital whites or khaki shirtwaists or the elegantly simple black silk dresses she wore to cocktail parties. But now, in a thick tweed trouser suit a bit too tight across the beam, she seemed shorter, stockier, provincial, and the thick bronze braid she wore coronet-style around her head looked rustic rather than regal. But her skin was as beautiful as he remembered it, and when she gave him her big firm minty-smelling mouth to kiss he kissed her back with genuine affection. 'I have missed you, Gay-org,' Vigdis said, meaningfully giving his name the Swedish pronunciation she always used in moments of intimacy.

After a happy if somewhat exhausting reunion at the hotel, he dozed while she bathed. But when she returned to the room she was ready for a little gentle interrogation. 'Have you had any luck with your search for a more suitable job, George?'

'Well, not much to speak of,' he replied evasively. 'These are hard times, you know. Actually . . .'

'It still seems to me,' Vigdis interrupted with a slight frown, 'that a man of your abilities could find something more useful and significant to do. I have been thinking more about it since you left Ghana. A job with the ILO, for instance, or perhaps with your experience you could teach business administration at the University . . .' George felt what was perhaps no more than a twinge of post-coital irritability. He wished Vigdis would put on some clothes – it was a little disconcerting to be hectored by a large naked woman. But he strove to keep his tone patient. 'Sweetheart, I'm a salesman. On a fairly big scale, but just the same that's what I do – I sell things. I know it's not a very noble profession . . .'

'Perhaps when we go to Sweden,' Vigdis said firmly. 'I have some contacts there.'

He let it pass in silence. The contacts would come to nothing; Vigdis was a good doctor but she knew damn-all about business. And if she cherished some secret notion of him as a sort of superannuated Peace Corps volunteer, that was her affair. He watched as she sat down at the dressing-table and coiled the great braid of hair around her head. She eschewed make-up – as with her lovely skin she well might – apart from lipstick and a little Vaseline on the eyelids. Watching her dab it on he suddenly remembered his mother. They were all to dine together that night at Henrietta's house. He cleared his throat. 'There's something I forgot to tell you about my mother. Some time ago she had an operation that didn't quite come off. I mean, one eye doesn't close properly so she always wears dark glasses. She's rather sensitive about it.'

'How very unfortunate!' Vigdis exclaimed. Her face expressed sympathy mixed with professional curiosity. 'Was a nerve severed? Has she not tried to consult a plastic surgeon? As you know I have strong views on cosmetic surgery; just the same such doctors can achieve good results when they apply themselves to cases of genuine need instead of vain and silly women.'

George could not recollect that Vigdis had ever before expressed her views on cosmetic operations. He had just known somehow what they would be. 'Actually the thing happened while she was undergoing plastic surgery,' he said. 'An eyelid lift.' He had an absurd and wretched impulse to laugh.

'Yes, I see,' Vigdis said. For a moment she concentrated on the application of her Beauty-without-Cruelty lipstick. But, being Vigdis, she could not let it go at that. 'When I say vain and silly, I mean vain and silly, George. But mostly I blame my colleagues who throw away their much needed time and talent on lifting chins and breasts for large sums of money. It is what the Americans would call a con game. It is part and parcel of what you do also. We have many times discussed how I feel about Africans spending their tiny incomes on the products you sell when they need protein and medicines. It is pandering for profit to people's weakness and vanity.'

George reflected glumly that she was right. Of course he was pandering for profit to people's weakness and vanity, just like the quack who had cobbled together his mother's eyelid. It sometimes seemed to him that the whole world was pandering for profit except for a few shining souls like Vigdis. It seemed to him that there was a positive aura around Vigdis's head until he realized that it was only the light bouncing off her braid.

The dinner party in Wandsworth was not entirely a success. Superficially it went off well enough, but George found himself in the uncomfortable position of seeing everything through Vigdis's strong blue gaze. She praised the food but he was certain she found it unwholesomely rich. She could not fail to notice the Irish wolfhound slobbering and gobbling under the dining-table, and probably other gross lapses in hygiene as well. After dinner the conversation turned to politics. Henrietta's husband was a self-made and self-employed businessman with extremely outspoken views on the iniquities of the welfare state. Vigdis was restrained in her defence of it but he could feel her stiffen as one after the other of her cherished socialist ideals was kicked into the dust. And to make matters worse, Henrietta suddenly started dropping references to Annabel's and Goodwood with an affected Smart Set snigger which was not at all like her; he could only infer that she had been driven to such silliness by way of reaction to Vigdis's unstated but palpable disapproval. His mother, on the other hand, said almost nothing at all apart from the first few social twitters. Perhaps she was comparing Vigdis to Vanessa with whom she had enjoyed an immediate rapport. Perhaps she was paralysed with awe. When the evening finally ended he saw Vigdis's eyes linger briefly on his mother's ancient leopard coat. A double fault: wanton extravagance coupled with an ecological crime.

On the way back in the mini-cab Vigdis said very little. There were none of the cosy port-mortems they enjoyed after dinner parties back in Accra. When they were in the hotel room George made certain overtures because anxiety always made him feel both hungry and randy and there was nothing to eat save for Vigdis's Swedish crispbreads which looked and tasted like pitted concrete slabs. But for the first time since he had known her, she was not in the mood. She politely said good night and climbed into the other twin bed, turning her broad shapely back to him.

The next morning as they were eating their muesli in the hotel dining-room, the quarrel that they should have had the night before erupted. Vigdis had decided to shop that morning and also photograph some churches for her architect son. And what were his plans? He had some appointments in the City, he told her. She looked up, alert and clear-eyed as a baby; unlike him, she was a morning person. 'About a new job?' He felt suddenly soured by her insistence as by the tasteless fodder he was spooning into his mouth. 'About the one I have, as a matter of fact. They want to brief me on their new advertising campaign.' At her look of dismay he felt his resolution harden. 'Listen, Vigdis, I'm afraid another kind of work just isn't on. It's all very well making idealistic plans over a few drinks back in Accra, but when it comes to the point this is all I can do. Besides which, I can't afford a cut in income just now.' Vigdis's mouth took on a mutinous set. 'I

told you, George, that I earn quite enough for both of us.
There's no reason why we need live on such an extravagant
scale as the others down there. I have always thought it rather
distasteful anyway. I am perfectly able to support you at least
while you get started on something else.' 'Be that as it may,'
George replied dryly. 'But I can hardly expect you to put my
son through school and support Vanessa. And I can't let
Vanessa live on welfare or scrub floors.'

He could see the twin Nordic lights of Calvinism and
Socialism burn fiercely in Vigdis's eyes. 'Why not? It seems
to me some quite worthy people have had to . . .' 'No,' George
said flatly. There seemed no way to explain that he couldn't
throw Vanessa, spoilt and silly as she was, middle-aged as she
was, to the wolves, not even to save his own soul. Which he
wasn't sure he wanted to have saved anyway. But he was
shocked by Vigdis's look of profound, almost heartbroken disappointment. How could she ever have taken that boozy
pillowtalk of theirs seriously? Well, he had almost taken it
seriously himself while in the never-never land of the expatriates' West Africa, but the first sight of Europe had
snapped him sharply out of it. It struck him that for all her
professional experience and sexual emancipation Vigdis was as
naïve as a young child, more naïve even than his own son.
Indeed, she was even looking at him with the uncomprehending
grief of a young child who has just heard a solemn parental
promise broken. And like most parents in such instances he
felt furious guilt submerge itself in furious exasperation. He
pushed his bowl of cereal away. 'I have to have something
more substantial than this to go on.' He summoned the waiter
and under Vigdis's now utterly tragic gaze ordered eggs,
sausages and real cream for his coffee. She waited till the man
was gone and then said in a low voice, 'I don't understand
what has happened to you, George. You seem entirely different
than in Ghana. It's as if I hardly know you. What has
happened to change you? Is it London – is it seeing your
family?'

He could follow her whole train of thought in all its wildly
innocent romanticism. There was he, once more brutalized by
the great soulless city, by Commerce, by the influence of his

frivolous self-centred relations. He tried to speak gently. 'My family aren't really as bad as they may have made themselves out to be. I think possibly you put them a bit on the defensive. Really, they're quite ordinary, decent people. Even Jack doesn't go around all the time grinding the faces of the poor.' But humour, even the mildest irony, had never been Vigdis's strong point. He was half relieved, half alarmed to see her woe-begone expression replaced by firm indignation. 'It is not for me to judge your people, George. But no, I do not find their attitudes compatible with my own, or their life-style or their greed for material things. I do not speak from inexperience or lack of choice. I could have gone to America and become very rich in private practice.'

George looked up interestedly from his dish of eggs; this was news to him. On the other hand, Vigdis was not exactly indigent down in Accra. Perhaps she mistook his interest for awe because her voice now took on a quite rhetorical clang. 'Oh yes, I had such offers. I could have sold myself.' The snap as she broke one of her mammoth crispbreads in two, resounded like a shot around the room. George rounded his shoulders against the discreetly fascinated gaze of the couple at the next table and hoped Vigdis wouldn't let herself get too carried away. 'You know I have the greatest respect for your principles,' he said lamely. She gave him a stern look. 'Do you, George? I'm afraid you are humouring me. I'm afraid my beliefs may now seem to you very simple, very unsophisticated. To respect the nature, to face one's social responsibilities, to do honest useful work . . .' 'Laborare est orare,' George muttered. 'What do you say?' she asked sharply. 'Just a Latin tag I learned at school,' he said. 'I do not understand,' Vigdis replied coldly. 'It seems I do not understand many things. The need for private schooling, the need to maintain a healthy woman who is perfectly able to earn her own bread. Or does your ex-wife also have to wear the skins of endangered species and pay to have her face lifted?' George stared at her, bewildered. 'Are you jealous of Vanessa? For God's sake, I don't keep her in luxury! It's just enough to take care of her because she's too damned half-witted to do it herself.' Vigdis took a deep breath. 'I am not jealous of Vanessa. It is you, George, I am thinking of. That you should sacrifice yourself to pay for such utter trivialities. That you should devote your life to selling make-up. That you can accept without the blink of an eye such a waste of money and surgical skill as your mother indulged in.'

'For God's sake!' he said again, but this time very angrily. 'I'd say there was bloody little surgical skill involved! As to my mother, she's just a poor silly childish old woman who has to live the rest of her life with one eye staring wide open!'

He could see on her set face the conviction that this was no more than his mother deserved. He looked with sudden dislike at her blunt features, her Vaselined eyelids, her splendid complexion. No paint or face-lifts needed there, nevertheless Vigdis had her own firm grip on the sweet bird of youth. What might that creamy skin not owe to the cosmetic benefits of a regular and vigorous love life?

The waiter coming with the bill to be signed put an end to the argument. George had to go to his first appointment. He and Vigdis discussed with chilly constraint a suitable place to meet before lunch. The knowledge that their quarrel was quite a different thing from the coyly playful lovers' spats they had allowed themselves in Ghana weighed heavily on both of them.

George had to put it out of his mind during his business meetings. But when he came to meet her at noon in the garden of St Botolph's-without-Bishopsgate she was not yet there. It was one of those amazing January days that sometimes drift down on London like a balm of blossoms from a mild and milky sky. As he sat on a bench and waited it occurred to him that she might not show up at all. Perhaps she had stalked off to Heathrow and hopped the first plane to Goteborg. He turned this thought over in his mind and felt a remarkable lack of affect. Perhaps it might be just as well. Oh, she had been very welcome company back in Accra, he conceded, a bit heavy-handed sometimes with her ho-ho-ho type whimsy but generally a very sturdy good sport and never before given to such pomposity as she had shown that morning. But perhaps they should have left it at that. Who had first suggested marriage anyway? – he couldn't remember. What would it be like to have all that solemn and sentimental high-mindedness

flowing over him constantly like a tide of treacle? At bottom
they had very little in common. Not even a liking for nature,
of which he suspected she would make a very big thing when
– or if – they visited her own country. Would she expect him
to stare transfixed at her precious lakes and woods as if confronted with the risen Christ? He looked around. He was an
urban animal; this small, elegant, stony sunken garden was
quite nature enough for him. His look around also took in the
City clerks and little secretaries turning their faces like pale
parched anemones to the sun. He remembered his fantasy in
the Godalming railway station. Any one of these girls might
be delighted to exchange her dull job, meagre wage and pimply
boy-friend for the relative luxury of servants, country clubs
and a free hand with the cheque book. Well, perhaps not the
very prettiest of them, he admitted realistically. But there were
plenty of others who were also nubile and manageable. He
checked his watch again, feeling both resentful and hungry.
A good starchy Lancashire hot-pot was what he craved and
possibly a good Lancashire lass as well. Anyway, it was not too
late. Even if Vigdis hadn't done a flit back to Sweden, he was
reasonably sure he could convince her he simply wasn't good
enough for her. He was as he was, he would tell her: a fat,
unprincipled, unregenerate, self-indulgent slob, a Hogarth
drawing made flesh, an exploiter of the ignorant black masses,
and if the poor buggers wanted to waste their pittance and
diminish their beauty with the muck he sold them, that was all
right with him.

For a few moments he wallowed with defiant pleasure in this
image of himself. Then he saw Vigdis emerge from the door
of the church. She was laden with shopping bags and camera
equipment. He started to rise and then checked himself. Although she sat down on a bench quite near him, she didn't see
him, she seemed lost in thought. She was wearing her dumpy
tweed trouser suit. She sat slumped on the bench, shoulders
bowed, fiddling dejectedly with her A to Z. For the first time
George saw her as middle-aged, a tiredly despondent, thick-
set, middle-aged Swedish lady on whom none of the other men
bestowed so much as a passing glance. He felt a curious
indignation on her behalf and at the same time he dispassion-

ately foresaw that she would find new lovers harder and harder to come by, even in West Africa. And what would become of her then? She had her work, true, but she also, with the ingenuous greed of innocence, craved love in both its companionable and carnal aspects. Without it she would soon become dour, dull, miserable and a social bore. Oh shit! George groaned in the heat of the sun, in his own thick suit and corpulent body, wrestling with some slim inner wraith, some parfit gentil knight that had always lived there, some chevalier always waiting to spring to the rescue, some gallantly tender, hopelessly out-dated lover of women for their unique unknowing vulnerability.

When he rose, she saw him. Her smile was reserved, but when he smiled back it became eager, welcoming and above all relieved. Of course he had a little missionary work to do, he told himself. He would have to stop her carping about his job and in the fullness of time he would tactfully have to make her understand that he was a fat man going on for fifty and not a prize stud. And that milkmaid's braid of hers would have to go. Taking into account Vigdis's mulish disposition it was an altogether onerous programme, but his step as he approached her was unusually light and confident for so portly a man; compassion, unlike pity, engenders its own authority.

# Fast Train
# To Brighton

Frobisher and his wife Madge stood at the back of the group
of American tourists who were lined up at Gate Fifteen at
Victoria Station for the fast train to Brighton. Frobisher knew
that Madge would far rather have been at the head of the
group with Huddy, who was regaling the others in his loud
flat Texan bray with observations as to the general inefficiency
of the whole Goddamn system. Madge allowed that Huddy
was sort of a loud-mouth, but he was also, she asserted, the
life of the party and they'd have had a lot less fun on this tour
if he hadn't been along. During the month that they had been
in Europe there had been a running flirtation between Madge
and Huddy. Nothing serious – just a lot of horseplay. Madge
would laugh loudly at Huddy's jokes and Huddy would
squeeze her around her broad waist. 'Hey, this is some doll you
got here, you know that, Fro, old buddy?' he would enquire.
His own wife, Shirley, would smile forbearingly. Frobisher
too would forbear to point out that Madge was a somewhat
overweight woman of forty-nine, a competent mother of three,
a pillar of the community in Milton, Massachusetts, a kindly,
affectionate, naïve flesh-and-blood woman occasionally given
to bursts of menopausal silliness. But not a doll. It was funny,
he thought, as they inched forward a bit in the line, how sensitive he had come to be about the nuances of language since
they came to Europe. Or Yoorp, as Huddy called it.

Madge sighed and jiggled next to him. 'You know, it is kind
of annoying,' she said. 'All this lining up for everything. Lookit
how they've got to let all those people coming off the train
through before they let us on. You don't get this sort of mess
back home. Huddy has a point.' Huddy, Frobisher remem-

bered, had been so irritated by the lines of people waiting to buy second-class tickets that he had led the whole group willy-nilly to the immediately accessible first-class window. He hadn't asked if anyone wanted to pay four dollars more per ticket to save a seven-minute wait in line; he had merely loped over there, waving them all on like sheep, and like sheep they had followed. The simile took on added meaning just then as Huddy, who was a head taller than anyone else in the group, looked back at them and waved demonstratively at the slow muddled crowd of incoming passengers. 'You know what these guys need?' he called out. 'A cattle-prod to get them going. About ten volts of electricity each to get them to hustle their cans.'

Madge giggled and Frobisher, as was his wont, shrank into himself. He wondered if Huddy thought that the natives of this country spoke Urdu. It hadn't been so bad on the continent, but even there he had sometimes been deeply mortified. At the Sistine Chapel, for instance. The rest of them had been appropriately reverent as they gazed up at the ceiling. But Huddy, disgruntled by the edict against cameras, had said loudly, 'Well, you folks can get a crick in your necks if you want. To me it's just a Goddamned bunch of scrambled eggs.' And a middle-aged Italian woman standing nearby had heard and gazed at them all through narrowed glittering eyes. 'Barbari selvaggi!' she spat out. Frobisher had understood the meaning well enough. Barbarian savages.

He looked around at the English also waiting in line with mild and patient resignation. If they had heard Huddy – and they could hardly not have – they gave no sign of it, although God knew what they were thinking. He himself entertained an image of Huddy swinging into action with his cattle-prod and uttering strange, loud, incoherent cries as he doubtless did on his ranch in Texas. He visualized the polite and gentle English thrown into pain and panic, scattering every which way. Like Jews at Auschwitz, he thought darkly, but then his sanity reasserted itself. The English were not helpless Jews and Huddy was not really a Nazi. If he applied his prod it would be fairly kindly and for their own good. And not at all to the old ladies.

'What are you thinking about?' Madge asked. 'You look so funny.'

'Huddy and his prod,' Frobisher replied, and suddenly laughed. Madge looked confused. She was an innocent woman; even the broadest of *double entendres* invariably went over her head. Yet she was aware, he realized, of Huddy's beefy shoulders and large hirsute hands and his disconcerting habit of sitting with his legs spread far apart.

They were at last allowed through the gate. Huddy led the way up the platform in search of a first-class compartment. Madge skittered ahead so as to catch up with him and Shirley. Frobisher declined to quicken his own pace but walked behind with old Doc Sonderheim and his wife. With any luck he would be able to sit on the train with the Sonderheims or others in the group whom he liked. But when he stepped into the compartment he saw that a seat had already been saved for him next to Madge and across from Huddy and Shirley. At least their group would have the compartment to itself, he thought, and he need not be anxious about Huddy shooting off his big mouth. Few English would pay nearly double for a short ride in a car that differed in no discernible degree of comfort or cleanliness from second class.

Huddy, it seemed, had just made the same observation. He was vigorously kicking out of the way a litter of paper plates and cups and cigarette stubs. 'Kee-rist!' he exclaimed. 'You ever seen anything so filthy? I mean can you imagine a Pullman car back home running over with this kind of sh . . . garbage?' Frobisher eyed him reflectively. It was funny about Huddy, he thought. He blasphemed like a trooper, or rather like the Marine sergeant he once had been. But there were certain words, even quite mild words by today's standards, that he never permitted himself in mixed company, as if fulfilling a Boy Scout vow. He respected women, he had once confided to Frobisher, and then in the same breath added that it was still a man's world out where he lived in Texas with none of this Woman's Lib crud. If Shirley or any of his gals had carried on like that they'd have got their little tails paddled pronto. Frobisher had recounted this to Madge, expecting her to be faintly revolted and amused as he had been. But Madge had shrugged and said, 'Well . . . I guess Huddy is sort of a dying breed. What they used to call a man's man.'

The dying breed, having kicked all the rubbish into the aisle, now sat back and spread his legs apart, forcing his wife to move closer to the window. Frobisher saw Madge's eyes drawn helplessly, uneasily, briefly to Huddy's flies. Did she *want* him to screw her? he thought with sudden anger. Did she want to get herself laid by this big, crude, loud-mouthed male animal who splashed both opinions and money about as if in token gesture of what else he could splash about if given half a chance? Not that it seemed to have done Shirley much good. She was a quiet, pretty, exhausted-looking woman. Of all the ladies in the group she was by far the best dressed – straight out of Neiman Marcus, no doubt. Large diamonds glittered on her thin fingers and twice a year she had herself done over at Maine Chance. But there was a resigned drag to her mouth, and when she spoke it was in a sad infantile whine that set Frobisher's teeth on edge. He looked at his own wife who, by then, had been able to drag her eyes away from Huddy's groin. They had lived together amicably for nearly twenty-five years. Did she now find him wanting? Did she compare his New England parsimony to Huddy's open-handedness, his reticence to Huddy's garrulity, his gentle, courteous, somewhat elderly love-making to whatever promise lay behind Huddy's straining Dak Slack zipper?

Just before the train started to move, another passenger got on. Frobisher's heart sank. It was an Englishman, a very staid and proper Englishman who took, moreover, the seat just across the aisle from them, which put him in a prime position to hear Huddy's observations. But Huddy was just then engaged with noisily flapping open his newspaper, and Shirley and Madge were talking about the exhibition of Regency furniture which they were going to Brighton to see. Frobisher stole another glance at the Englishman and saw him take from his attaché case a document which he recognized as a legal brief. His interest quickened. So the guy was a lawyer like himself, although there was no way of knowing where he fitted into the mystifying British legal hierarchy: solicitor or barrister or even Queen's Counsel. In fact he was altogether like himself:

slim, slightly stooped, well dressed, not young. Frobisher would have liked to talk to him – just a quiet chat between fellow professionals – but he could not think of any possible way in which to initiate a conversation. He had to admit that there Huddy had a great advantage. Had Huddy recognized another cattleman he would have immediately and effortlessly got things going, as indeed he had once done in a Florentine restaurant, with the result that they had all afterwards been invited to the Italian cattle baron's palazzo and had a grand time drinking vino and talking pidgin Italian. Quite naturally, the group had to give Huddy credit for his initiative and enterprise and the way in which he generally pepped things up.

His mind turned back to the one day he had spent by himself during the past week in London. The others had gone to Greenwich, but he had taken himself off and quietly wandered about Gray's Inn and the Law Courts. He had eaten lunch at a small restaurant patronized by jurists and had eavesdropped happily and unabashedly on their shop talk. Later, from a high gallery, he had gazed down into the pit of an Old Bailey criminal court as if at an Elizabethan theatre. The case in progress was a dull and routine affair but he had felt a childish pleasure, even awe at the pomp and ceremony, the wigs and gowns and m'luds. Such trappings were both old-fashioned and theatrical, he knew, but they conferred a solemnity which he had sometimes felt sadly lacking in law as he practised it back in Milton, Mass. He had even, at lunchtime earlier, felt a tiny shiver of enjoyment at hearing one of his fellow diners speak of someone taking silk. He knew what it meant, but it was such a lovely, eloquent little figure of speech. It was the happiest day he had spent during the entire tour. That evening he had told Madge about it and she had smiled and nodded. But later, when they were dining with Huddy and Shirley and the others at a fashionable Chinese restaurant, she had told all of *them* about it – not just what he had seen but what he had felt. 'Honestly, he was all shiny-eyed just like a little kid!' she chuckled. 'Imagine being carried away with all that corny old stuff! Can't you just see Fro in one of those cute curly little wigs?' And Huddy had draped a napkin over his, Frobisher's, head, and lifted his upper lip and assumed what he took to be an effeminate British accent: 'Could I have your Lordship's permission to go to the can and use the curling tongs on account of, dontchew know, I just washed my wig and I cahrn't do a thing with it.' Roars of laughter from all, even the kindly old Sonderheims. Frobisher laughed too – it would have been fatal not to – while his heart turned to stone at Madge's betrayal.

Now Huddy started to read aloud some newspaper item about Jimmy Carter. He read it loud and clear, dutifully enunciating each word. Frobisher hoped that his confrère across the aisle would be able to concentrate on his work. He himself shut his ears. He was what the Ancient Greeks would have called an incomplete man, totally uninterested in politics ever since Adlai Stevenson's second defeat. The long squalid Watergate debacle had left him disgusted but otherwise unmoved. He had been appalled by the Kennedy assassinations, but it was the prospect of civil anarchy that most horrified him – while the sight of Madge going about red-eyed and sniffling for three days secretly embarrassed him, as had the whole orgy of communal grief. He remembered Huddy telling them that he too had cried an entire day. 'We were doing some branding about that time and I remember my tears plopping down and sizzling all over the branding iron.' Frobisher had snorted with laughter and both Huddy and Madge had stared at him indignantly. 'It takes a real man to admit he could cry at a time like that,' Madge later told him pointedly.

Frobisher gazed past her at the scenery, which was rather uninteresting at that point as the track was laid in a deep trough with hillocks of vegetation on either side. Perhaps the reason why he felt so much at home in England was because there seemed to be less of that hairy-chested real-man he-man stuff that had so bedevilled his own generation. He had sometimes felt a positive envy of the androgynous young flower-bedecked hippies of a decade ago. That sort of feeling worried him when he was in the presence of someone like Huddy, although he knew he need have no serious fears as to his own masculinity. But it didn't seem to worry him here. Here Huddy was the outsider, not he.

Huddy folded and wadded the paper between his big hands

and looked out of the window and sighed heavily. But then
the Roman campagna and the valleys of the Loire had equally
incurred his displeasure, and the fields of Surrey and Kent
awakened his outright derision. Sure they were cute and pretty,
he admitted when the ladies timidly demurred, but what kind
of a half-ass way was that to run an agronomy with everything
cut up into little bits and pieces – little, anyway, when compared to his own spread at home – and the lousy broken-down
technology and the English squalling like scalded cats every
time a hedgerow was cut down. Huddy had all the facts at
his fingertips, even more than Paul Mannhurst who was the
economist of the group and had put in some time at the FAO.
Now Shirley patted his hand like a nervous mother quelling a
large unruly child. 'Never mind, hon, you'll like Brighton.
People say it's a real cute town.'

'What's to see there?' Huddy shrugged. 'Just a bunch of
old furniture and the beach. I met this Australian fella in the
hotel bar the other night and he told me the town was over-
run with queers.' He grinned at Frobisher. 'You and me better
watch ourselves when we go to the public johns, buddy.'

Frobisher smiled reservedly. He hated jokes about homo-
sexuals. Many years ago he had defended one against a
trumped-up morals charge. The boy had been pretty awful – a
screaming little faggot of the worst type – but he had also
clearly been the sacrificial lamb to a town clean-up campaign.
Frobisher had got him off. His professional colleagues who
knew the score had congratulated him sincerely on a tough
victory against very difficult odds. But in the small community
where he and Madge had then lived there had been jokes and
leers and sniggers for some time. He remembered them as he
remembered the distasteful and highly clinical cross-examin-
ation and the huge, teary, frightened lemur-like eyes of his
client.

He had had a bellyful of the subject at that time, but now
he saw with dread that Huddy had seized on it. 'That's another
thing about Yoorp,' Huddy said. 'The degeneracy. I mean,
Kee-rist, even when we were at St Peter's I caught this guy
giving me the eye. Fact. And this country's riddled with it.
Buzz Maplin back home – he's got a cousin in the CIA who

used to work over here and he's got stories'd curl the hair on your chest. Writers, politicians, guys way high up in the government, three-dollar bills all of them. They run the country – them and the commie unions.'

Frobisher saw that the Englishman across the aisle had put away his papers and was now sitting looking straight ahead and no doubt taking in every word of Huddy's inane polemic. Checking his watch, he was relieved to see that they were nearly at Brighton; in fact, just then the train entered a broad field of tracks and then unexpectedly stopped. It stopped in a very final sort of way right there in the middle of the waste of tracks, as if it was going to stay there for a good long while. Huddy, too, looked at his gold Tiffany watch. 'Jee-sus!' he exclaimed loudly. 'They can't even get the Goddamn train into the station. Whaddya expect with a bunch of reds and pansies running the show?' He suddenly took a new sociological tack. 'It's these boarding schools they got here. Buzz told me. It turns them out like boxes of salt-water taffy. The fairies, I mean.'

Frobisher felt himself redden with fury and embarrassment at the thought that the quiet listener across the aisle might take this half-witted buffoon, this caricature, to be the spokes-man for all of them. Huddy had been bad before but never as bad as this when his Neanderthal brain attempted analysis. 'They did pretty well during the war,' he muttered. And Madge warningly patted his arm as if it were he, not Huddy, who was making a fool of himself. Huddy rolled his eyes at him forbearingly. 'Listen, old pal. Who had to come over here and win the Goddamn war for them? Us, that's who. I mean they were just running around like a bunch of chickens with their heads cut off till we came along and put some sock in it.'

Frobisher had spent some time in England during the war as a young soldier. There had even been an English girl . . . He remembered the exhaustion, the weary good-humour, the incredible tenacity, the modesty, above all the modesty. The man across the aisle would also have been of an age to partici-pate and remember. 'Yeah,' Huddy went on reflectively. 'And after the war it was us who had to put them back on their feet and wipe their noses and pull up their little panties, you should

pardon the expression, ladies, as our Hebe friends would say.'
Madge giggled. Perhaps that was what did it. Frobisher
suddenly understood what it meant to see red. Well, not
exactly red but a feverish, dazzling, rosy flimmer as if he were
sun-struck. Among the objects he saw through that dazzle was
Huddy's big face multiplied dozens of times like the faces in
that long-ago courtroom, the heavy stupid condemnatory
macho faces, the branders and castrators and dockers of balls
when confronted with anyone or anything even marginally
different from themselves. And he said in a voice that he
meant to be cool and level but that came out hoarse and over-
excited and clearly audible to everyone around, 'Listen, old
buddy. Why can't you just for once keep your big fucking
mouth shut?'

Even old Sonderheim in the seat behind stopped rumbling.
Huddy's mouth fell open with astonishment. The two women
stiffened. But most of all, Frobisher was aware of the Englishman opposite still looking straight ahead. He wanted desperately to appeal to him: brother lawyer, fellow-respecter of
language, of the word, even the ugly word when justifiably
used, understand that it isn't you against me, English against
American, but us against them, civilized articulate man against
the xenophobes and jingoists, the ape-children. But the
Englishman didn't appear to be catching his vibes. Frobisher
was trained to read faces, even faces in profile. He saw not the
violent disgust he had seen on the Italian woman's face, but a
minuscule quirk about the lips of amusement mixed with disdain for all of them, himself included, as loud, ill-bred infants
giving vent to their squalid and raucous emotions in a public
place.

The train lurched forward. He had to look at Huddy. Huddy
was red and his big hands were balled into fists and he squinted
back at him menacingly like John Wayne. Frobisher wondered
what would happen if Huddy leaned across and punched him
in the mouth. In the physical sense he was not particularly
brave but now he feared the humiliation more than the possible
injury. Then Madge said tightly, 'If you ask me, Fro, that
really calls for an apology. *Right now*.' 'Never mind an
apology,' Huddy said. 'If that's the way Fro wants it, that's

the way it's going to be, old buddy. I don't mind a difference of opinion but I don't hold with abuse and dirty language. From now on we'd better all go our own way.' There was a curiously forlorn look of injured dignity in his voice and his face was aggrieved as a hurt child's. Frobisher shut his eyes against it and against the memory of his own almost hysterical rage a few minutes ago. Huddy was stupid, vulgar, bigoted and sentimental. If manipulated by shrewder and more ruthless minds he could be dangerous. But he was not Attila the Hun any more than those spiritual brothers of his at the homosexual's trial. Because in the end they had bowed, however unwillingly, to the law, to reason, to the word. As he himself had to forgo the bright satisfying flare of his anger and bow to reason and the realization that he had made a perfect spectacle of himself.

'C'mon, Shirl,' Huddy said curtly as the train stopped. The Englishman too left without a sideways glance, stepping fastidiously over the rubbish Huddy had kicked into the aisle. His slim elderly shoulders shrugged them all off as he and his had shrugged off millions of uncouth invaders before and would again. The others left also, and with plenty of sideways glances. But Madge remained sitting with the look on her face that meant she wanted to have a word with him. 'You know what this means, don't you?' she said levelly. 'It means the whole rest of the tour's spoiled. Scotland and everything. We won't even be able to eat with them at Wheeler's here in Brighton. We'll have to sneak off by ourselves to some hamburger joint. We'll be outsiders.'

'Is that such a bad thing?' Frobisher enquired sourly. And then, 'Okay. I'm sorry. But what's done is done.'

Madge looked at him curiously. 'I've never heard you use language like that before, Fro. Not in all the years we've been married.'

'Oh, for God's sake,' Frobisher said. 'It's just a word. Every time you open a modern book you see it. Scrawled all over the walls. Schoolkids, presidents, everyone uses it.'

'Not people like us,' Madge said coldly. 'Not people like Huddy and Shirley. Not even a big tough guy like Huddy. Huddy's a gentleman.'

Frobisher heard himself laugh. Then a phrase that had amused him by its comical meaninglessness when he overheard it in a pub, came to him. 'Huddy gets on my tits,' he said. He saw quite unexpectedly on Madge's round face a struggle between mirth and disapproval as she rose. And he rose too, a dry acerbic New Englander, chuckling quietly as he led her into the sunshine of Regency Brighton.

# Brent

They met Brent after they had been a week in Somerset. Each day Kay had dutifully taken her son to the beach. The weather was heavy, warm and grey. The sand, hard-packed and corrugated after high tide, stretched for half a mile to the flat spiritless sea. After they had staked their claim with towels and windscreen, Kay would settle down to her newspapers. But, looking up, she would see Jeremy standing with his back to her, plastic bucket in hand. He was searching – for what? Other children, the anticipated delights of a seaside holiday, the super fun she had promised him so gaily back in London? At six years old he still took on faith such resolute assurances; she was his single authority, his only parent. She remembered with what high-minded confidence she had made the decision to have and rear her child alone; the professional woman who had seen no reason why intelligence, organization and skill should not be as adequate to realize this project as any other. But she had not taken into account the helplessness she would feel when she saw the downy hollow between his shoulderblades, the broad backs of his knees and the new bucket all poised in wistful expectation. There might be groups of children playing nearby but she knew from her own secret shyness that to Jeremy they would be as impregnable in their solidarity as alien tribes. She would put down her paper and cry merrily, 'Come on, let's you and I build a sand castle!' Jeremy would accommodatingly consent; it was better than nothing. Between them there existed that grave and indispensable etiquette of people who have only each other and have the intelligence to know it.

Then came Brent. He was taller and perhaps a year older

than Jeremy. He introduced himself by the direct and simple method of kicking sand into Jeremy's eyes. Kay looked up, annoyed, a reproof on her lips. But perhaps it had only been an accident. She could perceive Jeremy's tense hopeful interest even as he sat kneading the sand from his eyes. The boy was a boy after all, and he was still standing there looking down at them expressionlessly. He was unusually handsome, with dark hair cut severely short, and long, startlingly green eyes. His body had already a flat masculine ranginess. The first sight of him evoked more of an appreciation of the man he would one day be than of the little boy he now was. 'Well, hello there – what's your name?' Kay asked with a shade more warmth than she felt. 'Brent Howard,' he said. She placed him then – he had come from a group sitting some yards away; three young women and two little girls. 'Would you like to help us build our castle?' she asked. He shrugged. His tanned narrow foot probed their citadel with a certain contempt. 'Yeah, okay,' he said. 'Are you American?' she asked as he squatted down next to them. 'Canadian,' he replied. 'Well, this is Jeremy,' she said. The two boys exchanged sidelong glances. 'Did you get that tan of yours on *this* beach?' she asked wonderingly. Brent gave her a hard green stare. 'This beach stinks,' he said.

Kay laughed uncertainly. Jeremy's conversational ability had perhaps spoiled her for other children. She withdrew to her papers; they were best left to each other. They seemed to get along, they even talked. She heard Jeremy's eager fluting treble and Brent's laconic one-word replies. But, after ten minutes or so, Brent rose. 'Let's go down to the water,' he said. 'This thing's boring. Let's squash it.' His deed as good as his word, he stamped a ruthless foot in the middle of the castle. Kay saw Jeremy gape for a second but then he joined joyfully in the orgy of destruction. 'Okay, you coming or not?' Brent asked impatiently. 'Put on your life-jacket and remember not to go in higher than your waist,' Kay told her son. Only a week before their arrival a child of his age had been caught in the undertow and drowned. She looked hesitantly at Brent, wondering whether to tell him that Jeremy could not really swim yet. On another such older bigger boy she might have

conferred a certain responsibility, counted on the rough toler-
ance of seniority. But instinct warned her that Brent was not
such a boy. 'Remember . . .' she called after them. When they
were tiny specks at the distant water's edge she kept her eyes
on them so intently that she jumped on hearing a voice next
to her. 'Excuse me, but I'm Brent's mother.' A nondescript
accent, a pleasant nondescript woman, quite young. It was not
from his mother that Brent had got his looks. 'I was wondering
whether your little boy would like to come over to us when
they get back – we've got lots of Coke and cookies and things
. . .' She grinned so engagingly that Kay felt her own smile to
be absurdly stiff. 'I'm so glad Jeremy's found someone to play
with,' she said. 'Oh, I'm glad, too!' Brent's mother exclaimed.
'I mean, for Brent. My sister's got her two little girls along
but of course he won't look at them. Listen! Whyn't you come
over, too? We've got lots of coffee and sandwiches.'

Of course she had to set aside her longing to finish the
papers and accept. It was worth it to see the joy in Jeremy's
eyes when he returned and found her with the others, her
presence there a fixative to his relationship with Brent. There
were introductions. Brent's mother was Judy, her sister visit-
ing from Canada was Jean, and the third woman, Sybil, was
English. They had all just got so fed up with the weather in
London, Judy explained, that they had rented a villa here for
three weeks and upped and left their husbands, who were all
elsewhere anyway, in Canada, Istanbul and Zurich on business.
'And I'll bet they're all getting more sun than we are,' Jean
sighed, and then added hastily not to get her wrong, she loved
England, she really did, except it was sort of funny weather for
July. Sybil smiled wryly at Kay. She was a small woman with
the smug round gloss of a pedigreed cat. She and Kay had, in
the instant of meeting, diverged from the neutral classlessness
of the two Canadians just fractionally long enough to place
each other. The fine steely antennae of social recognition were
stronger even than Kay's dogged egalitarianism. She had even
once met, in her capacity as a financial journalist, Sybil's
husband who had a seat on the Stock Exchange. 'Is your
husband coming to join you?' Judy asked with friendly interest.

'I've never married,' Kay said in the absolutely impersonal
tone she had perfected for this announcement. Judy and
Jean both blinked and then grinned very energetically like
stewardesses when the plane takes an unexpected lurch. Sybil,
as was to be expected, exactly matched Kay's tone with a smile
of incurious dismissal. But it was said, it was over and Kay
relaxed, although she wondered as often before what dour
self-mortification might underlie her principle of unabashed
honesty. The tiny awkwardness was quickly covered by the
rattling of coffee cups and unwrapping of sandwiches. Kay
dispatched Jeremy to fetch their own modest picnic hamper.
'Race you,' Brent said, and pelted off. Jeremy, shrieking with
delight, ran labouring behind. Judy looked after them fondly.
'Isn't it nice they got together? Brent's been an awful old sour-
puss since we came. He thought the beach would be more sort
of like Cannes.'

In the early afternoon the wind rose. Kay saw that Jeremy
was flushed with the exertion of playing with the older stronger
boy. Small shudders of cold and exhaustion shook him. 'I
think home and a little nap,' she said. 'Oh, Mummy!' he said
dismayed. He was too sweet a boy to nag or whine but she
could see his touching anxiety that the opportunity lost might
never be regained. She hesitated and looked at Judy. 'Perhaps
Brent could come over later to play for a while and have tea?'
They had already established the fact that their two houses
were no more than a hundred yards apart.

While Jeremy slept she drank a glass of wine and read with
such absorption that she forgot the time. Were it not for him
she would have relinquished the beach altogether and stayed
quite happily in the shabby little bungalow with its cast-off
bits of furniture and improvised warren of rooms. It was
humble and undemanding, as a summer place should be; she
was almost tempted to make the owner an offer for it. The
garden too had been conveniently neglected past the point of
redemption. A dusty tangle of rhododendrons run wild, a
sandy patch of grass, a high hummock, gave Jeremy his jungle,
his plain and his alp to tear about on without fear for the
herbaceous borders. Then Jeremy woke and instantly went out

to wait for Brent, and she had to hurry with the tea. She had not shopped that day – it would have to be baked beans and sliced ham and package cake. Brent appeared wearing clean shorts and tee-shirt, his short glossy hair brushed with water. He looked around him with his strange cold green gaze. 'What a funny-looking house,' he said. 'Take Brent to see your room,' Kay told Jeremy. For some reason the boy made her oddly nervous. Soon after, she sat them down to tea, the food already on the plates. She had dressed the table with a little pot of wild flowers and striped napkins. 'I hope you don't mind beans . . .' she said, and Jeremy proclaimed his usual gracious litany as host: 'You-don't-have-to-eat-it-if-you-don't-like-it.' Brent lifted a forkful of beans on high and then slowly and deliberately let the food slide off the tines and plop back down on to the slice of ham. It was a sensualist's gesture of enjoyably scatological disgust. 'Yuck,' he said. Kay saw the faint shock on Jeremy's face. This was not in his range of recognizable responses. As a guest one might giggle at the food but not openly insult it. Kay thought it best to leave them. She sat on the rickety divan in the lounge and lit a cigarette and realized that she too had been faintly shocked. We are slaves to our standards of decorum, she thought. Perhaps in Brent's home refreshing candour was the rule.

The next morning was heavily overcast. Jeremy pined for the beach and Brent; Kay racked her brains for something to do. At eleven o'clock Judy appeared at the door, pert as a teenager in a red plastic mac. 'We thought what with the beach being out today we might take a trip to Cheddar Gorge,' she said. 'Would you all like to come?' Kay, holding Jeremy's hand, could feel the wild charge of his delight and counter to it the negative charge of her own longing for a few hours of quiet work. Judy looked past her to the table spread with books and papers. 'Listen, maybe you're busy. I mean, we'd love to have you come along but if there's something else you have to do we could just take Jeremy. We thought we'd bring back some of that cheese and try making a sort of Cheddar fondue with it tonight. Maybe you'd like to come over for that?'

Kay accepted both offers with gratitude. That evening she

could see why Brent had thought her own bungalow funny. Judy's rented villa suggested in both size and decor that the long arm of Richmond had extended itself to the west coast. It belonged to a judge, Judy told her, and added, 'Oh, it's kind of cute but you'd think with all that lawn they'd have built themselves a swimming pool.' They sat on the flagged terrace and had drinks while the children played in the vast garden. Kay sensed vaguely that a pattern was being set; there would be more evenings like this and days together on the beach.

Later, when this proved to be the case, she was surprised at her own lack of resistance. Normally she had very little in common with the wife-and-mother type of woman. At dinner parties, when stuck with a group whose conversation orbited around refractory dailies or the stretching of carpets or the superiority of Andermatt over Saas-fe, she would feel lumpen and dull. Her professional training would seem conspicuously irrelevant, even embarrassing, like a sixth finger. She often found herself consigned to an intellectual bi-sexuality as delicate and demanding as the double role she had to play with Jeremy. But here it was different. For one thing there were no men to lure her with talk more compatible with her own interests. She sat with the girls on the beach, took occasional excursions with them, joined them of an evening for sugary daiquiris and gritty paellas. The atmosphere was easy and trivial and pleasant; like her ramshackle cottage, it was just right for a summer holiday. They were all young women together, and in the absence of sexual competitiveness they seemed more youthful, more humorous, more intuitive than in mixed company. It was as if they had uncovered a clear thin vein of feminine sensibility unadulterated by the alloy of status and position as conferred by their husbands. Kay was reminded of boarding school. There was even that indulgent atmosphere wherein at any moment the hair might be let down. But it never was, at least not by her – her reticence was too established a habit. She knew that Sybil was very curious about her beneath her attitude of well-bred disinterest, but Sybil knew the rules of the game. The discretion of the other two women she felt came from a sweeter source than mere good manners; a gentle solemn concern that she not be wounded. Sometimes,

when the conversation became too thickly studded with conjugal anecdotes, she would see Jean and Judy exchange a
warning glance. They did not want her to feel out of things
in her husbandless limbo. She was secretly amused because
the reason she had not married Jeremy's father was because
she knew that, despite his vehement assurances to the contrary, what he really wanted was a woman like one of these.
His subsequent marriage had proved her right.

She would have been quite content with the situation had
it not been for Brent. Brent – or rather Brent and Jeremy
together – worried her. She saw Jeremy's heroic efforts to keep
up with the older boy. Brent was a fast runner, a strong
swimmer, a natural athlete. Having challenged he would always
win, and having won would watch Jeremy's ineffectual
attempts at improvement with a cold, impersonal satisfaction.
Kay gritted her teeth to see her child wrestled to the ground
again and again, always with the same contemptuous ease, and
then rise with a game smile ready for more. Perhaps it was
good for him, she told herself. A father would probably have
said it was good for him: a lesson in the hard school of
competitive life. She tried to maintain an attitude of brisk
equanimity even when Brent, coming to play at the bungalow,
refused all food with a disdain which Jeremy now loyally
imitated, or physically assaulted the rough furniture, the trees,
even the walls of the house itself. When she remonstrated he
replied flatly, 'Why not? It's just junk.' If she pressed the
point he would say with the same remorseless calm, 'I guess
I'll go home now.' And Jeremy would shout in protest and
look at her in hurt and anger for having brought this disaster
about. She would smile weakly and suggest that Brent stay
after all as long as he stopped kicking the chairs. But meeting
his level gaze, she would know she was being had. At seven,
Brent was already a master at extortion. She saw that Jeremy
was drawn uneasily to the glamour of such quiet and self-
assured naughtiness and that he felt a confused equivalence
between his inferior physical prowess and his normal standard
of grave gentle good manners. 'Baby!' Kay had heard Brent
jeer at him when trying to incite him to some forbidden enterprise. 'You're such a sissy baby! A sissy baby girl!' She had

felt brief fury that Jeremy's maleness, which she had so carefully helped him define and assert, should be threatened by
this scornful juvenile machismo.

Had she not known Judy she would simply have dismissed
Brent as one of those atrociously spoiled unfortunates whose
behaviour can be put down to parental idiocy. But she saw
that in his mother's presence Brent was, strictly speaking,
'good', in fact a model child. He said Yes Ma'am, No Ma'am,
Thank you Ma'am, he ate nicely and asked to be excused from
the table, and once when he was sent to bed for some quite
minor infraction he went without protest apart from one single
chilling look at his mother before he left. His obedience was
remote and implacable. It was as if Judy's insistence on polite-
ness, while effective on the face of it, had nevertheless failed
to link up with some essential response in the child. He lacked
entirely the rudimentary social instinct without which the
pack animal cannot survive. Indeed, there were times when
Kay sensed in Judy's alert, even precipitous severity some of
the bravura with which the lion tamer enters the cage with
a fusillade of whip cracks to anticipate the slightest wayward
move from the treacherous beasts.

Oh, nonsense, she scoffed at herself then. Brent was only a
little boy. She could not, in all reason, subscribe to the fanciful
Jansenism of the Bad Seed syndrome. He was wilful and
curiously hard, but it was going too far to attribute to him real
evil. She reproached herself for always being anxious when
the two boys were out of sight and earshot. In her situation
she must be particularly on guard against the tendency to
stifle Jeremy with hysterical over-protectiveness. But it was
not always easy. One afternoon when they were all, except for
herself and Sybil, going to bathe in the sea, she called Jeremy
back to put on his life-jacket. Ordinarily he didn't object –
she had explained to him about the undertow – but this time
he scowled and muttered, 'Do I have to? It's what the little
girls wear. It's so sissy!' Brent's word, Kay thought grimly as
she tied the tapes. And Brent was standing some yards away,
arms crossed over his chest, watching Jeremy's humiliation
with his amused and narrow gaze. When they had left, she
told Sybil defensively, 'It's just that he can't really swim yet.

I mean he's not like Brent.' 'Brent's a right little horror,' Sybil said lazily. She propped herself up on one elbow; a soft sensual odalisque in her minimal bikini. 'It's odd really, because Judy's such a dear and so is his father. Both mild as milk. At first I thought it might be due to some weird North American theory of child-raising, but they're both quite strict with him and anyway Jean's little girls are perfect poppets so it can't be that. Maybe it's one of those extra chromosome things. Once I found a whole shoal of used matchsticks under his bed while I was helping to tidy his room here. He said he just collects them to build things with but it makes one think, doesn't it? Personally, if he were mine I'd send him off instanter to a good old-fashioned boarding school. Cold showers and six of the best – that sort of thing. And it isn't just me – my husband can't stand him either.' She giggled. 'John says he's an unmitigated little shit.'

Kay laughed weakly. She felt that Sybil's airy solution to Brent's behavioural problems fell somewhat short of the mark, but she felt also a strong relief at having her instinct confirmed. It was much the same sort of reassurance a husband might have given. A husband would have asserted forthrightly, as Sybil's John had, that Brent was a little shit and it might behove them to be a bit watchful, and that would be that. No, not just that, she had to admit to herself. A husband would also have been able to reassure Jeremy – as she somehow could not – that manliness was not just superior muscle power, and courage stopped short of irresponsible risk and arson. Yet the choice to make do without a husband had been hers, and she had to make the best of it. And try to keep her head about Brent. But that night Jeremy woke screaming from a nightmare and having wet his bed. As she helped him change and joked him out of his overwrought state, she could not resist the suspicion that Brent had something to do with it. Jeremy never had nightmares and had not wet his bed in years. She thought with a certain longing of his friends in London; those impish little boys to whom the depths of human depravity was a rude bathroom joke. She counted the days until they would return.

When the disaster finally occurred she had one stark awful moment of recognition. She had known it must happen. It was

their last day and Judy had invited Jeremy to lunch to keep
him out of the way while she packed. It was no weather for
the beach. There was a cold northerly wind and the sea was
whipped into a petulance of sharp little waves. Signs had been
posted to warn against swimming. The sky was dark, almost
autumnal. Kay was glad to be returning to London. She had
just finished stowing her book box into the car when Judy
came. 'My, you look busy!' she said. 'I thought I'd better
come take Brent off your hands. Are you sure you and Jeremy
wouldn't like to come over for a bite of supper?'

Kay dusted off her hands. Then very carefully she asked,
'Aren't they still at your place? Brent and Jeremy?'

'Golly, no,' Judy said. She was still smiling. 'They left right
after lunch and said they were coming straight here. That was
just a little past two o'clock.'

'Well, it's half past six now,' Kay said. There was a tiny
silence as each of them rallied her forces, tried to keep the
thing light and casual. There was reason for concern but not
panic. 'Why, the little scamps!' Judy said. 'I wonder where
they could have got to? Maybe they're exploring. Maybe they
went down to the candy store . . .'

'For four and a half hours?' Kay asked. Despite herself
there was a rasp in her voice.

'I guess we'd better organize ourselves into a search party,'
Judy said. 'They couldn't have gone far from here. I mean,
they wouldn't have taken a bus to Weston-super-Mare or anything like that.' She would ask Jean to take a look along the
dunes, she added. Neither of them mentioned the sea. It was
the unthinkable thought. Kay banished it steadfastly as she
searched and called. She heard the other women calling also.
Their voices were winsome, almost seductive, carefully devoid
of anger, or anything that could send the little boys into hiding.
The cold evening wind lifted her skirt but her skin was
clammy. She called over fences, into empty gardens, into the
dusty undergrowth on either side of the main road. Her own
voice sounded in her ears with the dreadful futility of an echo.
They met again at Judy's house; she and Judy and Sybil.
'Well, I guess we'll have to spread out a bit more,' Judy said.
Her voice was still resolutely cheerful. 'I could take the car and

look for them on the road,' Sybil volunteered.

'Listen . . .' Jean said. She had appeared quite suddenly and was holding her two little girls tightly by the hand. 'Listen . . .' They were all perfectly quiet. 'They've found something lying on the beach. Everybody rushed down there. There's a whole bunch of people looking down at something . . .'

Kay registered the waxy sheen on her skin and Sybil's sudden look of horror and an eerie yelp from Judy; she had once heard a dog cry thus when its foot was crushed in an escalator tread. Then her own mind opened to conceive the inconceivable. She saw as if in a silent blare of light Jeremy caught and dragged down by the wild grey rags of sea, his shrill screams for her, his incredulity when she didn't come, his terminal terror, his final intolerable pain. She began to run heavily but with great speed to the beach. Her lungs seemed filled with hot ash, her heart hammered against her ribs like an animal ablaze with anguish. She heard her own voice shouting strange loud beseeching profanities. She would barter anything against Jeremy without life, a life without Jeremy. The crowd of people stood in a dense circle almost at the water's edge. She pulled them apart, tore their shoulders apart like lumps of putty and pushed her way through to the space in the middle. The small form lay in the unmistakable dormancy of death. Because of the damage to the head and body it was difficult to identify at once – perhaps a seal, perhaps even a young dolphin.

'Well, take a good look seeing as how you were so eager for it,' some aggrieved voice said behind her. She did look, she stared fixedly, her eyes seemed to have an unslakeable thirst for what lay before them. Then suddenly she had had enough. She made her way to the outside of the crowd just in time. Leaning forward with her hands braced on her knees, she vomited with great violence. The people standing nearby stepped back in affront. As well they might, she thought; a pretty picture she must make with water streaming from her eyes and nose and bile from her mouth. She felt a tentative touch on her shoulder. 'Oh, Kay, honey, it's all right,' Jean said sympathetically. 'Sybil just saw the two of them running

towards your house. Here, take my hankie. It's my fault for
giving you all such a scare.'

They found the boys sitting on the stoop of the bungalow.
Their faces were flushed and sticky and they had an air of
pretended casualness. 'We just went to the Butlins down the
road,' Jeremy said. Kay heard Judy begin a cold, furious
interrogation. She herself sank down on the stoop and wrapped
her arms around Jeremy and rocked him back and forth with
unrestrained happiness. Later she would have to impress on
him the extent of his misdemeanour and extract solemn vows
that it would never happen again, but just now she could only
touch him. Her display of emotion was perhaps a shade exces-
sive for his taste but he endured it with fortitude. 'I'm sorry
you got worried,' he said. 'We didn't know how late it was.'
*We*, Kay thought, when Brent had strapped to his wrist one
of those egregious timepieces that tell the hour in every part
of the globe. She saw Brent standing stoically under the stream
of tearful reproaches from his mother. And Jean shouted
angrily, 'There was something on the beach – a dead seal. At
first we thought it might be you! Can't you imagine how
frantic we were?' To that he reacted interestedly. 'Can I go
see it?' He had not the slightest concern, Kay realized wonderingly, for the anguish he had caused. Perhaps Judy realized
it too, because her voice took on a hysterical tremor. 'What
you can do is march straight home and go to bed without
supper, young man! And stay there all day tomorrow!' She
reached for the boy but he slipped past her and ducked into
the house.

He was not in the lounge or the kitchen. Kay saw Judy
tremble with mortification. 'He's probably in my wardrobe,'
she said. 'That's where he liked to hide when they played hide-
and-seek. I'll get him for you.'

He was there in the farthest corner. He stood straight up;
not so much the trapped animal as the condemned waiting for
the handkerchief to fall. Kay felt an instant of pity for him.
'Listen,' she said. 'There's been enough fuss and worry. Your
mother has to take you home. Come along now.'

'Not unless I can go see the seal,' Brent said. He's bargaining! Kay thought, astonished. There was no fear in his eyes, just that ruthless and single-minded will. In what unholy compact were he and his mother locked? she wondered. I'll do you credit in company if you otherwise let me have my own way? This time, being only seven, he had misjudged the situation. But it was a mistake of inexperience – in later years he would become more proficient. Judy was still hovering wretchedly by the bedroom door, leaving the confrontation up to her. Kay gripped his arm and pulled. His resistance was amazingly strong but she was stronger still. She felt the force of his hatred and for one shocking instant the force of her own as her fingers bit cruelly into his slim childish bicep. 'Now you come, Goddammit,' she said quietly.

Later that evening when Jeremy was in bed, Judy returned alone. 'I just wanted to say goodbye for all of us as you're leaving so early tomorrow,' she said. She and Kay exchanged telephone numbers and addresses with the slight awkwardness that accompanies a purely token gesture. 'It's a shame all this hassle had to happen on your last day,' she added. 'We got Brent to admit that it was all his idea. He'd even fixed his watch so he was always giving poor Jeremy the wrong time. He wants you to know he's sorry.'

'That's all right,' Kay said. Persistent nagging might have elicited a confession from Brent but she doubted that even *la peine forte et dure* could wring from him the slightest twinge of remorse. 'I'll have to get his daddy to give him a real good talking to,' Judy said, but her gaze slid unhappily away. Kay could think of no reply to make. She was certain that behind Judy's ingenuous face lay the knowledge that Brent was both dangerous and endangered. He would not be able to count forever on the forbearance of adults, on the instinctive taboo that preserves the young against the unchecked hostility and strength of their elders. She had felt it slip herself during that ugly moment when she had truly hated him, truly wanted to hurt him.

Judy turned to leave, but at the door she hesitated. With some embarrassment she said, 'Listen, for what it's worth, I think – I mean we all think – you're doing a terrific job raising Jeremy alone.'

It was a graceful compliment and perhaps not an altogether easy one to give. Kay felt its warmth for some time after Judy was gone. But not for too long. She must not work the example of poor dreadful Brent and his hapless parents into some complacent self-justification of her own. For just a little while she did allow herself the balm of Judy's tribute, but only as one might allow oneself a single whisky on a cold afternoon.

# Mrs Wingate

It was a gesture of meaningless nostalgia, Mrs Wingate thought, that she and her daughter should meet here yet again. Years ago they used to home ritually in on this little patisserie, indulging themselves in its atmosphere of voluptuous gentility, its fragrance of hand-dipped chocolates, its fine coffee served in large thin tottery cups, its tiny cream-stuffed éclairs; an amusing treat after the ardours of Christmas shopping or the replenishing of school uniforms at Peter Jones. Or perhaps the amusing aspect had been apparent only to herself. Perhaps Allegra, never remarkable for her sensitivity to ambiance, would have preferred a Wimpy's or one of those rackety bistros on the King's Road.

The middle-aged waitress, experienced and alert to signs of crotchety hunger, hovered about her solicitously. 'I'm waiting for someone – I'll just have a cup of coffee in the meantime,' Mrs Wingate told her. She looked around at the other clients, carbon copies of herself with their chalky hair and silk toques and skeins of stone-martens and here and there the palsied quaver of a thin, liver-blotched hand. It was indeed a grand-motherly sort of place, she thought, suddenly depressed, but then she had always been a grandmotherly sort of mother to Allegra who had been born so long after Deborah and St John. She had greatly cherished the little girl, particularly after her husband's death when she had seemed almost like an intended memento, a final thoughtful gift from that eminently thought-ful and tender man. But when the child entered her teens, Mrs Wingate, by then in actual fact a grandmother, had looked at the jean-clad trendies who were the mothers of Allegra's friends and realized it would be ridiculous to compete on that level.

It had seemed to work well enough. People admired the composed and rather formal rapport she enjoyed with her adolescent daughter. And Allegra herself had been a placid child, quite content to bring her giggly little friends home from boarding school, quite content with the sedate holidays in the south of France, the small theatre parties and luncheons and shopping excursions arranged for her, all the elegant little treats indulgently bestowed on her. But *had* she? Mrs Wingate now brooded – had Allegra been given her due? Because she well remembered from her own girlhood as well as from her experience with Deborah (of which the less said the better) that at some point there must rage between mother and daughter the fury of the second birth, the unforgoable skirmishing in which one side was armed with experience and the other with awesome young pitilessness. But perhaps because she had simply been too exhausted to take it all on again and Allegra too docile, that aspect of nature red in tooth and claw had been quite absent in their relationship. Until a few months ago when, at the age of nineteen, Allegra had suddenly abandoned her secretarial course, packed up, left home without a word and gone to live in Notting Hill Gate with a student of Indian music. No, an Indian student of music, Mrs Wingate corrected herself with a sad and quite audible giggle.

Two dowagers at the next table glanced at her forbiddingly but the waitress, tolerant of such geriatric lapses, nudged a coffee cup in front of her and offered a bonbonnière of mint wafers. Mrs Wingate pulled herself together. But she still remembered her shock and astonishment that Allegra, always so meek and conciliatory and indeed languid almost to a fault in her relationship to young men, should have made a gesture so histrionic. Allegra had refused to let her visit the ménage in Notting Hill, in fact had refused at first to see her at all. Mrs Wingate had enlisted the aid of her older children. 'Oh, she's all right, Mother – it's the sort of thing girls do these days,' St John had said rather uninterestedly. 'Anyway it's time she broke away from home and got interested in a chap.' 'Pity it had to be a wog, though,' Deborah's husband had put in while Deborah simpered respectfully. She always appeared to enjoy Eric's masterful colonial attitude.

Since then Mrs Wingate had seen her daughter twice, both times by appointment and both times here. Allegra had been quietly sullen, wary and defensive, although she became somewhat friendlier when she realized that she was not about to be pried by force away from her love-nest. St John, after an unwilling reconnaissance tour, had reported to Mrs Wingate that it was *all right*: the two were living in a respectable bed-sit, Gunga Din seemed like a sober enough young fellow, and there was no evidence of drugs or white slavery or whatnot.

Even with her guard down Allegra had not been very forthcoming. She was quite happy, she assured her mother, she had a nice job selling art deco in an Antique Supermarket and whats-his-name was good to her. What *was* his name . . . ? Mrs Wingate tried desperately to recollect. Allegra's mumble had merely suggested to her something vaguely evocative of cosmetics or shoe polish. She had wanted to press, indeed there were times during those two previous meetings when she had wanted to scream at Allegra – questions, accusations; but the long-standing habit of courteous reticence was impossible to break.

And here was Allegra now, only half an hour late. Her entrance created a mild stir of interest among the clientele. Mrs Wingate looked at her in dismay. She had always taken such pleasure in dressing her; an interest in clothes seemed to be one of the things they could genuinely share. She had made tolerant concessions to the teenage crazes for denim and sheepskin and hobbling boots but everything had been smart and clean and of good quality. Now her daughter was sporting a curious new fashion: layer upon draggling layer of limp sad-coloured garments apparently drawn at random from a Salvation Army poor box and donned without an intermediate visit to the dry-cleaners. The whole ensemble, on this freezing January day, was topped by a hideous puce cardigan out at the elbows. Her normally thin but pretty hair had been hennaed, braided and frizzled into a kind of Renaissance fright wig. Her pale eyes were limned with kohl and she smelled powerfully of incense. Merciful God! Mrs Wingate thought despairingly. It seemed that all the adolescent excesses, all the lapses of taste she had imagined herself to circumvent through the exercise of tact and good sense, were now belatedly burgeoning forth. Not that it really mattered, of course – what mattered was that Allegra looked really rather unwell, pastyfaced and unhealthily plump. At their last meeting she had been 'into macrobiotics' and had refused to eat anything other than the watercress in the sandwiches, but that phase was evidently over. She slung herself down across from her mother, chatted perfunctorily for a few minutes and then applied herself to the platter of cream cakes, eating one after the other with unsightly greed and licking her fingers.

Mrs Wingate eyed her with increasing worry. She remembered that it had been Allegra who had asked for this rendezvous – perhaps she was in some sort of difficulty. *The* difficulty, the classic difficulty of her own girlhood era, flashed through her mind; but how to put it? Awkwardly she said, 'You're not looking quite as fit as I'd like, darling. You're not ill, are you? You're not – ' she hesitated, swallowed painfully – 'in trouble?'

'Oh, for God's sake don't be an ass!' Allegra spluttered angrily through a mouthful of custard cream. But then all at once her face became that of little twelve-year-old Allegra, flushed and abashed. 'I'm sorry, Mummy, but no, of course not.'

Of course not and God be praised for the Pill, Mrs Wingate thought. She poured them each some more coffee. 'You're still living with – ah?'

'Tanoo,' Allegra finished, and then shot her a suspicious look. 'Why are you laughing?'

'Nothing – no reason . . .' Mrs Wingate gasped.

'He thought St John's name was pretty comical too, I can tell you,' Allegra said sourly. 'But, anyway, the reason I wanted to see you was to invite you to a concert he's giving.'

'Tanoo is?' Mrs Wingate asked, and had to suppress another unseemly spasm of mirth.

'Yes, his teacher thinks he's ready,' Allegra said.

Mrs Wingate stirred her coffee thoughtfully. All at once

the prospects seemed somewhat brighter – if the boy really was a serious musician. She tried to remember what it was he played. She sternly repressed bigoted Eric-like associations with reed flutes and zithers. 'Will it be Indian music?'

'On the piano . . . ? Of course not,' Allegra said scornfully. 'Mostly Beethoven and Chopin. Anyway, here's the info.' She handed her mother not a ticket but a scrap of paper on which was scrawled a date and address, apparently some house in West Kensington. Mrs Wingate hastily scaled down her expectations from Wigmore Hall. 'Is it to be a private recital?'

Allegra nodded, looking very solemn. 'It's terribly important to his future – it's like a kind of test.'

'You mean like *The Alien Corn*?' Mrs Wingate asked apprehensively, but Allegra was not of a generation that read Somerset Maugham. 'His teacher insists on him doing it because he hates playing for the public.'

Mrs Wingate thought that a peculiar inhibition for one who presumably aspired to be a concert pianist, but said nothing. 'You will come?' Allegra said quite urgently.

'Yes, of course, of course. I should like very much to meet him.' Allegra's overture encouraged her to add boldly, 'You know, I haven't the least intention of interfering with your life, darling. I'll admit I was a little – ' she sought for the light non-emotive word – 'miffed – when you left as you did without a word. Obviously I kept wondering what I might have done wrong . . .'

'I thought it was time I got off on my own like everyone else. I didn't want a lot of argument and stuff,' Allegra muttered.

Once again Mrs Wingate suppressed the impulse to scream, 'What argument and stuff? Isn't there such a thing as civilized discourse?' Instead she merely said, 'Well, that's all water under the bridge. But I do hope that we can go on being good friends. We always were, weren't we?'

'Yeah, sure,' Allegra said dispiritedly. She concentrated on picking up crumbs of brown sugar with her wetted fingertip. No, Mrs Wingate thought sadly, they had not been friends. The modern mothers and daughters she knew were friends; enemies too sometimes, but that was the essential corollary.

She saw them slanging each other, sometimes teasing cruelly and even coarsely, but also talking, giggling, gossiping, conspiring, experimenting with fashions, hair-styles, food, comparing sardonic opinions about men, morals, sex and Women's Lib; and in that sharp intimate humour, sentimentality burned off, respect vapourized, but perhaps a new alloy was formed. Allegra too would have seen her friends' smart pally mothers – and their grandmothers – and possibly drawn certain conclusions, but Allegra had had to make do with their own grave, cordial relationship which would have been ideal, a very model, had it spanned not one generation but two.

She paid the bill. As they were leaving, Allegra said, 'I've asked St John and Deborah to the recital too.'

'Have you seen Deborah lately?' Mrs Wingate asked.

'We had lunch a couple of weeks ago, just her and me.' They were standing outside the patisserie on Sloane Street now. It was bitterly cold and she drew her pathetic cardigan closer about her. Mrs Wingate was wondering whether it might be *comme il faut* to suggest that they pop into Harvey Nichols and buy her a decent coat when Allegra, glancing at her rather slyly, said, 'She's not a bad sort, you know – old Debo. We had quite a long talk.'

It suddenly occurred to Mrs Wingate that Deborah had been eighteen when Allegra was born. By not too wild a stretch of possibility, Deborah could have been Allegra's mother. I'm becoming obsessed with this thing, she told herself. Then Allegra, still gazing at her furtively from between the smears of kohl, came out with a hoarse adolescent giggle. 'She told me all about how you tried to stop her marrying Eric.'

Mrs Wingate froze. She could imagine all too well the course the conversation had taken, the parallels drawn, the warnings given. She was sick with Deborah's unforgiving vindictiveness. After she had parted from Allegra and was in the taxi going home to Hampstead, she found herself thinking: would the child never let bygones be bygones? It had been her last great confrontation with either of the older children and admittedly she had made a mistake. But surely it was not so strange that in the grief and confusion following her husband's sudden death, she should have protested when Deborah calmly announced that she was marrying a man more than twice her age. Well, she had done more than protest, Mrs Wingate conceded. She had fought like a tiger to preserve her child from the clutches of that middle-aged roué, because it was such she knew Eric to be both by reputation and manner. He had been a social acquaintance of theirs, a guest in their house, and even then she had disliked his smug knowing air, his look of bluff, self-indulgent, self-satisfied sensuality. He was a stroker and a patter and a coiner of smutty *double entendres*; he had even, for God's sake, tried it on with *her*!

But Deborah had proved obdurate. She had been a lovely-looking child but greedy and obtuse. At certain angles she had looked remarkably like a beautiful young pig, and it was in Eric's chic sty that she was determined to root. In the end she had got her way, even down to the large fashionable wedding. As she came down the aisle, her face between its fallings of Alençon lace had looked shiny, pink, triumphant and more than ever like something out of *Charlotte's Web*.

So Mrs Wingate had lost, in fact doubly lost, because even her bleak prediction was wrong. Eric, whatever his other shortcomings, had turned out to be an irreproachable husband and father. She knew better than to attribute this to some miraculous change of heart. He had been an arrant womanizer but also a shrewd one – when he came to the point where his energies flagged behind his appetites, he had settled for the token virility symbol of a young and pretty wife. And not too token either; he kept himself extremely fit, as Deborah frequently assured her with just a trace of a leer. And Deborah had thrived in her chosen role as the rosy, simpering child bride, even with babies popping out of her nearly every third year. There were five now – more of a litter, really.

But that was no way to think of her charming grandchildren, Mrs Wingate told herself, no way at all. There must be something terribly wrong with her. Or did it happen to other women as well that at some point the veil of maternal infatuation fell from their eyes and they saw their offspring as they really were? Even St John, whom she had adored as a little boy, had disappointed. He had inherited his father's quite outrageous good looks but not, alas, his mitigating compassion and humanity. He was a prosperous family man, a successful architect and a very great bore, handsome as ivory and as bland. And sweet Allegra was bidding fair to become yet another scruffy half-wit hippy. But, dear God, she thought, if all her children had turned out to be prigs, poseurs and fools, it was not really good enough to settle for this attitude of carping distaste. Some of the blame must surely be laid at her own door.

They were at her own door now in fact. The driver had stopped the car and looked forbearingly over his shoulder at her; a silly old woman wool-gathering in the back seat. She paid him, but then stood a moment longer on the pavement looking at her home; a pale Georgian house set in a small deep elegant garden. It was the repository of her happiest memories from the time when the children were little and Walter still alive, but it was dark now and empty, a museum, a tomb.

On the appointed day a week later she made her way to the address in West Kensington. The house was of the same era as her own but very much larger and badly run down, as was the whole neighbourhood. On that late winter afternoon rubbish blew desolately in the streets and a sharp wind buffeted the peeling façades of the white buildings. She felt a moment of panic at finding herself in this strange place and, on quite uncharacteristic impulse, ducked into a shabby little corner pub and quickly knocked back a double brandy.

Thus fortified, she entered the house. There were already a number of people there, mostly young, drifting about and chatting. They collected in a large drawing-room quite empty save for a few rough benches and a boudoir piano at one end. There were no carpets, no curtains, no lights except for one ceiling bulb. After a few minutes she was found by Allegra who was wearing what looked like a cheesecloth shroud. Yes, Allegra told her casually, the house was a squat. Friends of theirs who lived there had cleared out their gear to make room for the recital. An uncle of Tanoo's had rented the piano and laid on the refreshments for after. Looking about at the other guests, Mrs Wingate suspected that it was the after they had come for. She felt more and more bewildered. Could she meet

Tanoo? she asked. Allegra gazed at her doubtfully. 'Well, he's pretty nervous but I guess so. Try not to put him off his stride.'

Tanoo stood alone in the little anteroom, flexing his hands. Her first startled impression was that she had been confronted with an enormous praying mantis, he was that thin and tall, with a small, dark, close-cropped, curiously vestigial-looking head. He looked down at her from his great and spindly height and gravely shook her hand and went back to his finger-flexing exercises, which put her disconcertingly in mind of a prospective strangler. His hands, like the rest of him, were remarkably long and lean. She supposed that their size must be an asset in his work as with Liszt and Rachmaninov. He looked kind enough in a gloomy sort of way, but not by the wildest stretch of the imagination could she connect him with Allegra.

Allegra found her a place on one of the benches; most of the other guests had to sit on the floor. After a moment or two, Tanoo entered and, without further ado, sat down and began to play. Although Mrs Wingate was not especially musical, she recognized most of the pieces – she could hardly fail to. His programme was entirely made up of the old war-horses most pianists keep for encores as a sop to popular taste. He played with prodigious volume and speed. His long foot pumped furiously at the pedal, his huge hands raced up and down the keyboard gobbling up octaves and arpeggios. After a while the sheer din of the thing, together with the cheap brandy rolling about in her stomach and the suspiciously musky smell of a neighbour's cigarette, gave her a severe headache.

Tanoo finished off with a tooth-rattling performance of the Revolutionary Etude, after which there was vigorous but brief applause and a rush for the adjacent room where punch and sandwiches were set up on a trestle table. Mrs Wingate stood up also, feeling stiff and hot and rather unwell. She wondered how soon she could gracefully extricate herself. Then she saw, standing near the exit, Deborah and her Eric, St John and his Ruth – they must have come late.

They were chatting cosily together, they were all good

friends. She hesitated before joining them, feeling ridiculously like an intruder. But Ruth caught sight of her and called, 'Why, there's Mother Faith!' It was a form of address that always made Mrs Wingate feel like some chuckly corpulent abbess. Still, she quite liked Ruth who was a thin, dark, nervous-looking girl, and felt obscurely sorry for her.

Her children greeted her and Eric kissed her smackingly on both cheeks. He called her Faith, as well he might; there was no more than four years' difference in age between them. 'I was just saying I think our Mowgli acquitted himself rather well,' he told her. 'Debo and I were thinking we might ask him out one evening to play for some friends.'

St John nodded. 'Not at all a bad idea. I imagine we might manage something along the same lines.'

'Do you really think . . . ?' Ruth demurred anxiously. 'I mean, our piano's awfully rickety and the lounge rather . . .'

'Don't be ridiculous!' St John snapped. Poor Ruth should have learned by now not to make deprecating statements or call the lounge a lounge, Mrs Wingate reflected. She looked at her son musingly. How had she ever created so colossal a snob? 'Do you think the boy's serious about a musical career?' she asked.

'Allie says he's studying privately with some Hungarian émigré or other,' St John replied. 'And I understand he comes from a quite affluent merchant family in Delhi. Who knows – the Japs and people like that are taking up Western music.'

'Anyway, it can't hurt to give the lad a push up the ladder,' Eric said with an indulgent chuckle. 'Perhaps we'll be in on the start of a brilliant career.'

Mrs Wingate thought not. In any case it seemed rather un-likely that success as a concert pianist would be much advanced by *soirées musicales* in Putney and Barnes. Deborah nuzzled girlishly against her husband's shoulder. 'Well, I suppose Allie could have done worse,' she giggled.

'At least the boy has a respect for the traditional disciplines,' Eric said with great authority. 'He's not some acid-head scribbler or faux-naïf dauber.' Mrs Wingate felt a surge of strong dislike towards him. When it came to faux-naïf, she thought, he might be well advised to tell Deborah that women

of thirty-seven did not look their best in Kate Greenaway
smocks and with their hair tied in bunches. There, I'm carping
again, she thought. Always secretly, always silently, but perhaps they felt it just the same. It was little wonder that they
ignored her and went on with their chat. Turning, she caught
sight of herself in a cloudy gilt-framed mirror that had somehow escaped the sack of the house. For a moment she was
terribly taken aback. Standing next to Eric she could have been
taken for Eric's mother – well, almost anyway – a short, stout
woman, dully and decently dressed, hatted and gloved, puffy
and powdered. How had she let herself get so old? she wondered. Not old in a way that could be altered by cosmetic
surgery or ridiculous clothes or doddering experiments with
sex, but atrophied in spirit, withdrawn from life as surely as
if she had entered a cloister. It had not protected her entirely,
not from the fiasco with Deborah, not from the well-
intentioned but repugnant efforts of her friends to jockey her
into a middle-aged romance, but in time the impingements had
fallen away. Indeed they had. When she murmured that she
was going to say goodbye to Allegra, the others seemed not
even to hear her.

During the next couple of months she made a resolute effort.
She put her house on the market – it was cumbersome and
costly to run and had clearly outlived its purpose as a family
home. She took a flat on Cadogan Place consisting of hardly
more than the former drawing-room and library of a converted
mansion, but they were beautiful airy rooms and she furnished
them with smart modern pieces. The activity thinned her
down, she bought new clothes. Not mutton dressed as lamb
but not mutton dressed as a well-hung old carcass either. She
took regular exercise swimming up and down the pool of a
neighbourhood hotel with her stately breaststroke. She dined
occasionally with an old friend widowed like herself, and
although his elderly whimsy was a little trying, it was nice to
be fussed over, nice to have a little mild flirtation. She abandoned Terence Rattigan for some of the more outspoken new
plays and found herself amused rather than shocked by their
solemnly insistent sexual candour. She booked a cruise for the

following winter to the far-off Seychelles. Sometimes she found
herself looking positively flushed and happy in anticipation
of the next day's, the next hour's living. At such moments she
felt an abashed sort of thankfulness that Allegra had made her
bid for independence. But she knew that her husband Walter
would have been pleased. Walter would have laughed and told
her that it was high time she climbed down from his funeral
pyre and put an end to her long, dully smouldering suttee.
And perhaps it was time also to mend her fences with the
children, who were no better or worse than other people's
children. It was not their fault that they were not Walter. She
would invite them all to cocktails and dinner. Tanoo too, if
he was still in the picture. Allegra had telephoned her some
time ago to say wanly that they were off on a short holiday to
France.

She rang their number first. A truculent West Indian voice
identifying itself as the caretaker said yes, the Indian chap still
lived there but there was no young lady. She had disappeared
weeks ago.

Mystified, Mrs Wingate rang St John. There was no reply.
She rang Deborah. 'Wasn't she going off to France or something?' Deborah said vaguely. 'I haven't talked to her in ages.
I don't think St John has either. I've been awfully busy
decorating the weekend place.' She tittered. 'Also, I'm preggers
again.'

As she put down the phone, Mrs Wingate felt the first faint
tremors of guilt and alarm. She had been so busy lately, so
self-absorbed. She had assumed that the other two children
were keeping an eye on Allegra, the wish being father to the
thought.

That evening she tried ringing Tanoo again but the phone
was constantly engaged. When she did finally get through a
new voice answered and said yes, he would see, and never
returned. For ten minutes she heard distant rackety shouts,
harsh music, and then a quiet sinister click as the receiver was
replaced without a word. When she rang again the phone was
once more engaged. She felt sudden panic. A picture flashed
in her mind of Tanoo's closed dark face, his long dark
throttler's hands. All the way to Notting Hill Gate in the taxi

she fought back her terrible misgivings.

Tanoo, looking slumberously surprised, opened the door to her. Glancing past him she had the impression of a large, badly lit room, sparsely furnished. A plump young Indian girl was cooking something pungent and smoky in a brazier on the floor. But the domesticity of the scene reassured her somewhat. 'I've been trying to get in touch with Allegra,' she said, and gave him an unthreatening social smile.

He didn't ask her in. 'She left some weeks ago – I don't know where she is,' he said flatly.

She tensed with the certain knowledge that he was lying. 'Nonsense – she couldn't just have disappeared!'

He shrugged. 'I came home one day and she was gone. That's all I know.'

Her panic returned. He looked different from the way he had at the concert, where he had worn a black suit comically too small. Now he had on a long saffron-coloured robe, and in his native dress, tall and thin as he was, he had a troubling exotic presence. She was aware of him as a man, Allegra's lover, perhaps Allegra's demon lover. 'Look here, this really isn't good enough . . .' she began, trying to keep her voice firm, but he broke in irascibly, 'I'm sorry, I'm sorry, but it's no use. You had better go.'

He was trying to close the door on her. She gasped with the force of her own fury. Not all her timid recent attempts at rejuvenation had done as much for her. She slapped the door open with the palm of her hand; she was quite prepared to fly at him like some small rabid pouter pigeon in a flurry of rage. 'I shall go at once to the police!' she shouted. 'I must warn you that both my son and my son-in-law are persons of influence. Don't imagine for a moment . . .'

'She has a room in Brixton,' Tanoo interrupted curtly. He stood back. 'She told me not to give you the address but I want no palaver with the police.' With an odd touch of hauteur he added, 'I don't wish to bring shame on my family.' He said something to the Indian girl who rose and scuttled past them down the hall. He scowled forbiddingly at Mrs Wingate. 'She's pregnant – Allegra. And it's too late for an operation.'

She felt the colour drain from her face. 'That's impossible . . .'

All at once he became furiously angry. 'She didn't tell me till it was too late. She says she didn't know herself. I would have helped her to make arrangements. Is it my fault she can't count or remember to take a pill? I am not irresponsible. I gave her all the money I had – a whole month's allowance from my people. I didn't throw her out – she wanted to leave. She knew from the beginning there could be nothing between us. She knew I would be returning soon to Delhi to take a teaching post in music and that I have been affianced for many years to a girl of good family.'

Stunned and still incredulous, Mrs Wingate glanced automatically in the direction of the girl who stood meekly waiting at the end of the hall. 'That one is the daughter of my uncle,' Tanoo said shortly. 'She has come here to make a marriage, also arranged. In our family such things are done in the traditional manner.' He looked down at her with morose and arrogant disdain. 'You English! Why can't you take care of your young girls? You let them loose, you let them sleep with anyone like animals in a field.'

Mrs Wingate looked back at him across the gulf of their two quite irreconcilable cultures. Try as she might, she couldn't really hate him for what had happened. 'Let me have her address,' she said.

It was dark and rainy outside. The taxi, moving by fits and starts in the choked evening traffic, took her through seedy urban districts she had never seen before. She, who rarely went out at night except in her own quiet fashionable neighbourhood, felt the tempo, the contained alarm, the nervous tension of a great unfamiliar city. The entrance to Allegra's building was squeezed between a laundry and a fried-food shop. As she stepped out of the taxi, rain blew into her face together with steam and the reek of hot lard. The place was horrible, a mean dead slum lacking even the squalid cosmopolitan élan of Notting Hill. She felt the burden of her own deplorable innocence.

Allegra was home – if it could be called that – a long narrow room at the back of the building. When she saw Mrs Wingate she burst at once into tears. 'Oh, the bastard!' she exclaimed.

'I made him tell me where you were,' Mrs Wingate said. Her relief at finding her daughter was followed at once by a strange dispassionate curiosity. She saw that Allegra, now sobbing and snuffling, wore a grubby pink quilted housecoat already much too small for her. They had bought it together for her last year at boarding school. She seated herself on the bed. 'This is ridiculous,' she said calmly. 'What are you doing in a place like this?'

'I didn't know how long my money would hold out. The job at the antique stall was just temporary.' She hiccuped pathetically. 'There's a lot of unemployment about, you know.'

'I know about the baby,' Mrs Wingate said.

This triggered a fresh outburst of crying, through which Allegra blubbered, 'It's too late, it's too late to do anything about it. Legally anyway, and I'm scared of the other way. You know how stupid I always was about dates and remembering to take my vitamin pills and things.'

'You must put it up for adoption,' Mrs Wingate said. She was amazed at the steady briskness of her own voice. 'There won't be any problem about the mixed blood – people are wild to have babies. I'll get in touch with Mildred Lancing; she runs a large adoption agency.' Wryly, she thought with what relish her old friend Mildred would take on this particular case.

Allegra slumped down on the room's only chair. 'I guess so – I don't know.' She giggled drearily. 'I've got myself into a fine pickle, haven't I?'

Not wholly by accident, Mrs Wingate thought. She looked about the room. There was a quite dramatic pathos about its ugliness and poverty. Allegra was proving how far she could sink, like a small child that blunders from mishap to mishap and finally subsides into total demonstrative despair: Do with me what you will. And like that child, she had fully expected to be found, redeemed, forgiven.

'Well, you can't stay here,' she said. 'You'd better come home with me.'

She was surprised that there was not even a token gesture

of resistance. Allegra stood up at once and took off her robe and pulled on one of her cheesecloth smocks. Quite cheerfully she asked, 'What's it like? Your new flat, I mean.'

'It's very small . . .' Mrs Wingate said. 'There's a dressing-room I could make into a bedroom for you – or perhaps you could share my bedroom . . .' All at once her throat crowded. She could imagine Allegra lumbering disconsolately around the little apartment, getting bigger and bigger by the day. She could foresee her own forced steady cheeriness, and her modest flutter at a fresh start strangled at birth. She was deeply ashamed of her revulsion to the idea but she felt it nonetheless. 'Or perhaps,' she amended, 'I could find you a nice little flat nearby. If you'd prefer to be on your own, that is.'

Allegra paused in the act of trying to button her jeans around her already thickening waist. 'Oh . . .' she said. Tears began to leak once more from her eyes. 'I get awfully depressed when I'm alone. What would I do all day?'

'Of course I'd much rather have you with me,' Mrs Wingate said hastily.

'I don't want to sit around thinking about the baby,' Allegra said plaintively. 'I'm afraid of getting all soft and soppy when they show it to me in the hospital. They always do that to give you a chance to change your mind.'

Not if she and Mildred had anything to do with it, they wouldn't, Mrs Wingate thought grimly. She could not allow this baby of hers to blunder about with a baby of her own. 'I'll keep you busy,' she promised. 'We'll shop and go to the theatre and try all the nice little restaurants around us.' The round of grandmotherly treats, she thought. Because that was what Allegra was used to, that was perhaps what she had fled from and, having made a mess of it, that was what she wanted to fly back to now: the calm, orderly, trustworthy detachment, the elderly nest. She helped her wrestle down from the top of the wardrobe the venerable Vuitton case that had served her at boarding school. 'You're an awfully good sport, Mummy,' Allegra sniffled. 'I was scared you'd go all shocked and reproachful on me.'

The consequence of her ineffectual rebellion, the long dark skinny Indian baby growing inside her, meant nothing to her,

Mrs Wingate realized wonderingly. Not yet, anyway. 'Oh, it'll be super to be home!' Allegra cried, and out of sheer relief aimed an awkward bumpy kiss at her cheek. Mrs Wingate held her delicately for a moment and the frowsy unwashed-smelling hennaed head rested against her shoulder in solemn tribute to the moment's high emotion. 'This won't be an altogether easy time we have ahead, you know,' she warned. 'With or without me, you'll sometimes get depressed. We'll get on each other's nerves. This is a nervous painful business you've taken on.'

Allegra drew back. 'Oh sure, I know,' she said without the slightest conviction. She was not interested in pain. What lay ahead, waiting to exact its due from them both, was not yet evident to her. Once again, Mrs Wingate felt a curiously hot rebellion of her own. It occurred to her that she might heartlessly wash her hands of the whole tedious pitiful affair, settle merely for giving financial support and get on with what was left of her own life. Her native scepticism eschewed whatever solace another woman might have drawn from a lachrymose pride in making a mother's sacrifice. And she knew that as things now stood she would have her scorched fledgling hanging about for a very long while before it essayed another flight. Allegra, innocently unaware of what was being weighed, was already tossing armfuls of clothes together with their jangly hangers into the case. But then she looked up and met her mother's considering gaze. 'What's the matter?' she asked anxiously. 'You look so serious.'

Mrs Wingate shook her head. She had suddenly, bitterly, remembered the agony of fear that swept her when she thought something might have happened to the child. Allegra back in her care would be a big burdensome lump: there was more than one pregnancy in play here, she thought with grim humour. But Allegra bumbling about helplessly on her own – the mere thought of it – would be unremitting torment. 'I'll help you pack,' she said. She knelt down at the floor of the wardrobe and began making neat pairs from the jumble of rubbishy shoes. Fecklessness, like all things else, must be learned, and she was too old a dog for such jaunty new tricks.

# The Village

❦

Corinna lifted the baby and told him to wave bye-bye to
Daddy. She herself smiled radiantly. She hoped Philip would
take this pleasing picture to town with him. At breakfast he
had been distinctly surly, snapping at John for not icing the
water, at the baby for drooling his porridge and at her for
sanctioning these transgressions. Corinna had held her tongue.
She was very young and had been married for less than three
years, but of all the precepts impressed on her by her mother
the most inviolable was, 'Never send them off to work on a
quarrel.' Rather let the equatorial sun set on your wrath than
rise on it, her mother always said: in the heat of the day little
conjugal tiffs could come to a fast and furious boil within
minutes. So as Philip got lethargically into the car, she kept
the baby waving and herself smiling gamely like Madam
Butterfly, meanwhile reflecting how silly it was of him not to
hire a driver. As Daddy pointed out, an accident with a
Nigerian at the wheel was one thing, with a European quite
another – even a killed chicken could give rise to months of
hysterical litigation. When the car paused before her, she
reminded him gaily, 'Don't forget to come home at noon – it's
Saturday and Mummy and Daddy are coming to lunch!'
Philip didn't seem to be greatly cheered. He stared at her
morosely for a moment and then said, 'Oh yes, meant to tell
you. Mind the baby when he's wandering around in the garden
– Crozier said he's certain he saw a green mamba yesterday.'
It was all she could do not to scream 'Rot!' at him as he drove
slowly off.

Inside the bungalow, John was clearing the breakfast table
with his usual slow care. She looked at him appreciatively; all

her friends envied her John, who had been small-boy to her mother's cook-steward and thereby trained to an almost European standard of proficiency and cleanliness. She passed through to the little verandah and the nearly-green lawn leading down to the creek. The creek had been what decided Philip to rent this modest bungalow in the Apapa suburb of Lagos rather than one of the more imposing villas in Ikoyi. Philip had been enchanted by the proximity of running water, even though she and her parents had pointed out to him humorously that its turgid yellow current ran with a number of things, including alligators. She put the baby in his play-pen and seated herself with her petit-point. Glancing next door, she saw the Croziers' gardener dribbling water from a rusty can on to the parched earth which constituted their lawn, and her lips tightened. If there was any serpent in this Garden of Eden it was not the green mamba, but the Croziers who had moved into the neighbouring bungalow three months ago.

She and Philip had found them installed there when they returned from home leave; their first home leave, which had been spent in its dreadful entirety with his family in Bristol. Exhausted as she had been, she had still felt impelled to make the first sociable approach and invite them to dinner. It would be nice for Philip, she had thought, because at thirty or thereabouts, the Croziers were closer to his age than hers; but she too would have plenty to talk about with June Crozier, who was massively into her first pregnancy.

But from the start she had had misgivings. The couple were here on a one-time posting; it was their first time in West Africa and would bloody well be their last, Ian Crozier said in his furious Scots gargle. They detested everything about it, and the European life-style in Lagos was a particular object of their amused and aggressive derision. 'Folie de grandeur!' Ian Crozier said scornfully. 'A lot of glorified clerks living like the Raj – big houses, servants, country clubs, the lot. It goes without saying, it's a paradise for third-raters. What the hell would they have to settle for back home?'

'A semi-detached and a pint at the local, like us,' June Crozier giggled. 'Bloody right!' Ian agreed, and they both laughed immoderately. Corinna saw Philip looking unhappy, probably because of the inadvertent slur against her parents who were both old African hands – her mother was third generation. These two must really be put right, she decided, before they dropped any more clangers. She explained firmly that there were two kinds of Europeans down here: the sojourners like the Croziers themselves who weren't really expected to settle in, and then the permanent residents often born and bred in the tradition of colonial service, to whom Africa was home. Ian guffawed. 'You mean like first offenders versus hardened lifers?' 'It does take a certain kind of mentality to live here,' Corinna said a little stiffly. 'What mentality?' Ian jeered. 'Most of the old hands I know have to fish their mentality out of a pool of gin each morning. And who's to blame them after a decade or two in this sink?' Then he addressed Philip directly – his wife and Corinna might as well not have been there. 'When are you wending your way back to civilization?'

Corinna held her breath, watching Philip hesitate. Finally he said, 'Well, as long as I stay with this company, this is where we'll be. They don't like to exchange home office with field personnel – '

Ian nodded sympathetically. 'Indentured servitude. Didn't you know that when you took the job?'

Philip seemed strangely embarrassed. 'Actually, I got the job when I was already down here – Corinna's father put me on to it. Originally I was down here just for a lark – a few months as a replacement with a shipping office from home.' 'Home?' June enquired. 'Bristol,' Philip said. 'Now that's a grand city!' Ian exclaimed warmly, and Philip looked at him with a certain pleased surprise. 'Wasn't there anything you could have turned your hand to back there?' Ian asked. 'Well, it's hard to find a decent opportunity . . .' Philip mumbled. In point of fact, he had left university in his first year and then roamed aimlessly from job to job. Ian, bristling with the Protestant work ethic, said, 'Enterprise, man, enterprise. Decent opportunities have to be made, not found!' 'Yes, well actually . . .' Philip began again. He hitched his chair a little closer to Ian's. 'Actually, my brother-in-law's on to something quite interesting. A little plant turning out glass-fibre hulls for sports boats

– we discussed it on home leave. He's just starting in a small way but in time there might be scope for a bit of export trade.' 'Damned right there might be!' Ian exclaimed. Mercifully June had interrupted this ominous line of speculation. 'You remember that wonderful brisk, salty air in Somerset, Ian?' she asked longingly, and the three of them joined in a paean to the air which Corinna also remembered – icy draughts of it that circulated in her mother-in-law's dreary little house with its perpetual odours of fried herring, chlorine and damp wool.

She had consulted her mother the next day and Mummy had said sagely, 'Ah, Corinna, one always meets people like that here. They *have* to go back, you see, to their wretched little lives, and they want to drag everyone back with them.' Worried, Corinna had persisted. 'Philip seems quite impressed by them. He says they're very well educated – university and all. And she's a social worker back in Glasgow.' 'Over-schooled,' her mother said firmly. It was one of her favourite terms of censure. She twinkled at Corinna. 'Make friends with the wife, dear. You'll find an ally there. The women always adjust quickly, especially if they're pregnant.'

June Crozier had already adjusted, it seemed. To Corinna's surprise, she admitted that she was delighted to be having her baby in Lagos. But then she added, 'I mean, as Ian says, what else is there for women to do down here but sit on their back-sides and breed. No wonder everyone you meet is in pig. But I'm having a grand time just vegetating for a change.' She patted her huge stomach amiably. 'Soon enough we'll be back in Glasgow and I'll be boiling nappies for this lot and beating my way through the sleet to the Co-op, not to mention getting down to some real work.'

Corinna had gazed at her with uneasy resentment. She had met women like June before – and like Philip's sister in Bristol; big, cawing, confident women who scrubbed and shopped and slung children around single-handedly, and as often as not held down a job as well – coarse-skinned, garrulous women who swore and discussed politics and drank like men, the *new* Englishwoman, as her mother was wont to say with a delicate sneer, who had Socialized and liberated and over-schooled herself out of every last vestige of feminine grace. While in

Bristol, Philip had proudly referred to Corinna's graces – her exquisite needlework, her sound management of household staff – but his mother and sister had gaped uncomprehendingly; it was a genre of domestic accomplishment clearly not within their ken. Once she had spent an entire morning baking for them the superb vol-au-vents which were the pinnacle – in fact the whole – of her culinary skill, and Philip's sister had chuckled, 'Good gracious, Corinna, how do you find the time for all that fiddly work?' And indeed time had been a problem there in Bristol, Corinna had found. All she was expected to do was to care for her baby, but that unassisted chore of laundry, feeding and walks in the freezing cold reduced her each day to a secret frenzy of exhaustion. Philip's relatives had been understanding – looking at her wan face, they said with maddeningly kind inanity, 'I expect growing up in the tropics thins your blood for you – why don't you take a nice iron tonic?' Iron was the word, Corinna had reflected bitterly, iron men and women breathing the iron air of that ugly iron town.

But if June was a model of competence in that world, she was a dunce in this one, utterly clueless. It restored much of Corinna's amour-propre to instruct this older woman with kindly tact, to tell her which Indian trader sold the best silks, which soap to use against prickly heat, which solution of potassium permanganate to disinfect salad greens, which tribe produced the best night-watchmen, which country club had the best films and which native night-club the best High-Life, which subjects to avoid when socializing with Africans, what degree of pilfering she must expect from her servants and which were the symptoms she should be alert for – again with the servants – of syphilis, tuberculosis, leprosy and yaws.

To all that June had listened with gratitude but also with a certain unmistakable ribaldry, as if being initiated into the rites of some weirdly comical coven. Once, not long ago, Corinna had felt bound to point out to her that in among the hideous six-foot-tall sunflowers which were her gardener's idea of a herbaceous border, there also grew a flourishing crop of Indian hemp. June had stared down at it, apparently fascinated. 'My God, I never knew it was that easy to grow pot!' And that evening Corinna had seen her and Ian both saunter over to the flowerbed and look down at it, laughing up-roariously. The next morning their gardener had uprooted the stuff, whistling unconcernedly because he would immediately replant elsewhere, and without risk of discovery since Ian and June never inspected the staff compound as Philip did rigorously once a week. Corinna shuddered to think in what squalor their villainous-looking servants lived with their families behind the partition that separated the compound from the front garden – clearly the piccaninnies hadn't even been taught to use the latrine because both she and Philip had seen them peeing into the grass and even the driveway. But June shrugged and said, 'Oh, I know it's Tobacco Road back there, but I really can't bring myself to start poking around in their things,' and Ian said with unexpected liberalism, 'After all, it's their home, poor bastards.'

That was the trouble with people like the Croziers, Corinna had told Philip. In their inexperience, they didn't hesitate to attribute the most unspeakable depravity to the natives (June had asked her worriedly whether it was true that African males regarded intercourse with white baby girls as an infallible cure for venereal disease); on the other hand, when actually dealing with them, they fell back on the woolly assumption that Basic Human Feelings were the touchstone of inter-racial communication. Philip had agreed, he had emphatically agreed, on the fact that the Croziers were letting their nice little place degenerate into a kind of equatorial slum and that their laxity was shocking. Philip understood the dangers of laxity very well; even Corinna's parents admired him for his firm and immediate grasp of the importance of standards. Corinna didn't know how he dealt with the African staff at his office but at home he was masterful almost to a fault with the servants. Funny, really, that he should be such a martinet, she mused, when one remembered (as she had discovered with secret shock in Bristol) that his own mother had been a char-lady in her early days.

But if Philip disapproved of the Croziers, he was also curiously drawn to them. Their arranged meetings were very few; the Croziers invited them to one large and rather drunken cocktail party and they had asked the Croziers to one of their

cheese-and-wines. And, of course, she had to ask June to her
morning coffee parties, where she sat the whole time, neither
sewing nor knitting or even talking much, but just listening
to the others from behind her heavy, mottled, amused-looking
face. 'They're sweet girls but don't you find their conversation a little – well, obstetrical?' she asked Corinna once. So
the vision of cosy little dinner parties together had quickly
faded. But more evenings than not, at sundown, when they
were having drinks on the terrace, Ian would be seen to
wander down to have a look at the creek, and then Philip
would amble down on his side of the little hedge, and before
long June would come along, drink in hand, her flanks perspiring wetly through the heavy drill maternity skirts she wore,
and then Corinna would have no option but to join them.
Often she was there in presence only because the other three
would be talking about England, about telly and taxes and
soccer and strikes, about comprehensive versus grammar
schools, about royalty and rates and the latest gaseous exhal-
ations from Whitehall. Sometimes, as the light drained from
the sky with a sudden dead collapse of day into night and the
densely curled mangrove bush on the other side of the creek
began its nocturnal rustling, she would hear in the murmur
of their voices a companionable nostalgia that made her
desperately uneasy.

June often tried to draw her into the conversation; England
failing as a subject, she might bring up Nairobi, where
Corinna's father had been legal adviser to the government both
before and after the troubles. 'The troubles!' Ian cackled
delightedly once. 'Are you perchance referring to that little
spot of bother when Kenya bid its shy adieu to the British
Empire?' 'Don't be mean, Ian, that would have been well
before her time,' June said practically. 'But didn't you mind
being sent off to school, Corinna?' 'Oh, there was a perfectly
adequate little Catholic school in Nairobi,' Corinna said
eagerly. She felt at home and happy with this topic. 'Then
when we came to Nigeria, my sisters and I had a tutor. But
we also each had a year in Switzerland.' 'Switzerland!' June
sighed. 'What I wouldn't give for some Switzerland right now!
How could you bear to come back to this climate?' 'I didn't

mind,' Corinna said airily. She had hated Switzerland. Then Ian had looked at her with the bemused expression of a man who had just hit on the last vertical of *The Times* crossword. With an odd kindliness he said, 'I shouldn't think that a year isolated on a Swiss alp would have seduced you dangerously towards Europe – no, not at all. Where are your sisters now?' 'Sylvia's married to a Dutch doctor in Ibadan and Chloe's husband is in Accra with Barclay's Bank,' Corinna replied. 'We often take local leave together and we all come to Mummy and Daddy for Christmas.' She shared her mother's pride in the accomplishment of having kept the family together. For once, Ian seemed to understand. 'Remarkable,' he murmured. But her recollections of an African girlhood never held him for long and he would beguile Philip to more talk of 'back home' or, worse still, of business. He was an economist with a special interest in small businesses, cottage industry and the like, he had the theoretician's fanatical zeal for his subject, and a little family enterprise such as the glass-fibre boat-building plant in Bristol seemed to hold an unholy fascination for him. Always after such conversations Philip was flushed and excited and distrait, he would eat his dinner with a far-off look in his eye, and if he talked to Corinna at all it would be in the glottal argot she had heard him use with his relations.

Corinna had again sought her mother, who scoffed, 'Of course, it would be madness for him to expect you to lead that kind of life – a girl that's been gently reared!' Neither of them so much as smiled at the charming anachronism of the phrase. 'But don't bring the subject into the open, Corinna, never, never,' her mother went on. 'You mustn't on any account try to push him into promising he won't go back there. You must make him want to stay here.' 'How?' Corinna cried. 'Little by little,' her mother said mysteriously. 'A woman has to do these things by instinct.'

Corinna mused with some perplexity on her mother's advice – she mused on it now in the unhappy recollection of Philip's growing bad temper. Her reflections were like a soft worrying descant to the languor of her activities that morning. An observer watching her waft about the house, play slowly with her baby, untangle the scarlet and violet silks of her embroidery, would have been struck by a certain progressive somnambulism, a preservation of energy curious in so young a woman. This eerie faltering tempo could have been observed in all the pretty jerry-built bungalows facing the creek as the heat increased. Women listlessly turned the damp pages of magazines, lay supine in tubs of tepid water or half-dozing in darkened bedrooms. The servants, unsupervised, slowed almost to a standstill as if in the entranced palace kitchens of Sleeping Beauty. The heat of the day imposed its own clockless rhythm like sex or childbirth, widening in silent pulses towards noon when the sun whitened the sky and the dazzled gardens were quite empty and the Englishwomen and their African men-servants were equally reduced to gentle stupefaction. But with the return of the husbands for Saturday lunch, there was a frisson of renewed activity, slightly confused, even mildly anxious. The women splashed eau de cologne on their skins and briskly instructed the servants who, with a matching show of industry, chopped and sliced and stirred as if there had been no hiatus at all. There were energetic smiles all round for the weary, often testy masters.

At Corinna's house, her parents arrived first – it was their turn to be guests at the traditional curry meal. Her mother paused on her way through the house and inspected the dining-table. 'Very nice, John,' she complimented the cook-steward and added with a winsome smile, 'But won't Madame allow you a blushing hibiscus for the centrepiece? Surely there's one left on your bush, Corinna?' 'Madame next door's cook borrowed it last night,' John said. Corinna and her mother stared at each other indignantly. It was understood in the neighbourhood that servants could raid each other's bushes for the rare flower so prized as a table decoration, but only on special occasions and only with permission. Corinna's father chuckled dryly. 'You must enlighten Madame next door on the Code Napoleon for hibiscus blossoms.' 'No, but really, Nicky, it is too bad . . .' her mother demurred. 'Fetch me my grandson and a glass of wine,' her father told the cook. The single glass of wine he permitted himself once a day represented his triumph over an all-but-forgotten 'drinking problem'.

On the terrace he sat down slowly in his accustomed chair. He often moved with a suggestion of unspecified pain although his health was good, apart from a malfunction of the sweat glands, so that the heat that he was bound to endure in the small, spare and mercilessly dry carapace of his body seemed to have leached him of all colour. By contrast, Corinna's mother was almost embarrassingly radiant. When surrounded by her three pretty daughters, as she often contrived to be, she conveyed the perfection of a chocolate-box tableau; in fact one Singalese artist with a shaky knowledge of the classics had painted her as Cornelia and her jewels. In the expatriate colony, anxious for talismans of survival, her accomplishments as a hostess, wife and mother were exemplary if not already legendary.

As the small-boy, smelling violently of Lifebuoy soap, served the drinks, Corinna heard the distant thunder of Philip's return. She could imagine him hurling his damp clothes on to the floor and turning the shower on full force. She prayed that his mood would have improved. Her mother always put husbandly bad temper down to the wife's failure to provide a frictionless home environment, an inability to cope. Just recently, when a popular Italian doctor had fractured his wife's jaw with full, if drunken, intent, Corinna's mother had calmly told her friends in the scandalized European community, 'Well, the woman only had herself to blame, didn't she? – she obviously didn't know how to cope.'

But Philip, when he appeared, was in the best of spirits. He shook his father-in-law's hand vigorously and kissed Corinna's mother on both cheeks in the continental manner – 'Danielle, you look lovely!' She dimpled and so did Corinna, who took a funny little pleasure in hearing her husband and mother address each other by first names; it gave her a sense of being childish, cherished, in the company of Olympians. 'It's marvellous to relax!' he sighed as he accepted a drink from the small-boy and sank back into his deck-chair. Corinna felt a responsive wave of happiness; in fact all of them seemed charged with a blissful consciousness that this was the finest hour of the finest day of the week. In the deep shadow of the verandah objects sparkled darkly, picking up sun from the garden – the garden burned with the bare primal heat of mid-day. The sky was flawless blue but the creek drew its heavy humid colour from the coarse grasses at its bank and the dwarf jungle of mangroves on the other side. Nothing moved. The slightest exertion silked the skin with sweat. Admittedly the heat was immense, the heat and humidity together had reached that point where people like the Croziers mewled with anguish and fled to their air-cooled bedrooms. But Corinna, sitting in a drowse of content with her frosted glass held against her cheek, was comfortable with it; to her, heat was a natural fact, an extension of her own corporeal warmth, blood heat, whereas cold, such as she had experienced it in England and Switzer-land, was the absence of heat, a negation, a bitter inimical deprivation. Of course, one had to take care, one had to refrain, for instance, from jumping up with quite unnecessary violence as Philip did now, crying, 'Come on, everyone – let's take the boat up the creek and see if we can find a breeze!'

Corinna's mother gave a tiny sigh and said humorously, 'Oh, Philip, such vigour! When will you learn not to fight the climate? Well, you can go without me – I'm very nicely settled, thank you.' 'And so am I, thank you,' Corinna said, folding her arms with cute obstinacy; but Philip, still with his jolly scout-master smile, reached down, grabbed her wrist and jerked her rather hard to her feet. Corinna hoped her mother hadn't noticed – to cover up she said quickly, 'Oh, look, there's poor June Crozier. Let's ask her along, do let's, darling!' She twined her hands appealingly around his bicep. 'Suit yourself,' Philip shrugged. Unexpectedly, Corinna's father padded quietly after them to the bank where the little outboard motor boat was tied. Her mother was left sitting on the verandah with the baby on her lap and a smile of amusement at their folly.

June was delighted to come. She had never been up the creek, she told them – wasn't there a native village or some-thing around the bend? Ian was working late in town and they were skipping the ghastly curry and she was nearly going out of her mind with the baby nearly two weeks overdue. Corinna did feel a certain sympathy as she watched the two men hand that clumsy, perspiring bulk into the boat, but June had only herself to blame – she had let herself get very fat and she would wear ridiculous things like slacks instead of pretty voile shifts. 'Babies are always late down here,' she reminded June, who replied glumly, 'Like every other damned thing.'

But June fell silent with the rest of them as the little boat got under way and put-putted gently up the middle of the creek past the neat modern bungalows. There was a tiny breeze, Philip had been right. From her seat in the middle of the boat, Corinna gazed up at him where he sat at the tiller, looking quite commanding and very handsome in his starched whites. When he looked like that she could easily recall the emotion verging on adoration which she had first felt for him when they met at a dance at the Ikoyi Club. Of course, she had been barely seventeen then and her father had objected because of her youth and inexperience, but her mother had quickly pointed out that eligible young men were thin on the ground in Lagos and had coaxed him to use his extensive contacts to find Philip a good permanent job. The wedding and reception had been lavish, even by Lagos standards; it was said by people who knew that they could not have carried it off better at the Savoy. She and Philip had honeymooned in Cape Town. They had been wonderfully happy. Even bed, over which she had worried because her mother had made such a point over its importance as a compensatory gratification to men down here, had been quite lovely.

She looked admiringly at Philip's hand on the tiller. What little reading she did was confined largely to gothic romances in which grim jaws, saturnine smiles and shapely masculine hands had a coyly hidden sexual significance. Such romantic literature might also have affected her expectations of his life in England. Of course, she had known that his family didn't live in a wind-blown mansion on a cliff, that his widowed mother's circumstances were modest, but she hadn't known quite how modest. And back in Bristol, Philip himself had seemed different – smaller and somehow diminished in his dull winter clothes. She had been baffled by the colloquial speech of his friends and their rough, down-putting slangy humour. Whenever he had referred to his way of life down in Lagos, they had screamed with laughter – You're quite the great white master down there, are you, Phil? – and he had just

grinned sheepishly. His manner with women was unrecogniz-
ably different from, say, the boulevardier gallantry with which
he addressed her mother – he treated them with a coarse jokey
egalitarianism which they returned in full measure. He changed
even towards her. In Lagos he called her Kitten-Face, my
sweet, my sweet, dainty Cora; but in Bristol, her kitten-face,
pinched with misery as she sat shivering in the icy little back
bedroom assigned to them, seemed to appeal to him less. There
were times when she caught him looking at her with an alarm-
ing combination of anxiety and dislike. Even his love-making
lost the romantically autocratic touch which thrilled her; it
had instead the callow, slap-dash, adolescent quality of his
bantering with the local barmaids. Of course everything would
have quickly returned to normal when they came back to Lagos
had it not been for the colossal bad luck of finding the Croziers
next door, with their insidious jeering and their continual
whines for life 'back home'. Even now, June Crozier was
speculating plaintively as to what people were doing back home
at this very moment, and although Philip said nothing, Corinna
feared greatly that he too was entertaining a memory of the
table laid for high tea with its plastic cloth and archipelago of
sauce bottles, and the men shouting at each other across the
soccer game on the telly.

'We're coming up to the native village,' she told June
sharply over her shoulder as they rounded the bend. There
was a silence and then she heard June say hoarsely, 'Well, I'm
damned!' Corinna turned around in her seat to see what all
the heavy breathing was about. June's face was unattractively
flushed with excitement. 'Just five minutes away from our own
twee little suburb!' she marvelled. So at last she had found
something to be enthusiastic about, Corinna reflected wryly;
how typical that it should be this eczematous native settlement
which had existed since God knew when at the point where
the creek narrowed and disappeared into the bush. The dozen
or so huts, shuffled together from leaves and cardboard and
corrugated iron, sagged precariously towards each other over
a scratchy central path or leaned over the creek on spindly
bamboo stilts. A few scrawny chickens and a vulture pecked
at the droppings of one of the huge, white, bony, starveling

Yoruba cattle. The women, sitting crouched between their haunches, shielded their faces angrily against a possible camera, but the piccaninnies waved, and one of the men washing himself in the murky waters at the bank, straightened up, naked as a jaybird, and grinned at them. June's eyes were bugged right out; perhaps she was one of those women excited by that sort of thing, Corinna thought with distaste. When Philip turned the boat around in a slow circle for the return journey, June cried longingly, 'Oh, please, just a minute more! I never could go along on Ian's trips to the bush because of the baby. I never knew there was anything like this just around the corner from us. It's a different world from ours!'

'Like most of downtown Lagos,' Corinna's father murmured. He seemed vastly amused by her.

'That's just like Calcutta and places – urban slums are all alike,' June said impatiently. 'But this is a real indigenous village – I mean it's the real thing, isn't it?'

'Most of these natives are related to the neighbourhood servants; when it comes to that, they mostly live on what the servants pinch from us,' Philip said shortly. His good mood had suddenly evaporated as it so often did these days. Corinna was glad when he revved up the motor and turned them around the bend again towards the long bright row of bungalows. But even with the native settlement behind them, June went on. Her voice now had the high-pitched irascible clang of Ian's when he was at his most sententious. 'It's the contiguity, don't you see? I mean, there they are, almost on top of us with an authentic community, and here we are with this silly pretence at gracious living . . .' As they passed the low, spacious houses, each with its large square of lawn, each terrace now occupied by people taking their pre-prandial drinks, she encompassed it all with one richly scornful wave and the neighbours flapped their hands amiably in return. '. . . this entire façade, this whole ridiculous Potemkin's village of a street!'

Corinna's father chuckled. 'This blessed plot, this earth, this realm, this England.' He patted June's knee, humouring her, of course, Corinna thought. 'Would you like to see us living in tin shanties?' Philip enquired sullenly. 'We live the way we'd

live back home.' June roared with laughter. 'The way we'd
live if we won the pools, you mean.' The boat eased to a halt;
Corinna was profoundly relieved that they were home. As the
men hauled June out of the boat, she determined not to ask
her back to the house for a drink. Her mother, cool and composed as if at a garden party, drifted towards them. 'Welcome
back to civilization, children. Did you enjoy your little excur-
sion into the bush, Mrs Crozier?' June blinked at her. She
seemed to have lapsed back into her dark astonishment. 'You
know, I've often wondered what it was like down here during
the worst of the Biafra thing,' she said. 'I mean, was it business
as usual with curry chop on Saturday and dances at the club
with people starving to death all over the place?'

'People are still starving to death, Mrs Crozier,' Corinna's
father said with the strange quiet mirth which June seemed to
arouse in him. 'And it's always been business as usual.'

'My dear, you have to accept that Nigerian politics are best
left to the Nigerians,' Corinna's mother sighed. 'Of course,
one was terribly aware . . .'

June came out with a kind of strangled laugh and Corinna
was suddenly furious that they should all be put on the defensive for what the damned Africans did to each other. 'Well,
you have slums and poverty and things in England, don't
you?' she demanded. 'And old people dying of cold. But just
the same, life goes on . . .'

June stared at her. 'But, Corinna, for God's sake, it's a
question of scale – priority. Things happen right under our
noses and we act as though we're living in Wimbledon. Last
week my cook's wife delivered herself of a still-born baby right
there in the servants' compound and I didn't even know. They
didn't even tell me till they needed time off to bury the thing
– they didn't think I'd be interested.'

'Why should you be?' Philip muttered. Corinna and her
mother exchanged an eloquent glance. Newcomers like June
so often disrupted social gatherings with just such melo-
dramatic non-sequiturs, and the rhetoric of outraged social
conscience usually came to a boil with the third gin. June was
not drunk but she was well into her tenth month, and Corinna
could remember the theatrically heightened sensibilities of

attenuated pregnancy. 'You mustn't think it meant all that much to them,' she told her kindly. 'They don't even count a child as living until its first birthday because of infant mortality. Just the same, I imagine it must have been an unpleasant shock to you.' June looked at her wonderingly as if she were speaking in tongues.

Philip straightened up from his business with the boat. His face was flushed and heavy. 'I don't know what the hell you've been going on about,' he told June rudely. 'But I do know that right now, one of your cook's living progeny is urinating all over your flowerbeds.'

They all looked over to the Croziers' garden. A boy of about four was wandering alone on the lawn. He wore a short white vest and nothing else. He held his minuscule sex clutched in his hand. He made his way to the bank of the creek and peed again, looking absorbedly down at himself. June chuckled. 'He does it in driblets like a puppy, doesn't he? Maybe he's establishing his territorial imperative. When you come to think of it, it's his bloody country.'

'And it's your bloody house!' Philip shouted suddenly and very loudly. 'And your bloody garden and our bloody neighbourhood, and we'd appreciate it if you could exert some discipline over your bloody servants before they over-run the place.'

There was an embarrassed silence. Corinna hardly knew where to look. Philip had been very uncivil, he had violated the cardinal rule of good-neighbourliness, but she could understand his irritation and, to make matters worse, June was giggling frivolously. 'Well, Phil, really – it's just a wee black babe, not Genghis Khan and his ravaging hordes.'

'Filthy little bastard,' Philip said. He wasn't shouting now. His voice was normal, almost conversational, its quiet hatred shocking to an extreme. He was still looking at the child, now squatting on the bank. 'The children are vermin,' he said. 'Every day I drive into that sewer of a town and they come scrabbling over to me like rats with their filthy claws out for money. They don't have anything to do with being children. I hate them more than anything else about this place. I used to be like you,' he told June, who was gaping at him open-mouthed. 'When I saw pictures of the Biafrans and tried to imagine what their parents must feel; even when Andrew was born, I tried to imagine what it would be like to watch him die of starvation . . .' Corinna looked at him aghast but her mother said in a rather faint version of her smoothing-things-over voice, 'Well, it's quite natural to feel some empathy, Philip . . .' Philip laughed quite chillingly. 'The hell it is. Oh, I used to have a right old wallow in empathy and what-have-you; when I first came here, there wasn't a leprous beggar in town that didn't get his shilling off me, but now I know they don't have emotions like us, they don't feel like us, they just imitate us like cancer cells, so if they die starved or still-born like your cook's brat, so much the better.'

This time even Corinna's mother had nothing to say. The echo of Philip's bleakly insane declaration sizzled quietly like a fuse towards detonation. Corinna knew what her parents were thinking. Like them, she had sometimes heard similarly bizarre outbursts from people who, as the old hands sympathetically put it, '. . . were not really stable enough for the life down here'; it was a lack of emotional equilibrium to which they also attributed drunkenness, physical violence, sexual misconduct and that peculiarly special aberration known as 'going bush'. Even June, from the depths of her almost criminal ignorance, was looking at Philip with a kind of queasy compassion, and Corinna suddenly discovered that she herself could feel hatred. She felt it for June who had blundered into their restorative repose with her fat, sloppy ways and her big, loud, fat, sloppy moral indignation, who had nagged and stung and provoked Philip to his morbid revelation and who could still presume to feel sympathy. She found herself thinking of June in terms both cruel and profane, she hoped she would go into labour now and stay in it for fifty hideous hours, and she knew, moreover, that only the stirrings of her rabbity Christian conscience kept her from wishing something worse. Then her mother said soothingly, 'Why don't we all go back to the terrace and have something cool to drink?' But Philip was already loping towards the house. June muttered, 'Well, I'll go and tell the cook to remove his bairn.' And then Corinna heard a voice – her own – shriek balefully, 'And you can tell him as well to keep his damned black hands off my blushing hibiscus!'

June stared at her, she stepped back a pace, she appeared to stumble. She turned and wobbled back to her own garden, her shoulders shaking peculiarly. It was a moment or two before they realized that the sounds wafting back to them were peals of mirth. Corinna was humiliated, shocked at herself, even more shocked to see her father smile.

Philip was standing on the verandah. He seemed to be waiting for them; quite unrepentant, even challenging, he appeared to loom in the shadow with something very like menace. It occurred to Corinna that Philip, in the grip of whatever was happening to him, might be capable of a loutish brutality quite removed from the gentlemanly high spirits she had attributed to him before. She was cravenly glad to have her parents on either side of her. 'Oh dear, what a fuss!' Corinna's mother said a little wanly. 'That stupid woman . . .' As they approached the verandah, she added in a low, confidential tone, 'But you must tell Philip to mind his tongue when he's talking about the nationals, Corinna. You know how touchy they are. It doesn't do to antagonize them. People have been sent home for less.'

'Philip wants to go home,' Corinna's father said loudly and cheerfully. They had reached the verandah. 'Isn't that right, Philip? He wants to take Corinna and the baby and go back home to England.' Philip's amazement and Corinna's horror paled in contrast to her mother's reaction. 'This is Corinna's home!' she cried. 'This is the way of life she's been reared to!' In the shrill clamour of her voice, Corinna heard something long forgotten, from back in the days when she and her sisters had been tiny girls and before her father had confined himself to a single glass of wine: the occasional screams and shouts and horrifying thumps that could be heard from her parents' wing of the villa in Nairobi. Her hands twitched helplessly at her sides and she felt tiny tears of terror and bewilderment ooze from her eyes. But her father said calmly, 'Corinna is twenty. I think she might just still be able to make the adjustment.' Corinna's mother swooped down to the play-pen and picked up the half-sleeping baby. 'They won't even be able to afford him a decent education!' 'Our girls didn't get an education at all,' Corinna's father said. The baby yelled and Philip, looking rather bewildered now, made an uncertain gesture towards it. 'Take him, take him!' her mother said with great bitterness. 'Take Corinna away too before you even give yourself a chance to settle down here!'

'And before he breaks her jaw for her like your Italian friend,' Corinna's father said equably.

He sat down. With exhausted and quite ludicrous meekness they all followed his example. Of all of them, Philip now seemed the most self-possessed, perhaps because the interchange had passed largely over his head. He was gazing at Corinna's father as if suddenly confronted with the benign countenance of Jove. 'Actually I have been thinking along those lines, sir.' He dumped the baby casually on Corinna's lap and turned back to her father. 'I wouldn't want to go back home if there wasn't something with a real future to it. But in point of fact, a relative of mine is on to something quite interesting – ' And he drew from his breast pocket the grubby little wad of papers over which she had sometimes seen him deliberate with Ian. He must have been carrying it around with him like a psalter.

As he talked, Corinna looked at him in dull wonder. She felt that she had never seen him before. She felt that she had just been given in marriage all over again, not to the noble novelettish Philip of her courtship or even the uncouth, callow Philip of Bristol, but to an imperfect stranger in the person of this red, drenched-looking, excited young man who was prattling about glass-fibre moulds while her father listened sleepily. She looked at her mother, but her mother was staring silently at some point across the creek. She tried to think about Bristol and her mind veered away like a frightened hare, but she had to dredge something from her tiny store of courage, some hope. Timidly, she said to her mother, 'Actually, London might not be too awful. If Philip could get a job there . . .' She tried to remember what she knew about London, which was very little and mostly derived from dated copies of *Queen* and *Country Life*. 'Maybe we could get a little house, one of those pretty little mews houses and a cottage in the country and a pony for Andrew . . .' Her imagination came gallantly to the rescue. After all, London would be nothing like Bristol, she thought. She briefly conjured up fires sparkling in grates, tea at Rules, the stony smell of snow. But her mother looked at her coldly. 'Don't be an utter fool, Corinna.'

Corinna swallowed with painful dismay. She understood that for some unspecified failure on her part she was being abandoned as totally as her baby would have been had she tossed him into the creek and let him drown for not knowing how to swim, for not being able to cope. Her father too had retreated like some weary old turtle back into his dry impregnable shell. There was only Philip left to make what disposition he would of her, merciful or otherwise. No African virgin sold for a brace of goats could have been more woefully dependent. She dragged her chair closer to him. She tried through her blurred misery to pretend a show of interest in the figures he was writing all over his wretched little pieces of paper. Philip was so engrossed in his role as a captain of industry that at first he didn't even notice her, but then he did glance around and took in her proximity and put his arm around her with a kind of friendly abstraction as he talked; and she realized with desolate gratitude that wherever he went or whenever, he would at least let her come along.

# Certain Standards

꘏

Arthur's shopping list was written on the rough expensive paper his wife used for casual notes. In a hand so dashing as to be almost illegible, it commanded him to buy stracchino, chorizo, quiche lorraine, popadums, pumpernickel, Brie . . . whatever had happened to real food, he thought dourly, remembering those scraps of butcher's paper on which his mother had written 'half pound yellow cheese, ditto marge, pound sprats'. His mother had always specified the exact quantity and had, in fact, suspiciously balanced the greasy little packets on the palm of her hand, testing for true weight. Monica, on the other hand, always left it out as if the measure of such delicacies was predetermined, fixed and immutable like the albedo of stars. He had to make a guess – the Pakistani assistant was waiting, knife poised over the powdery wheel of cheese. 'Half a pound, I suppose,' he said, and remembered just in time to have the man box it.

As he moved on to the delicatessen counter he reflected that he was being unfair to Monica in harking back to his mother's frugality, which was as much the product of a dull imagination as a virtue wrested from necessity. She had been an abominable cook; he remembered the plates of burnt sausages and lumpy mashed potatoes banged resentfully on the table as she eyed the clock to calculate the time lost from Bingo. Whereas Monica took cooking very seriously, her casseroles were mysteriously redolent of saffron and bitter chocolate, and this weekend she was clearly planning to outdo herself in honour of his sister's visit. At breakfast she had told him, 'Well, darling, after more than twenty-five years in America, Em's bound to have got beyond the toad-in-the-hole stage. I don't

want her to think you've married a frump. Do you think we'll
hit it off? Although I do get on well, don't I, with Gavin and
Sheila? To tell you the truth, I'm all in a twitter.'

A mumble from him had been sufficient reply. Monica's
affectation of nerves was as contrived as that arch cosiness
with which she 'got on' with his older brother and sister on
the mercifully few occasions when they met. For ever would
he remember Monica gaily having a 'woman's natter' while
helping Sheila wash up, her pale hands reverently lifting the
soapy Tesco crockery as if it were Spode. Or Monica tripping
down the back stairs of Gavin's council house with cries of
admiration for his twelve-foot-square garden. In the early
days he had tried to joke with her about them, because a
recognition of the fact that Gavin, Sheila and their mates were
vulgar, comic, touching, would also, at least, have had to
allow for the fact that they were real. But Monica had gazed
at him, wounded. What did he mean? she cried, of course
they were real, that's why she adored them! She would not
permit humour to leaven the hard shiny loaf of her patronage.
Mummy, Nanny and Roedean had instilled in her the conviction that the lower orders, like children, must be wooed by
relentless enthusiasm, wide-eyed rapture over their goods and
chattels, their little bits and pieces. And, rather horribly, it
worked. Sheila shyly modelled her new simulated-leather coat
for her, and Gavin went on at length about his herbaceous
border. They responded much more happily to Monica's
whimsical mateyness than to his own strained and awkward
attempts to re-create the family bond.

Still, Em might be something else again, he speculated as
he moved into the vegetable halls to buy endive and small
hairy raspberries priced like rubies. Because Em was now
American – at least, that was what her passport would say –
she was rich, a property-owner, she had married and divorced
a flyer named Orsini. Try as he might to attribute this
glamorous change of condition to the morose heavy-set girl
he remembered, his imagination failed him. Still waters run
deep, they had all said of Em when, after secretarial college
and two years in the City, she had joined one of the earliest

migrations of secretaries whose English accents were coveted
as a status symbol by American businessmen. After two more
years in New York she had married her Air Force captain,
Orsini. The name had evoked to Arthur an image that was as
irresistible as it was absurd; he had seen in his mind's eye one
of those early aviators climbing into their wobbly crates, white
silk scarf streaming in the wind and white smile flashing –
gallant, reckless, doomed. But the wedding photographs had
put paid to that notion. The figure standing next to Em was
no dashing Enrico or even Henry but plain Hank – hair cut
*en brosse*, tall, square-jawed and with that look of smiling but
implacable probity peculiar to military men. When they
divorced some years later Em had taken a settlement in lieu
of alimony, and a quite substantial one as it happened because
Hank, in the surprising way of Americans, had turned out to
be very rich, the scion of a nationwide chain of florists' shops.
Em had bought first one, then several buildings in Palo Alto
and converted them to flatlets for swinging singles. The term,
new to Arthur at the time, had suggested some bizarre new
affliction, a form of sexual vertigo. In fact there was something
altogether vertiginous about Em's success, spiralling dizzyingly
from one venture to another, from her secretary's chair on
Park Avenue to Orsini the flyer-florist, to blocks of flats in
California; something erratic and far-fetched as compared to
his own slow sedate upward climb. Still, she had done well.
   They had both done well, he thought as he left the store
with carrier bags dragging on either arm. Perhaps they had
been at the tag end of the last generation to whom that term
really meant anything. Even when young they had done well;
as opposed to the two older children they had won places at
grammar school, and that was in the days when such a distinction could split a family into two factions as irreconcilable
as the Guelphs and the Ghibelines. He and Em had, perforce,
been thrown together. He had often thought her quite boring
with her eternal washing of hair and ironing of blouses and
shaving of legs, particularly as none of these rituals had miti-
gated to the least degree her heartbreaking plainness. But
there was undeniably a bond between them as they toiled over

Latin and logarithms at the kitchen table. Sometimes, when Gavin and Sheila tore through the room with glottal jeers and their father belched companionably over the racing form and their mother clawed the steel curlers from her hair, their eyes would meet. In Em's gaze, pale and glittering behind her little National Health Service spectacles, he would read his own fanatical resolve.

Brompton Road was glutted with Friday-afternoon traffic but he had allowed for more than enough time to get to Heathrow. What he dreaded was the long ride afterwards to the country cottage. He wished he had not given in to Monica's whim that they entertain Em there rather than at their flat in Westminster. Monica had insisted that, after so many years abroad, his sister would appreciate the quintessential 'Englishness' of the cottage; he had forborne to point out that Em's previous experience of Englishness had been confined to two-up-and-two-down on a back street in Nottingham. As he drove past the luridly ugly terrace houses on Talgarth Road, he wondered whether Em had retained any happy memories at all of her youth. In retrospect he suspected that she had suffered the quiet but intense unhappiness of girls who are poor, bright and very plain. Her wedding pictures had suggested a marginal improvement of the plainness, but even then she had been rather overshadowed by her Action Man bridegroom. He wondered how she had changed. With passionate curiosity and more than a little apprehension, he wondered how she looked now.

'Well, aren't you the cutest thing!' Em exclaimed to Monica in that extraordinary new voice of hers, loud, emphatic and self-assured, steam-rollering the vowels, pushing some syllables into mysterious prominence while others disappeared altogether. As Arthur stood behind them in the tiny hall of the cottage, still sweating from the weight of her suitcases, his sister and his wife touched cheeks, wrists carefully poised on each other's shoulders, strangers to each other, and one of them certainly a complete stranger to him. All the way from the airport he had sneaked covert glances at her – this large handsome woman in whom he could find no traces, *none*, of dour dumpy Our Em. Where were the poor, slinky little strands of hair in that stiff and shining fall of streaked yew, where the astigmatic grey squint in those abnormally large and glossy blue eyes, where the unhappy pout in that dazzling grin, where the wan acne-pitted skin in that dermal wonder of velvety apricot set off to advantage by the bisque-coloured mink coat and chunks of gold jewellery?

He could see that even Monica, with no previous memory of Em, was startled by so much glamour. But she rallied and suggested that they go directly to the guest room; the tour of the house could wait till later. 'Not that there's much to tour,' she said deprecatingly as they toiled one after another up the narrow little staircase. 'It's rather a poky old thing, it used to be a farrier's cottage, but then it's been around for rather a long time. Fifteen eighty-six; wasn't that the date, Arthur?' 'It's just darling!' Em said, stooping to avoid a crossbeam.

The guest room had been converted from the little attic. It was quaintly furnished, charming and extremely cold. Monica hurriedly switched on another bar of the electric heater. 'This will take the chill off. I'd've given you one of the children's rooms but they'll be here tomorrow. Anyway, this has a super view of the downs.'

Em bent down to peer briefly through the dormer window at the darkness beyond. 'I'll bet it's just gorgeous in the day-time. I can't wait to see the kids.' Straightening up again, she appeared to loom in the tiny chamber. She showed no inclination to take off her coat.

In the sitting-room Arthur built up the fire to a towering blaze. Em joined them for drinks wearing a snug cashmere trouser-suit. He eyed her with renewed amazement; had she really been growing breasts like those under her starchy blouses those many years ago? 'We have a reasonably drinkable sherry but I know Arthur's been dying to show off his dry martinis,' Monica offered. 'Shaken or stirred?' Arthur asked Em, holding up the pitcher. In his nervousness he was taking on some of Monica's deplorable archness. 'Oh God, I just empty the ice-maker into a jug and pour on the poison,' Em laughed. 'This is Beefeater's,' Monica said with a gentle cough.

Em had brought down with her a carry-all containing gifts. A handbag and a bottle of Joy for Monica, a Mark Cross attaché case for him, a cloisonné cigarette-box for the house, a portable tape-recorder for their son. For their daughter a small mink shrug dyed the palest of pink. 'Well, my goodness, Em . . .' Monica said falteringly. All at once the small hot room was filled with the subtle bouquet of opulence: cowhide, musk, tame silky fur. 'Yeah, well, I sort of splurged on the kids, especially the girls,' Em said. 'I mean, I got shrugs for Sheila's daughters too. You know how teenagers are . . .'

Arthur hoped his own teenager would rise to the occasion. Sheila's girls certainly would. But Bess, when home from boarding school, donned either an outfit of sapphic severity – narrow jeans, man-tailored shirt and hacking jacket – or costumes of such bizarre slovenliness that she could have been welcomed as a soul-sister by derelicts sleeping rough. He somehow couldn't see those mille-feuille layers of Moroccan ethnic and Victorian rag-bag topped with the pink mink. But Monica was still exclaiming over the fur. 'It's utterly divine! Why, I'd have given my right arm for something like this at Bess's age . . .' Em stretched out her legs, crossed her feet encased in suede bootees, and smiled at Monica. Her glance flickered then to Arthur and he wondered if he read in it – no, surely he was wrong – a certain irony.

They dined British that night – haute cuisine anglaise. It was not altogether a success. Em raved over Monica's jugged hare but ate barely half of it before she sat back and lit a five-inch cigarette. Arthur saw his wife's mouth crimp; that was a damned expensive port lying awash there on Em's plate. She also declined the Queen's Pudding. 'I have to watch the old waistline,' she said. 'Nonsense, you have a lovely figure,' Monica replied with some asperity. 'Only because I hie myself to the fat farm twice a year,' Em chuckled. 'You really look marvellous, Em,' Arthur said for the sixth time. She gave him the full force of her smile and then he realized what above all else was so bewilderingly different about her: what had happened to those teeth, crooked, forward-crowding, overlapped, which had given young Em's face the look of a disconsolate chipmunk? 'You've changed your teeth!' he cried stupidly. Em nodded. 'You'd better believe it. Extractions, crownings, cappings, the works. Three thousand dollars' worth. And this too . . .' To his horror she suddenly tapped her eyeball with her fingernail – there was a dull little click. 'Contact lenses. You remember those God-awful glasses I had to wear when I was a kid? And this . . .' she grazed her knuckles across her creamy cheek. 'I had all the acne scars de-embrazed.' Monica leaned forward, fascinated, her chagrin over the jugged hare quite forgotten. 'Is it true what they say about Californians and plastic surgery?' 'It's true,' Em said laconically. 'Most of the gals I know got more skin tucked in back of their ears than in front of them. And when they make a fast move you hear the silicone slosh like Niagara Falls.' She grinned and patted her large shapely bosom. 'I never went that far, though. A poor thing but mine own.' 'Well, this youth cult business you have over there . . .' Monica began. 'Cult, schmult,' Em said forthrightly. 'It makes sense to put your best face forward. Particularly if you're a working girl.'

Monica giggled and poured herself another glass of wine which she took with her when they returned to the sitting-room for coffee, while Em excused herself to go to the 'john'. Arthur realized that Monica was letting herself get tiddly; a rare lapse and one that he generally enjoyed because when in her cups she became quite endearingly randy. She would even permit herself growly little jokes about his base origins so as to goad him into some demonstration of working-class machismo. Like many women of her own class, Monica assumed the proletariat to be thrillingly over-sexed; like most of them she would walk past enclaves of hooting, lewdly appreciative construction workers with her face set and aloof, but trembling inwardly with quivers of mirthful excitement. But, of course, she was also a child of her generation. The business, to be interesting, needed a fillip of intellectuality. It was not the construction workers she desired, or Mellors the gamekeeper, but Jimmie Porter looking-back-in-anger with Richard Burton's sexy snarl.

He perceived that she was working herself up to one of those vigorous encounters now. After pouring the coffee, she came to sit next to him on the sofa, stretched sensuously and placed a casual hand on his thigh. Em, coming in just then, saw and glanced quickly away with a bright smile at the mantelpiece. Arthur understood that among all her other acquired characteristics was that curious prudishness he had observed in other middle-aged Americans, a kind of naïve and wistful delicacy in sexual matters. Em might look like a Madam and talk like a cow-hand but never in deed or thought would she be even faintly blue.

'Well, here's to absent friends,' she said, lifting the glass of Cointreau he poured for her. 'I figure on hiring a car when I drive up north to see Gavin and Sheila. I don't guess the trains have improved much since I left.' She hesitated. 'I was sort of kicking around one notion. Maybe I could drive them back to London – I mean with their spouses, naturally, and we could all have a night out together . . .'

'What a super idea!' Monica cried merrily.

'Well, I thought you people might know some nice nightspot with a good floor show where we could all swing it a little and have ourselves a ball . . .'

'Talk of the Town?' Monica suggested. Arthur glanced at her sharply. But her face was blandly innocent and her suggestion, of course, perfectly sound under the circumstances.

'I'll see if I can talk them around to it,' Em said. 'It's about time we all had a get-together. I've been trying to make it back here for years but something's always come up – the business mostly.' She gazed down into her tiny glass. 'I felt real bad about not getting over here for the old folk's funeral. But, like I wrote you, I was in the hospital myself just then.'

'Well, dear, there really wouldn't have been much point,' Monica said compassionately to cover Arthur's embarrassed silence. 'I mean, it couldn't be what you might call a proper funeral anyway, what with the wretched plane exploding in mid-air like that. It's such a pity they never even got to Majorca. But at least we can be sure they never knew what happened.'

'Yeah,' Em said glumly, and for just an instant Arthur caught a glimpse of the old Our Em. 'The only exciting thing that ever happened to them and they Goddamn well had to miss it. If you'll pardon my French. You know something, though? I think it was really nice that you people christened your kids after them.' She smiled tenderly at Monica who simpered back, taking full credit for the happy conjunction of finer feelings with the fashionable swing towards honest artisan names.

Next Em offered to show them some photographs of her life in California. The pictures were transparencies but she had also brought a viewer which they passed from hand to hand. They saw her apartment houses which looked like small luxurious Caribbean hotels, and also the real hotels in Vegas, Acapulco and St Kitts, in front of which she posed surrounded by large tanned grinning playmates. They saw her baby-blue Cadillac and tennis court and the huge bland cobalt wink of her swimming pool. Arthur was touched by the ingenuous pleasure with which she showed off her toys but he could sense Monica growing more and more silent. Her hand was no longer on his thigh. She sat between them, shoulders hunched, legs tightly crossed as if disdaining physical contact. When Em showed them the new house she had just built in Palm Springs – a vast redwood atrium – she smiled thinly. 'It must cost a fortune to keep up. How much staff do you have?'

'Oh, just a gardener and a Jap houseboy.' Em shrugged. 'Everything's automated. All Iko has to do is push buttons and make the chow. To tell you the truth, I've forgotten how. You're lucky to have got yourself such a good cook, Artie.' She shook her head admiringly. 'That rabbit tonight – real Cordon Bleu stuff!'

'Well, I'm afraid over here one has to learn,' Monica said waspishly. 'It's impossible even to get proper help any more, let alone afford it. And still you're expected to keep up certain standards. When you entertain, for instance . . .'

Arthur looked at her, astonished. Expected by whom . . . did she mean him? It was she, for God's sake, who had steered him through all the mysterious do's and don't's that ruled their social life: never decant an inferior wine, better no flowers at all than those not fresh.

'Yeah, well, things are more informal back in the States,' Em said comfortably. 'We do a lot of patio entertaining, barbecues, sitting around the pool, stuff like that. I really wish you folks could come over some time with the kids! I mean I could put you up at the shack in Palm Springs or you could have a couple of my apartments – anything.' Her eyes were bright with enthusiasm. 'Imagine little Tommy at Disneyland! Why'n't you think about it for this summer? I'd get a real bang out of showing you off to my friends, they're a real nice bunch. They'd just love you, honey!' she said to Monica, who responded with a cool laugh. 'Oh, dear me, I'm afraid our bank manager would take a very dim view of that project. The four of us flying over and back when we still have the restoration to finish on this place and the mortgage and the overdraft and the children's school fees going up each term! It comes down to the dreary old business of priorities, I'm afraid.'

Em looked embarrassed and Arthur felt an angry humiliation. Among their own friends, of course, it was the in thing ruefully to cry poor. Everyone understood the frame of reference. But Monica should surely understand that the famous priorities meant nothing to Em. She might think that they really were hard up. She had never been initiated into the incalculables of A Decent Education, the acceptability of plonk on-certain-occasions, the subtle distinction between old and shabby and good-quality old and shabby. It was now Em who changed the subject and lightened the atmosphere. She moved on to politics, asking innocent questions which gave Monica the chance to expound her high-Tory principles, her defence of which was couched in terms so orthodox, blinkered and passionately clichéd that Arthur could only sit and listen in helpless silence. But Em nodded soberly to everything she said. She, the capitalist and entrepreneur, was also decidedly right-wing. To his secret amusement the evening ended on a nice little glow of rapport.

He still felt indulgent and good-humoured as he lay in bed watching Monica take her usual precautions against the erosion of a night's sleep. It occurred to him that some time, very long ago, he had probably visualized just such a scene as this: a pretty woman sitting at a pretty rosewood dressing-table, stroking her hair with a silver brush and preparing for bed – his bed. He often indulged pleasurably in such half-recollections, and why not? It was not to his discredit that he should have had the imagination to dream such dreams on that dreary Nottingham back street or that he had had the intelligence and drive to realize them: the wind bellying the sail of his little yacht, his table set glittering for guests, his articulate and self-assured children, his decorative wife. Not very noble goals perhaps, but not utterly contemptible either, and he had worked very hard for them. He wondered what comparable visions Em might once have entertained and whether she found any correspondence to them at all in her own banal and sunny way of life. Had Monica been more discursive by nature and – well – a little more intelligent, he would have enjoyed discussing it with her a bit before making love; as it was he would have to settle for making love.

But Monica was still dithering endlessly. Just now she was inspecting her bottle of Joy. 'Do you think Bess will like her fur?' he asked. 'It was awfully sweet of Em,' Monica said vaguely. He recognized the evasion and sat up in bed, alert and frowning. 'Yes, but will Bess like it?' Monica began delicately to rub cream into her neck. 'Well, darling, it's a lovely gift but it's not really the sort of thing young girls wear, is it?' She meant young girls like Bess, of course, light-years ahead of Sheila's girls with her public school éclat and with-it fashion sense; Bess who was already 'into' Fiorucci and Liberty's, having left Laura Ashley and the King's Road far behind. Monica was smiling when she rose from the dressing-table but the smile was wiped clean from her face when he said harshly, 'Well, see to it, damnit, that she makes a fuss over the thing. I don't want one of those supercilious simpers of hers. You hear?'

That tore it, of course, as far as any love-making was concerned. Monica liked working-class masterfulness well enough, but in one area only, and to that she was now instantly, glacially closed. 'I believe that Bess has been well enough brought up to show a proper degree of appreciation,' she said flatly as she got into bed and turned her back to him. 'Good night, Arthur.'

He woke several hours later to a thump followed by a scraping noise from the attic above them. Monica still slept. Then there was the sound of agitated footsteps. He went upstairs and found Em crouched in front of the little electric heater. 'Oh gosh, Artie, I'm sorry if I woke you,' she said repentantly. 'I was going to switch this thing on higher but I guess I must have tripped over the wire or something. I hope I haven't busted it.'

He set the heater aright and turned it on full. The room was freezing. He saw that Em had spread her mink on the bed. Damn Monica, he thought angrily, with her idiot economies and demonstratively spartan ideas of 'fun' country living. Gavin and Sheila lived more warmly than this, and even their childhood home had been impregnated with a moist humble coal-lit fug. 'I'll go down and make you a hot drink,' he said. 'Oh shoot, Artie, you don't have to do that!' Em protested. 'Listen, you go on back to bed.' 'I often wake up like this,' Arthur lied. 'Me too,' Em confided. 'I don't hold with pills, though. You start with Nembutal, next thing you know you're popping uppers and downers every time you turn around. It's better to stick to booze. Hey . . . you want a snort, Artie? I got some pretty good stuff in my bag.'

It was the last thing he wanted, but she looked at him so appealingly that he nodded. He watched as she rummaged through her suitcase. She was wearing man-tailored white silk pyjamas and in them her body looked looser, fuller, younger. The stuff clung to her big opulent haunches as she bent over, and he was startled and amused to find in himself a mild stirring of sexual interest. His mind knew she was only Our Em but his glands registered a strange foreign woman déshabillée in the middle of the night. She took from her case a long leather bag designed to hold a single bottle, and a matching container with nested, stainless steel cups. He saw that she was trying to control the impolite chattering of her teeth as she poured them each a drink. She sped back to her bed with alacrity. Once under the blankets and the mink coat, she winked at him happily. 'Well, here's mud in your eye, Artie. It's just like old times, isn't it?'

Arthur seated himself on the little gossip stool which quaintly complemented the rustic decor of the room but made no concession at all to middle-aged spread. 'I can't recall that we ever sat around at four in the morning drinking Jack Daniels,' he said dryly. Em giggled. 'More like that God-awful malt thing Ma used to make. But you never had to burn the midnight oil much anyway. I was the one that used to have to sit up all night before those darned exams.'

It was true, he remembered. Many times, coming down to take their turn washing at the kitchen sink, they had found her asleep among her books. 'You worked so hard, Em,' he said. 'I often wondered why you didn't go on to university. You could have had a scholarship, you know.' It was her turn to look at him dryly. 'Not to Oxford, like you, I couldn't have.' She shook her head and laughed wonderingly. 'Oxford – Jeez – it seems like a thousand years ago! No, it wasn't in the cards for me, Artie. I knew the best I'd end up as was some dumpy old-maid schoolteacher. Maybe a grammar school principal – headmistress. You had the brains in the family. And the looks.'

And that was true also. He had got through with relative ease the lessons over which she toiled and plodded. And while she had taken after their mother he had inherited their father's looks, or rather the look of his father before the beer bloat set in: short and bandy-legged, but with a sharp feral handsomeness. He could see the common sense behind her decision. Not all the scholarships in England would have given her the glamour and affluence for which she had longed. But apparently longed-for in secret. During all those childhood years he had never guessed that her goal was more than a modest hitch up the ladder. 'Were you very unhappy back then, Em?' he asked curiously.

Her big, handsome, high-coloured face gazed at him wistfully from above the ruff of pale mink. 'Oh, heck, Artie, you remember what I looked like. I mean the teeth and the glasses and the acne and the flab. I wanted to be pretty and have pretty things. I didn't want to be looked down on all my life.' She laughed suddenly. 'You remember the girls from the snob private school on the other side of town? Sometimes you saw them shopping or horse-back riding or going to the movies – they looked like cream poured out of a silver jug. God, how I used to envy them!'

Arthur was silent for a moment. He too remembered those girls walking in groups through the town in their smart forest-green capes and berets, their skin fresh and their hair sleek, their shoulders slim and level, their thighs strong from clenching the sides of ponies. His emotion towards them had been not envy but simple unaffected lust. 'I didn't exactly want to be like them,' he told Em. 'I just wanted to have one of them for my very own.' Then Em really did laugh. Flashing her beautiful three-thousand-dollar teeth, she rocked back and forth, hugging her mink with uninhibited shrieks of mirth. 'Well, I'll say you really managed it, Artie! You really pulled it off!'

Arthur knew Monica would be ill-pleased to have her famous school put on a par with what he now knew to be a very déclassé little establishment, but he laughed too, although a little reservedly perhaps because Em stopped suddenly and looked at him with great remorse. 'Oh, don't misunderstand me, Artie! I think Monica's a real honey. I mean I can see how nice she keeps this place and I know she's a wonderful wife to you and mother to the kids . . .' Arthur cut short this eulogy to Monica by pouring them each another drink. As he sat down again he drew his robe tightly around him because the frail glow from the heater barely touched the chill of the room. He would have liked to dive in under that mink with Em, not in the spirit of vile incestuous passion but for plain warmth. 'Why didn't you ever marry again, Em?' he asked.

'Oh, well . . .' she shrugged. 'After Hank I was kind of put off the idea. Not that there was anything really wrong with Hank. He was just – sort of – ' she hesitated, grimaced, then dimpled apologetically – 'well, actually, he was sort of dumb, Artie. It used to get on my nerves. He was a good enough pilot, I guess, but most of his spare time he used to spend chewing gum in front of the box. Anyway, after the divorce I found out I had a pretty good head for business and I guess I got used to being independent. There is a guy, though; I mean there has been for the last six years. But he's married with a couple of kids. And he's a Catholic.'

'That's hard luck,' Arthur muttered, and wished for more eloquence, but Em said quickly, 'Yeah, well, you take what you can get. And I get to see quite a lot of Al. And the business keeps me busy and I've got a lot of friends. It's just that as you get up in years you start thinking of family. I'd have liked kids but it's too late for that now. That's another thing . . .' She looked suddenly rather embarrassed. 'I live pretty high on the hog but I can't spend anything near like what I earn. There'll be a fair hunk of cash when I pop off. So as I haven't got any heirs of my own, I'm leaving it to your kids – and Gavin's and Sheila's naturally, even-steven.'

Arthur stared at her. It had never occurred to him . . . or had it not? Because in one tiny corner of his brain something had already made a sly lightning calculation: his two children, Gavin's two, and profligate Sheila's four. Eight in all to share the loot, or was it seven? – because Gavin's eldest was his wife's by a previous marriage, but of course Em wouldn't discriminate – he swept it all away in a wave of self-disgust. By rights he should tell Em to cut Tom and Bess out. He himself would be leaving them no substantial assets, but with the kind of education they were getting they ought to damn well be able to accumulate their own. But the imp in his brain prodded him cunningly. Was it right to deny his own flesh and blood their share of what might be a quite considerable fortune? Just how did Californians define a fair hunk of cash: in terms of ten, hundreds of thousands, perhaps *mill* . . . he shut himself off hastily, but Em must have registered the conflict on his face because she said quickly and humbly, 'Oh gosh, Artie, I didn't mean . . . I guess I'm in pretty lousy taste, huh? Listen, honestly, I'm not trying to be the rich American auntie coming over here to lord it and the poor kids forced to fawn on me – oh God!' There were tears of distress in her eyes. 'I don't want Gavin or Sheila to know – or anyone – but I had to tell somebody on account of we live so far apart. And if I get knocked down by a bus or something out in Palo Alto, one of you ought to know so's to keep an eye on things. You can't always trust these fancy shyster lawyers. So can we just keep it between ourselves? I'd hate to think of it spoiling this visit. I've been looking forward every which way to meeting my nieces and nephews.'

Arthur went to the bed and kissed her firmly. 'And in time

your grand-nieces and grand-nephews I hope,' he said, meaning it.

He stayed for an hour or so longer; they reminisced and sipped whisky. On his way back to his own bedroom he stopped and looked out of the little window on the landing. He saw the dawn of a cold, very early spring day. The ground was scraped with frost and wavering green threads of ice. Tatters of mist from the downs beyond caught on black twigs. There was a small heavy dun-coloured flutter; a hare or moorhen. A bird screeched in the sky's cold young pallor. This was how he liked it best, before it became enamelled with Monica's flowerbeds, these scratchings of black and white and thin glittering greens and the trees just barely beginning to thicken muzzily with grey buds. Leaning his forehead against a diamond of bubbled glass, he wondered: Did Em never miss it? Out there in her eternal honeyed California sunshine with the banal palmettos and blue pools and buildings like wedges of pink and white ice-cream, did she never think back on these chilly English springs, green as young girls and as sour in their reluctant unfolding, cool, thin, shy, dilatory, but sweetly doomed to blossom just the same? No, probably not, and certainly not in those terms, he told himself dryly, recognizing through the bourbon blur of sentimentality the familiar priapic itch. Anyway, how could Em miss what she had never known, because such scraps of wintry spring, such fresh and casual rural views had been no part of their ugly urban childhood.

He slept late into the morning. When he came downstairs, Monica had just returned from the station with the children. There was the meeting with Em: cries of amazement, inspection at arms' length, hugs and kisses to which Bess and Tom submitted with the usual sheepish smiling constraint. Then Em gave them their gifts. Tom was clearly delighted with his tape-recorder; at eleven he could not have dissembled if he tried. Arthur kept a wary eye on Bess but she too looked ecstatic. She stroked the little fur and preened and posed in it. He winced slightly at her affected soprano warble: 'Oh, Arhntie, it's absolewtly soo-pah!' but she seemed sincere enough, and Em was pleased, and he could not forbear from

giving Monica a telling smile. Of course Bess liked it; what
little girl would not respond to its extravagant prettiness, however much indoctrinated with this or that strangulated notion
of 'good taste'? He was quite unprepared when, a little while
later, he went into the pantry to fetch a pre-prandial sherry and
heard his wife and daughter in the kitchen preparing lunch.
Bess's voice was pitched lower now in the hard petulant whine
he was coming to know so well. 'Oh, Mummy, what am I
going to do with the thing – I can't possibly wear it. Nobody
my age wears mink, and pink mink at that! The girls at school
would absolutely howl!' Then Monica soothingly: 'Yes, I
know, darling, but never mind, it was kindly meant. It's a
sweet little evening wrap. When you're older you may find
a use for it at a dance or something.' Then Bess offered the
intelligence that *nobody*, not even Fiona Egerton who was
very flash, would be seen *dead* in a thing like that . . . and
Monica, her voice slightly edged, said, 'Yes, well, darling, we
can pop it into storage for the time being but don't go on
about it now, please, I've already had quite enough palaver . . .'

Arthur stood in the pantry, cream sherry in hand, heart
touched by ice. How had Bess at fifteen so perfectly mastered
the technique of social hypocrisy? When he came into the
kitchen for glasses, Monica was alone, wiping endives at the
sink. They looked at each other. She knew he had heard and
now it was she who wore the telling smile along with a look
of narrow-eyed warning. He had no cause for reproach; she
had primed Bess as he commanded for that show of ingenuous
enthusiasm.

It began to rain during lunch, so the proposed walk
afterwards had to be cancelled. Tom begged for a game of
Monopoly. Monica hastily excused herself and went to take a
nap but Em good-naturedly agreed, as did Bess with an air
of great ennui, so Arthur consented to make up the number
although he detested the game with its inevitable longueurs,
and of course the children would insist on playing to the bitter
end.

It was already growing dark when they finished. Arthur
brought a cup of tea to the bedroom. His mood was much

lighter. During the course of the game it had become obvious that Em and Tom were striking up a boisterous rapport and even Bess, caught up in the excitement of the play, had shed her laconic affectations and become a nice funny child again. They had had a good time.

He sat down on the edge of the bed. Monica was still sleeping, and dreaming it seemed. From the faint flush on her skin and the small kittenish stretching of her body as she turned, he could guess what her subconscious was up to although she never admitted to erotic dreams. By the same token she would never admit to how deeply she was irked by Em's vulgar American affluence which resisted like a big bland stone the drip-drip-drip of her kindly condescension. Still less would she ever be able to acknowledge that she was simply jealous on behalf of what *her* taste might have done with all that lovely loo-lah: the effortlessly chic little dinner parties, the bits of Sheraton, the standing order with Fulbrook and Gould. He decided not to tell her about the bequest to the children, not until Em was safely back in the States, and perhaps not even then. It would be an ironic little joke with which he could amuse himself as he watched her write out the annual Christmas card as she always did to Gavin and Sheila, crossing out the printed names and appending a personal message in the spirit of bright chirpy seasonal noblesse oblige.

She half woke and looked at him sleepily. 'Mm . . . what time? Is it still raining? Who won the game?' Her eyes shut again; her questions had merely parried for another delicious minute or two. 'Em tried to throw it to Tom but in the end she won. She had all the good properties,' Arthur said. 'Yes, I'll just bet she had!' Monica chuckled, and he was caught by that note of unthinking drowsy malice. He had a sudden irrational impulse to hit her lightly across the face. Which, of course, he resisted. She was a silly woman but not a bad one, a devoted wife and mother, a loving custodian of the little treasures his success had brought him, a reliable guide through the maze of social niceties through which the arriviste must otherwise bewilderingly lurch alone. In short, exactly what he had always wanted, planned for, lusted after. And a reasonably good lay to boot, the coarse unrefined Arthur of his childhood reminded him. He smiled and firmly turned her face towards him, cupping her cheek with his hand, a token blow to him, a caress to her. Her eyes opened and stayed open this time, shining invitingly as his hand moved down her neck, her shoulder, slipping free the silk straps, cradling her breast with the hard warm businesslike dispatch she knew and liked so well.

# Romance

He was not likely to be recognized in that part of town and the restaurant before which he was waiting was not of the type frequented by people he knew; only tourists were lured by its Merrie England decor and vulgarly lavish menu. Nevertheless, he felt uncomfortably conspicuous as he waited there for Doreen, a foreigner in his own city among the gusts of Americans and flurries of Japanese. Even the doorman, preposterously costumed in slashed doublet and hose, was Greek. He felt, as he always felt when he was abroad, conspicuously English – which indeed he was; middle-aged and well-dressed, grave and quite portly, a man to whom one would instantly and correctly attribute decency, an embarrassed capacity for heroism, a horror of emotional fuss. He felt, moreover, a faintly ridiculous association, by propinquity, with a young American who was also clearly awaiting someone and who gave him a commiserating grin when he glanced at his watch.

But it was he who had been early. Doreen appeared on the dot of the appointed hour. He watched her come down the street, moving like a hobbled colt on the frightening super-structure of her shoes. She wore a pink leatherette suit very short in the skirt, a relic of her home town where girls still wore the mini. She had been wearing much the same ensemble the first time he met her in – of all places – a temporarily stalled lift. He could still remember the exact sequence and intensity of his reactions at the time: first a bored apprehension that she would become hysterical, then amusement at her quaveringly brave siege mentality, and finally, when they were forced to sit awkwardly jammed together on the floor with the sepulchral shouts of the repair men echoing on all sides, a

quiet astonished appreciation of her prettiness. He had invited
her for a drink afterwards for no better reason than that he
might gaze a little longer at that remarkable combination of
cloudy dark hair and startlingly, incandescently blue eyes.

Something dire had been done to the hair this time – some
ruthless hand had moulded, lacquered and interlaced it with
one of those towering postiches so loved by provincial house-
wives. She held it protectively as she kissed the corner of his
mouth. He smelled hair spray, wine gums and wildly expensive
perfume. She stepped back and awaited his comment. 'Stun-
ning,' he said. 'It is, isn't it?' she agreed delightedly. 'I'm
wearing the scent you gave me. I wanted to look really posh
for you. Am I late? I was waiting on this customer and she
wouldn't let me go till she'd tried on nine pairs of gloves.
I nearly went bonkers.'

He had a sudden flash image of his wife; she too would sit
at the counter, her elbow propped on the supporting cushion,
her hand stiffly upheld like a jonquil, insisting pleasantly but
firmly on faultless stitching and a neat fit at the wrist. He took
Doreen's arm and led her into the restaurant. 'Have you ever
eaten here before?'

'You must be joking!' she giggled. She looked around her,
awed by the Tudor tat. 'It's quite famous, isn't it?' They were
led to a banquette table and handed a yard of parchment
scroll. 'This will cost you a bomb, Charlie,' she whispered.

'I have something to tell you,' he said when they had
ordered. 'Margaret's going away for three weeks. It's a very
last-minute thing. A friend of hers had to drop out of one of
those mid-winter cruises and she's taking her place.'

Doreen looked solemn as she always did when he referred
to his wife, rather as if he had mentioned a passing encounter
with the Queen. 'Where's she going?' she asked. 'Morocco,'
he said. 'Oh . . .' Doreen breathed longingly. 'I'll bet she just
jumped at the chance!' Margaret had, in fact, balked maddeningly at the idea. She didn't really like travelling with Sara,
she had told him; Sara always got so silly after a couple of
drinks – the mind boggled at what might happen in Morocco.
In any case, wasn't there always something a bit louche about
middle-aged women careening around together? Rubbish! he

had assured her robustly; as for Sara's proclivities, that need have nothing to do with her, let Sara sleep with the whole Foreign Legion if she fancied the idea. 'I rather think she'd confine herself to the officers,' Margaret had said dryly. 'Just the same, I'm rather surprised that you'd let me go with her.' He had stared at her astonished. '*Let* you go?' Margaret had seemed suddenly and unaccountably embarrassed. 'Yes, well . . . I will go then.' She had leaned over and kissed him on the mouth. 'You're sweet, Charles.' He had patted her thigh absently. He was already making plans.

'You see, don't you?' he now told Doreen. 'It means we could go away somewhere for a week or so. Some quiet place.'

Her initial look of rapture was quickly replaced by uncertainty. 'I'm not sure I could get the time off from the store.'

'Oh, for God's sake, forget the damned store!' he exclaimed testily. 'You can have your own store. I'll buy you a boutique.'

She looked away from him with meek wounded propriety. 'You know I couldn't let you do that, Charlie. You know I'm not that kind of a girl.'

'Never mind, we'll work out something,' he sighed. He had been forced to concede early on that she was not that kind of a girl. Whatever that sinister classification meant, it precluded any of the conveniences which might have ensued had she become his mistress in status as well as in fact. At first he had cynically speculated that she might be holding out for something more substantial, and to forestall any misunderstanding he had gravely impressed on her the inviolability of his marriage. She had agreed most earnestly. She understood, she assured him, that a person had responsibilities and could still feel tied to a person even after the magic had gone out of a person's marriage. Her conversation abounded in such monumentally silly clichés culled from the agony columns and true-life romances which were her only intellectual sustenance. She could discourse for hours on the Search For Love, a pursuit which seemed to absorb her to the complete exclusion of those rather more austere goals of self-fulfilment and identity which his daughter and her friends stalked relentlessly. Doreen was an anachronism. Her search for the touchstone of romantic love was as pure and uncomplicated and single-minded as the

quest for the Holy Grail, despite the miserable little mis-
adventures which had befallen her along the way. He knew that
she had been unmercifully pawed since an early age, endlessly
pursued by adenoidal whines of 'Come on, Daw-reen, give us
a kiss then?' and that those desperate grabs by randy ado-
lescents had been inflicted on her just at the time when her
own notion of carnal love was faint-heartedly confined to
smarmy Hollywood fade-outs. When he met her, she had
been in that state of befuddled sexual illiteracy inadequately
described as demi-vierge because some lout actually had perpe-
trated a kind of beery half-rape on her. She was, she had
warned him sadly, frigid. He had only just been able to contain
his amusement although there were also times when he had
been sorely tried by her skittishness and quite incredible
ignorance. She would always keep her eyes squeezed desperately shut, trying, he was certain, to visualize twittering leaves
or pounding surf. Confronted with even the mildest innovation
she would giggle doubtfully, 'I've never really done anything
like that before, Charlie . . .' as if he had suggested that she
climb the north face of the Eiger. But she did trust him, just
as she had trusted him in that lift (she told him later) to
prevent by the sheer fact of his presence and authority the
ultimate plummeting catastrophe. When finally, by dint of
patience, skill and a little judicious bullying, he seduced her
successfully, she had been awed as if by some unprecedented
tour de force. His achievement struck her as something fan-
tastical and rare – like the Code of Courtly Love it bridged
the huge anxious gulf between the actual and the ideal. For
himself, the quaintly seigneural role into which he had been
cast gave to his feeling for her a curiously rich medieval
flavour, a chivalrous, totalitarian, possessive zest.

He looked around with a certain distaste at the crowded
room, the barnyard gabble of diners. He intercepted the young
wine steward's appreciative leer at Doreen and chilled it to
quick death. He was bored to distraction with places like these
and the smart little clubs where he dined with his wife and
their friends, of the City and the city with its endless extensions in Las Palmas and Cortina d'Ampezzo and the Midi.

'I woke up this morning thinking about our place in Wales,'

he told Doreen. 'That's where I'd like to take you for a while.'
He smiled at her. 'Say forty or fifty years.'

She had been prattling about her friend Heather – the affairs
of her girl-friends had the intricate inconclusiveness of television serials. But she stopped at once, delightedly ready to
play. The game of Make-Believe was one of her favourites.
'Wouldn't that be super, Charlie? I'd love living some place
like that. What's it like?'

'Not much to speak of,' he shrugged. 'The house is old.
We haven't been there since the children grew up. I imagine
the whole place is rather run down.' He always spoke of it
deprecatingly. Like many men of his type, he was vaguely
embarrassed by the depth of his feeling for his own country
where it was country. It seemed stupidly chauvinistic to make
comparisons as one gazed at the Alps, but the Alps chilled
him with their savage inhuman beauty and he always longed
to get back to the English landscape with its sweet dowdy
villages, its stoneless fields, the astonishment of its entranced
quiet ruins, its blooded, parcelled, stamped, heraldic look of
survival. He knew he was trying to convey something to
Doreen's somewhat limited intelligence when he added, 'I
think I've been happier there than anywhere else in my life.
I once thought of retiring early and moving out there for good
but . . .' But Margaret hated living in the country just as he
hated the idea of joining some boozy gang of expatriates in the
Algarve. 'It's very isolated,' he told Doreen. 'You'd hate it.'

'I wouldn't!' she said indignantly. 'I love the country. I
nearly joined a commune once just because it was out in the
country. I thought it might be some big old house with roses
and things. I thought it might be fun growing your own food
and all. But it wasn't like that,' she concluded sadly. 'All they
were trying to grow was pot.'

'People tend to become disenchanted with the simple life,'
he told her dryly.

'I wouldn't get disenchanted,' Doreen said. 'It'd be just my
cuppa.'

Perhaps so, he mused, perhaps so. She was adaptable,
young, still too young to have any deeply entrenched ideal of
the three-piece suite and accessible Bingo parlour. And money

had a nice way of smoothing over the grosser simplicities. In Wales Doreen, half hippy, half chatelaine, could pad about in bare feet and long draggy skirts and train roses to climb up the wall. He could fish and read. She might want children; they could have a child or two to keep her happy. They could embower themselves in slow cool days, in mild work, in unspoiled children, in fish-rich rivers, in books and ale. Even her youthful silliness, engaging now but potentially wearying, might change and deepen till she became like one of those earth-sweet Lawrence women, rich in the heavy bloom of sensual content, dreamy, quiet, wise. He would awaken every morning to her blue blue gaze. For the first time, the idea struck him as possible. Upsetting in terms of his family and associates, cataclysmic even, but not out of the question. He covered Doreen's hand with his and she looked up, pleased because he was rarely demonstrative in public. 'Shall we think about it some more?' he said.

'About what?' she asked. 'You mean about if we had a place in the country?' She was willing, as always, to take another sojourn to the Never-Never land. She looked about her at the fake plaster beams and plastic tankards. 'Wouldn't it be fun to take an old house and do it up like this? We could travel around and pick up antiques.' Her eyes were bright with the limitless happiness of fantasy. 'We could travel, couldn't we, Charlie?'

He hesitated, sought his footing again. 'Why not? There are places I'd like to show you.'

'I'm scared to death of flying,' she confided in him. 'Heather said I ought to be an airline stewardess but that's why. But wouldn't a cruise be super? Or a *yacht*!' she breathed, in for a penny, in for a pound. 'We'd want a place in London too, wouldn't we?' She frowned. 'Maybe the country house ought to be closer in to London so we could have people for the weekend. I mean when we weren't in Majorca or places. Or skiing. Listen to me . . .' she giggled with endearing self-deprecation. 'Really full of myself, aren't I?'

He had listened. His ageless Lawrence woman glided mournfully away. He looked at Doreen in her latticed hair and little pink suit and realized that precisely what she was not, was ageless. She was a baby, and to keep her he would have to become one of those elderly Flying Dutchmen, one of that legion of young-old men he had seen from Cowes to the Cap with their tanned faces and wattled necks, their elfin grey haircuts, trendy jeans and amusing striped jerseys, their lithe boyish strides and, trailing behind them, their artsy-craftsy child-brides and perhaps even a toddler or two to prove that the yoghurt and wheatgerm and dry martinis could still do their stuff.

She had finished her dessert – he passed his own to her. 'I'll get fat,' she protested, but took it anyway. 'I've been thinking, Charlie. I think I could get a Friday and Saturday off if I switch with one of the other girls. So we could have a whole weekend.'

'Where would you like to go?' he asked her. 'Anywhere at all would be all right. Where would you really like to go?'

She was sitting quite tensely now. Her eyes seemed filled with their wonderful volatile blueness. 'Would Paris be all right?' she asked. 'I couldn't go on the school trip because my mum was down with her asthma.'

'Paris would be all right,' he said.

He left his office early that afternoon and walked through Hyde Park. It was already growing dark, the nursemaids and children melting away. As the late winter afternoon deepened, the night sojourners appeared, single men who loitered under lamp-posts, sad, strangely menacing. On shadowed benches the derelicts settled into the cold dark mulch of their clothes. He felt depressed by the nocturnal poverty that bloomed silently about him. He was glad to break into the heavy sparkle of Knightsbridge, glad that he was to meet Margaret for a drink and dinner and grateful for her brisk, reliable companionship. Margaret would be in a good mood, having spent the day buying cruise clothes. That morning she had demonstrated a suppressed excitement about her trip. He had come upon her trying on beach pyjamas and a long wig, looking quite unlike herself, evoking a curious nineteen-fortyish image of glamour. She had blushed rather touchingly, she had been uncommonly tender towards him at breakfast.

Now he saw her before she saw him, through the arched

smoked-glass windows of the modern little pub on Sloane Street. She sat alone, of course, at a little table right next to the window, and even as he recognized her some detached perception registered the unconscious element of display, the dreaming line of her arm and shoulder, her elegaic middle-aged prettiness, her still, bemused, entranced availability, and he knew that whatever she was waiting for, it was not really for him.

# Gifts

Mrs Prout insisted on accompanying Philippa right into the hair-styling department and at once created one of her ghastly little scenarios. '*May* I leave this young lady in your charge?' she beseeched the manager. 'We're in town just for the day and I'm madly pressed for time. Lady Liddedale particularly hoped Mr Maurice could do the cut.'

Mummy had particularly hoped nothing of the kind, Philippa recalled. She had just said casually, 'Oh, get one of those Crispins or Maurices or whatever to snip off a yard or two.' Now one of the young men approached and the manager told them that Mr Maurice was tied up but Mr Dominic here could take the young lady right away. Prout raised her eyebrows in bewildered hauteur. 'Oh, really? Lady Fiona did say . . . well, I suppose it'll have to do. All right, Philippa? Meanwhile I'll pop around to Bond Street and do some errands. Then we can get your uniform sorted out and have a spiffy lunch.' To Mr Dominic, who was just standing there with his hands groping for his non-existent hips, she added chummily, 'It's been ages since I kitted anyone out for school. But poor Lady Fiona's up to her ears so I volunteered to take Child along with me to town.' She left them with a gay little wave of her podgy fingers and a swirl of her horrible lapin coat, having managed, Philippa reflected, not only to drop Mummy's title three times but also to impress on the proletariat that she was in town for a day of harried skirmishing after life's basic necessities at Fortnum's, Harrods and Asprey's. Whereas in all probability she would be spending the next hour hunched over a cup of tea at the nearest Lyon's.

While her scalp was being kneaded over the shampoo basin,

Philippa stared morosely at the ceiling and brooded over the wasted day. She had been so close to persuading Mummy that she might – at nearly fourteen – come into town on her own. She might even have been able to winkle her best friend, Solange, from the parental purdah that had been imposed on her for failing three exams. Solange's parents approved of her and her own brilliant school record. She had marshalled all her arguments and Mummy had actually hesitated, but then old Prout, who had been taking tea with them, had bulged her bulgy eyes out still further and moaned, 'Oh, would you let her go in alone, Fiona? Would you *dare*? Actually, I've been thinking of going into town myself. I could take her in with me.' And Mummy's face had taken on that creamy look it always assumed when someone volunteered to do a tiresome chore for her. Which was often.

That evening Philippa had overheard her parents talking about it. Her mother said, 'Of course I'll be laying on transport and lunch and so forth. Anyway, it gives poor old Flo a chance to get into London. With that miserable army pension of hers, she can barely manage tea and a cream cake on the High Street.' Then Philippa's father said dryly, 'In that case, I think you might discourage her from bringing you all those pricey little gifts.' 'God's teeth!' Mummy exclaimed, 'I only wish I could. I positively cringe whenever she comes trotting up with yet another pomander ball or what have you. I suppose it's her way of paying me back for the odd tea or bridge party – she doesn't like asking people in to that dim little flat of hers. It's sad really, Rupert – I mean, all those years of sweating it out with her husband in Nigeria and then when they were finally coming home for good, the poor old Colonel had to go and die on the boat . . .' 'Just keep her away from me, that's all,' Philippa's father had warned. 'That genteel *Gemütlichkeit* of hers makes me break into a cold sweat.'

Philippa had crept away and vengefully violated the parental edict on long-distance calls by ringing Solange in Wimbledon. 'Aren't parents gross?' Solange had commiserated. 'You should see the way mine are acting! It's been like that for the whole holiday. And all because of three filthy little exams. Listen, though. You can make the day absolutely miserable for the old bag. If you act absolutely filthy, she won't offer to take you again.'

Philippa had tried. All the way in on the train she had maintained a sullen silence, but old Prout hadn't even noticed. She had just brayed happily on about Lagos and the Colonel and the little giggle she had shared with dear Princess Alexandra on Independence Day. Once she had even squeezed Philippa's arm and cried cosily, 'Aren't we having fun, though?'

Now Mr Dominic was at her with his shears. Afraid that he might try to converse with her, Philippa opened the book that she had brought. She held it awkwardly far down on her lap because experience had taught her that the reading of – not to mention the writing of – poetry, was regarded as a hopelessly wet activity. But he just snipped along in a bored sort of way at the boring fringe that hung damply over her long boring face – Daddy's face down to the last pore except that on Daddy it looked clever and humorous. 'Well, I suppose she was handed Rupert's looks along with his brains,' she had heard Mummy sigh once. Not that Mummy was really pretty either but she had *something*, so that even when lounging about in an old hacking jacket with her hair skinned back in a leather thong, she conveyed that nervy high-style gloss so prized by *Vogue* which had, in fact, recently pictured her: 'Lady Fiona Liddedale seen here with her daughter, the Honourable Philippa . . .' Oh gross, Philippa groaned to herself in recollection, but then Mr Dominic asked, 'Would you just turn this way, please?' and she had to swivel around to a position which brought her directly eye-level with his flies.

She snapped the book up to her scarlet face. There was Yeats serenely, 'You need but lift a pearl-pale hand, And bind up your long hair and sigh . . .' Philippa did sigh. The lines reminded her of Solange. Solange had her hair cut at Vidal Sassoon's. Solange had stayed at the Paris Ritz instead of sawing down every winter to dreary old Kitzbuhl. Solange knew which boutiques were in and which pop stars were out and could discuss with authority the marginal difference in wetness between Marlborough boys and Etonians. That Solange should graciously put up with her own rustic innocence on such matters was still a cause for humble amazement on Philippa's part. She remembered how wretched she had been at boarding school before Solange, when all her childhood friends had seemed to be emigrating to a different climate that was humid, faintly troubling and wildly desirable, a different and mysterious country for which she didn't even have a passport. She had worked that image into a poem on the set theme of adolescence; it had gained her an A plus and one of those covertly interested looks from her English teacher. But that was small consolation. She was used to A pluses and English teachers had been looking at her like that for as long as she could remember. Meanwhile, she had prowled disconsolately around the outer fringes of the ruling clique – of which Solange was the centre – longing to take part in the fascinating comparisons of bust measurements and Laura Ashley dresses – of which she had neither – until that miraculous day when Solange had actually approached her. 'Hello, old Phil,' Solange had said with her amused, sleepy smile. 'Come and talk to me. Come and help me cram for this filthy French test.'

Mr Dominic passed her on to a lesser deity for the blow-drying. When it was done she tipped everyone awkwardly but scrupulously, slipping the coins into their pockets as Mummy always did, except for Mr Dominic whose pockets looked like a rather risky proposition so that she had to give the money to him directly. At the touch of his young male hand she flushed even though she knew, from Solange, that they were all poofs.

Old Prout was already in the ante-room engrossed in a tattered copy of *Queen*. She clapped her hands together when she saw Philippa. 'Ravishing! Absolutely ravishing!'

'Yeah,' Philippa muttered, and hunched herself into her old mac. It struck her that Prout looked curiously hot and excited and was acting even sillier than usual. 'I've been a very busy girl,' she giggled at Philippa, and lifted her bulky shopping bag. 'Now we'll go and buy your uniform.'

Of course, that was sheer death. The school uniform department was crowded, the staff harassed, and old Prout at her absolute worst. She slung herself on the only available chair, cawed superciliously at the saleswoman and struck up a clearly unwanted conversation with another customer, scattering names and titles with wanton abandon. When it came to actually assembling the uniform, she acted as if Philippa were being fitted for inaugural vestments, imperiously waving garments away as being too large or too small – as if it mattered with navy-blue gym knickers and white Aertex blouses. She even insisted that the summer-term dresses be tried on so that Philippa had to stand there for all to see, long bony arms and legs sticking out from her white cotton slip. Her bust didn't fill even the modestly darted bodice of the dress. All that was supposed to change when you got your period but she hadn't even got her period yet. She was probably permanently sterile.

At last the things were collected to be sent and Mrs Prout said cheerily, 'Well, I'm feeling a wee bit peckish. Shall we go and have our chop?'

'I thought we were going to Luigi's?' Philippa said, alarmed. Was she even to be done out of her cannelloni? Prout trilled with laughter. 'Oh, silly me! Chop was the word for food in Nigeria. Lunch chop, tea chop, dinner chop. Italian chop if you like, dear child.'

Luigi's was where she and her mother always lunched when they came to town and such occasions with Mummy could be quite fun. Which was hardly the case now. Prout dithered girlishly over the menu, asking Philippa's advice, asking the bored young waiter. When the order was finally completed, she giggled and said, 'I think I'm going to be awfully naughty and have a teensy aperitif.' To the waiter she added, 'Gin-tonic. Une double, s'il vous plaît.' Philippa looked down at her hands, profoundly embarrassed that even old Prout could descend to that *pas devant les enfants* stuff.

There was also a bottle of wine. Prout seemed to be more interested in that than in her food. She poked at her loin of pork with a certain elegaic amusement, and Philippa sensed that an anecdote was being born. It was some involved account of a dinner party at the Governor-General's residence in Lagos. Like many of Mrs Prout's stories, it had to do with the comical witlessness of the native servants. 'Mind you, my own staff was always very reliable,' she concluded. 'We had five, you know – cook, small-boy, chauffeur, gardener and watch-night. And, of course, a nanny before Oliver was sent home to school.' She stopped suddenly. Philippa remembered that the only child, Oliver, had been killed in some freaky accident at boarding school. She put her fork down reluctantly. It seemed somehow uncouth to go on chomping at the cannelloni.

With the dessert and Cointreau, Mrs Prout went off on another tack. She seemed suddenly overcome by plaintive affection for the little restaurant. 'Isn't it grand to have a little treat like this once in a while? I hope you appreciate it, Philippa. I mean, this way of life – the little touches that make life worth living. Enjoy it while you can. Gather ye rosebuds while you may.' She swigged down the rest of her liqueur and leaned back with one arm slung over the back of her chair. The mouldy little skein of furs she wore around her neck slipped rakishly askew. Her voice took on a dark prophetic timbre. 'Within a generation it will all have greyed to nothing-ness. Beauty, breeding, quality of life all taxed, socialized, equalized out of existence.' Her all-encompassing wave at the room suggested that the tumbrils were already at the door. There was an audible snort of laughter from the next table. They probably thought that Prout was her grandmother, for God's sake, Philippa thought wretchedly. She glanced at her watch. 'I think maybe the waiters want to close up,' she said. 'Yes, yes,' Prout agreed sombrely. 'They want to close.'

When they were on the street Prout told her they had to make one more stop before catching the train home. She had to buy a little giftie for Mummy for giving them this lovely lovely treat.

Philippa trudged dispiritedly after her up and down the aisles of the gourmet food store. The musty aromatic odours of herbs, potpourri, grains, teas, sat badly on the rich meal she had just eaten. But Mrs Prout, her equanimity mysteriously restored, wanted to take her time. She inspected the items closely, holding her spectacles up to her eye, and chirruped enthusiastically, 'Colonel Skinner's Chutney! I haven't seen that in years. And those heavenly little pickled mussels. And brandied chestnuts! Now, that might be something for your mother! Go find out what those things on the epicure shelf

are, Philippa.' Philippa moved down the aisle and gazed
revolted at the jars of Braised Baby Bees. She turned to rejoin
Prout and then stopped stock still. She gaped idiotically as she
saw the jar of chestnuts disappearing into the shopping bag,
slipping into it so deftly, so almost demurely, that she could
hardly believe it had happened at all. The pores of her body
prickled with damp heat. She forced herself to look back
rigidly at the bees. 'Shall we go?' Prout called to her gaily.

The aisles leading to the door were crowded. Prout made
her way without haste, even pausing to inspect a basket of
mangoes. She's done this before, Philippa thought, stupefied.
She was horribly aware of the photo-scan camera's round eye
snaking from side to side searchingly. She had heard that they
couldn't do anything until you actually left the shop. She
could visualize it all; the hand dropped on Prout's shoulder,
the forced march back through the store past the staring
customers, the scene in the manager's office, the constable, the
ride to the police station, the telephone call to Daddy. And,
of course, the search through that knobbly shopping bag which
would reveal God knew what else. Perhaps they would think
she was in on it too as some sort of a decoy, even a partner.
'Peer's Daughter Held For Questioning.'

Prout opened the door and they were on the street. The
sharp sunny wind blew in their faces. Philippa shut her eyes.

'Well, come along, child, the taxi's waiting!' Prout called
to her impatiently.

Philippa huddled in her corner of the cab. Her common
sense told her that the danger was past but it was not until
they were actually sitting in the train that she relaxed. She
stole a glance at Mrs Prout who was quiet for a change. Her
face had an exhausted but curiously peaceful look.

Of course, it was an illness, Philippa told herself uneasily.
Like poor fat Dierdre Winstanley rifling people's lockers at
school and being nastily blackmailed for it by Emma Poole.
She supposed that in a way she herself now had Prout in her
power. It was an exotic and troubling thought. The word was
not in common usage either at home or at school except in its
remote political application. People preferred to talk solemnly
about responsibility. Only poets seemed fully at ease with it.

Look at Yeats with Leda and the Swan: 'Did she put on his knowledge with his power?' Yeats didn't waffle on about responsibility which, in any case, wouldn't have scanned. She wondered when Prout had first started pinching things and whether she only pinched things to give to other people and, if so, whether that made it less bad. As a moral problem it had a certain correspondence to the little understanding whereby she wrote Solange's poems and essays for her – not that it was always easy to make the metre trip or flatten the good lines so as not to give the game away. Was Solange stealing what was freely given or was she, Philippa, stealing from herself so as to give? Scowling deeply into her book, she was startled to hear Prout say, 'My goodness, how much you look like your father sometimes, Philippa! Are you reading? Is it verse? Your mother says you write it sometimes. It's a charming hobby, isn't it? I suppose it passes the time.'

Philippa squeezed her Yeats angrily between her hands. She entertained an image of Prout passing the time in Holloway.

'I'm told you have quite a nice little gift,' Prout went on archly. 'Speaking of gifts, have you seen my little goodie for your mother? Do you think she'll like them?' There, held up for inspection, was the purloined jar of chestnuts. It was, in fact, the sort of delicacy that her mother did enjoy. Philippa could imagine her spearing them out with a little silver fork, nibbling with dainty greed, saying, 'Well, it is quite touching of the poor old thing, Rupert.' With much the same amusement as she would say, 'Yes, Phil does have quite a nice little gift for verse.' She felt a sudden black irrational rage. 'She wishes you wouldn't,' she blurted out.

At once she regretted it, but it was too late. Prout made big incredulous eyes at her. 'I beg your pardon?'

'I mean I think she's afraid you can't afford all these presents,' Philippa blundered on. Worse and worse. An ugly colour crept over Prout's jowls. She looked as if she had been firmly slapped. 'Well, Philippa,' she said finally, 'I think I must be allowed to be the best judge of that. I'm sure Mummy would agree. It's true, Heaven knows, that the socialists leave one little enough after a lifetime of service and sacrifice, but one still tries to make the little gesture now and again. I know you're considered to be a very clever little girl but if you don't mind my saying so, I think Mummy would be rather surprised at your want of tact.'

Philippa stared down at her little bitten nails. It was not the first time she had felt the crushing weight of her own inexperience. Then she heard Prout again, frostily intimidating, the way adults always were when they wanted to give the screw one more turn. 'Need we mention it any more, Philippa?'

'For God's sake let's not mention any of it!' Philippa exclaimed wretchedly. 'I mean I won't mention any of it either.'

'What?' Prout asked. For an instant they looked at each other in perfect and terrible understanding. 'Nothing – nothing!' Philippa stammered. Then Prout exhaled – a long, thready, unhealthy wheeze. She pulled at the skein of little dead animals around her neck. She's having a heart attack! Philippa thought, panic-stricken. She shot to her feet and wrestled the window open. But all that happened then was that Prout patted her podgy bosom and said in a voice that was frail but otherwise normal, 'Why, thank you, Philippa. It was very close in here. You're a very clever girl. A very clever, gifted, kind girl. I'm sure you'll write very wonderful novels. Writers have to understand people, you know. They have to have compassion and understanding.'

Philippa nodded abjectly. She would agree to anything in order to reassure Prout, even to writing wonderful novels full of compassion and understanding. But at least the crisis seemed to be over. Prout was subsiding in a restless sort of way; she patted and fussed with her dim little furs, she darted nervous smiles out of the window, she couldn't seem to keep still. Philippa was reminded of something she had seen once on an oil-slicked beach – a sad greasy small bird hopelessly shaking and preening itself. Her eyes narrowed; yes, that was exactly right for Prout. Her mind seemed to shunt itself suddenly to a plane of absorbed but dispassionate detachment. Hesitantly her ear sought a metre to fit the words before they locked into each other, intuitively she warned herself to keep it loose till she got home, briefly – but with a certain strange recognition – she experienced a cold shocking excitement.

'Well, we seem to be here,' Prout said dispiritedly.

Mummy met them at the station. Prout declined her invitation to tea and she didn't offer the stolen jar of chestnuts. She seemed anxious to get away. Afterwards, in the car, Mummy asked curiously, 'Did anything happen, Phil? You both look rather drained. You didn't quarrel with poor old Flo, did you?'

'Nothing happened,' Philippa said. She glanced at her mother's thin, handsome profile. Of course, she wouldn't tell her about old Prout. As to the other, the thing that had happened when she conceived her poem about the bird-Prout, that premonition of brilliant possibility, that moment of spectacular happiness; it had come somehow with its own pre-packed warning: I never last long. I am not to be talked about.

'How was the uniform-buying bit?' Mummy asked.

'Gross,' Philippa replied.

'God's teeth!' Mummy exclaimed. 'I sometimes think you children have no feeling for language at all.'

# Wifey

Ella, riffling through the morning post, stopped short with a hoarse yell of amusement. 'I'll be Goddamned!' she said. 'You got another letter from Wifey.'

'Throw it away,' Julian said.

'No, that's your privilege, honeybun,' she sniggered. She tossed it across the breakfast table. One edge caught in the butter dish. He looked down without touching it. It was the same as ever: the cheap pale-pink envelope, the round banal handwriting, the i's dotted and t's crossed with the laborious tongue-sticking-out-of-the-corner diligence of near-illiteracy.

'Was there anything else?' he asked casually. Ella always made him ask.

'Just bills. I don't guess you want to look at those, do you? Nothing from Felix if that's what you mean.' She shrugged. 'What the hell did you expect? He nearly broke his ass trying to get you to go on that tour. It would have meant four months' work. But no. What isn't good enough for Lord Larry or Sir Ralph isn't good enough for you.'

He buttered a piece of toast very carefully. 'I couldn't by-pass the chance of that part in the Beeb serial.'

'The serial, the serial,' she jeered. 'They needed a guy thirty years old for the serial. I told you you were wasting your time. After all these years you still don't recognize a brush-off when it hits you in the face. The tour would've been a sure thing. It might even have been kind of fun, not to mention helping to pay these.' She fanned the bills out for him. Studiously dropping his gaze he found himself staring at the pink envelope and felt bile come to his throat. His revulsion was aroused partly by the predictable contents of the letter

and partly by Ella's idea of fun: the cheap seaside rooming-
houses, the boozy late-night parties, the arrogance of the 'star'
secure in his tenure of next season's third-rate television sit-
com, the lachrymose reminiscences and pathetic pluckiness
of the supporting cast, the buffoonish script milking every
prattfall for laughs, steam-rollering every *double entendre* so
that nothing might escape the audience, and the audience –
never to forget the audience – with its huge collective face
chomping on Toffos and rewarding them for their efforts with
gusts of hot obedient chocolate-scented laughter. He looked
up again and caught Ella's gaze glittering at him derisively.
Of course Ella too had known better things, but she had her
American toughness, she had the survivor's incalculable ability
to adapt.

'Aren't you going to read your wifey's letter?' she asked.
'It might be good for a laugh and God knows we haven't had
too many of those lately.' Mercifully, the doorbell rang.
'Maybe it's a telegram from Bertolucci I-think-not,' she said.
'Actually it's the milkman so I got to go take some money from
your pants.'

He looked after her as she left the room. It gave him some
bitter comfort to reflect that she had not aged well. Her
ingénue freshness, her cute stubby girl-next-door's face had
softened to dough, mean little folds and pouches, pinch-lines
of greed and petulance around the plump mouth and freckled
retroussé nose. Her figure was still passable, at least in the
dated styles she still wore to enhance it: clinging sweaters to
show off the bosom hoisted to perky points, skin-tight stretch
trousers to encapsulate the hips. But it was precisely that: the
illusion of youth encapsulated, not real youth as one saw it
in young girls on the street, their thighs fluent in jeans, the
soft wobble of their unconfined breasts under thin shirts.

There was still the pink envelope. He could have thrown it
away but a morbid curiosity stopped him . . . that she should
still care enough to write in the face of his relentless silence,
after the years and years of his contemptuous indifference!
He slit the envelope open. He held the notepaper to his nose
because there were actually times when she daubed it with
cloying Woolworth's scent. And once or twice, in the early

days, with tears. It began as usual. 'My dearest darling Hubby
– I guess you have been wondering why you have not heard
from me so long. But I have been troubled something awful
with my lumbago what with the weather so bad. But I think
about you every day and every night when I go to bed and
your picture is next to me and in my heart. I want to tell you
about Julian Jr. He looks more and more like you every day
and this is the exciting thing which is he is soon getting
married! Heather is a lovely girl and I know you would love
her as I do. She works at the same garage where he is at.
There was one of your pictures on the telly last week. It was
All Banners Down and I nearly missed it because they did not
write in the papers it was going to be on the telly and I nearly
went to Bingo!'

There was more, but just then Ella returned. He hastily
let the letter fall but she saw and snickered. 'Having a nice
ego-trip? She still loves you, huh? So how come she hasn't
written in such a long time?'

'She's been ill,' Julian said.

'Aw, gee, that's too bad,' Ella grinned. 'What's the latest
on Julian Junior?'

'He's getting married,' Julian said unwillingly. But to ignore
her ridicule was to invite her sudden savage wrath. Ella
shrieked, she rocked back and forth with laughter. 'No kid-
ding! Hey, that means pretty soon you'll be a grandpa!
Maybe we ought to go to the wedding. After all, he's the only
kid you can call your own. You think she'd mind having me
there? I mean all along she's sort of made out like I never
happened. So what else is new?'

'Nothing, just the usual rubbish,' Julian mumbled. 'She
saw *Banners* on the box.'

Ella snapped her fingers. 'Hey, I remember that one! They
lapped it up out in the sticks. They sure used to go for that
veddy veddy British accent of yours. You remember your big
scene with Ariadne?' She stiffened to a pose of militant rectitude. 'My dulling, I have a battle of my own to fight. I cahrn't
ignore my feelings for you any longer . . . Or words to that
effect.'

Julian looked away, embarrassed that even at parody she

should be so inept. But then even at the long-ago time when he had helped test her for Metro it had been painfully clear that she couldn't act her way out of a paper bag. Not that it mattered because she had dropped her career as soon as he took her up. 'It was an imbecilic script,' he muttered.

'It was box-office,' Ella snapped. 'Or it might have been if you hadn't bitched things up by fighting with Hymie all the time.' She shook her head wonderingly. 'Jesus, what a prima donna you were then! And all on the strength of one lousy season with the Old Vic and a couple of two-bit films with Ealing. You know, of all the guys they brought over from England about that time, you were the biggest shit, Julie. All poor Hymie was trying to do was put together a moom pichure and make a fast buck, but you, you had to screw it all up with artistic significance!'

Julian said nothing; there was nothing to say. As usual she had got it all wrong. By the time *Banners* was filmed he had given up all aspirations to significance of any kind, let alone artistic. His battle with the director had been one of grim survival to ensure that the camera was at least occasionally on his own face rather than Ariadne's marzipan profile and heaving cleavage. Because although Ella didn't seem to realize it, his career had already been on the wane. Now she squinted at him thoughtfully. 'Come to think of it, that was about the time you got involved with all that fancy-pants theatah. Desire Under the Whatsis at the Pasadena Playhouse. Yeah, now I remember: O'Neill and O'Casey and O-kiss-my-ass, not to mention that egg you laid off-Broadway.'

'All right,' he said wearily. 'Could we just forget it now?'

'Sure,' Ella said. 'Why not? Everybody else has.' There was a pinched, curiously livid look to her face but he could see she was trying to control herself. She feared her temper as much as he but for a different reason – her heart was bad. She gestured towards the letter. 'Did she send any pictures of Our Julian this time? I really get a honk out of those pictures. You know it's funny she never sends one of herself.'

'I know well enough what she looks like,' Julian said ironically.

'Not money either,' Ella mused. 'I mean she's never asked

you for money. Which is just as well on account of we ain't got none.' Her voice changed then, became unctuous and conciliatory. 'Listen, Julie, whyn't you just give Felix a call anyway? Just to remind him you're around. I mean that's what agents are for. I'll bet he could find something for you even if it was just a commercial on the tube. You're still a real cute-looking guy, sugar.'

He sat perfectly still around the sclerotic core of his own loathing. More than any of her other moods, the sullen, the sarcastic, the drunkenly abusive, he hated this recourse to wheedling obsequiousness; and when there was something she wanted badly enough she was not above taking a dive into her old bag of tricks, her starlet's repertoire of cute wriggles, giggles, twitches, crinkled nose and big rounded eyes, so that on her puffy face he must see that horrible charade of teasing teenage sexuality. 'I'll call him,' he said. 'You do that, honey-lamb,' Ella said. 'I'll leave you alone.' With a grotesque affectation of delicacy, she tip-toed out of the room.

He twiddled the pink letter between his fingers and then remembered that he hadn't finished it. There was not much more. 'Well, my Dearest Darling Husband, I do not have anything else to write. Julian Jr. and me are fine and I hope you are likewise. Nothing can ever change my love for you and no other man has ever owned my body. With all my kisses and loving heart, your loving Wifey. I will write again soon.'

And so she would, Julian thought. Until death, his own or hers, he would never be rid of her, and it was the same with Ella. It was as if the three of them were all that remained of his life. All the others, the glittering hundreds of others, had fallen away, leaving the three of them locked together and spinning alone in some ghastly desolate outpost of the universe.

Not bad that, he thought and was fractionally cheered. Perhaps he should have tried writing his own words instead of braying the clichés of others. Look at Coward, Ustinov, Emlyn Williams. And perhaps a call to Felix wouldn't be entirely wasted. He was not, as Ella had put it in her revolting Americanism, a 'real cute guy', but neither was he a pig. He had not let himself run to fat; on the contrary, he was almost cadaverously thin and very tall. Surely some use could still be made of that distinguished stoop, the eyebrow sardonically quirked, the clipped authoritarian diction. Other actors had risen phoenix-like from the sour ashes of Hollywood. It would only take one decent piece of luck – a long-running series, for instance – and he could buy Ella off with a settlement and move out of this hole. He looked around him with distaste. This was the only decently proportioned room in their dingy Bayswater flat and Ella had ruined it entirely with her pretensions to flatulent Hollywood grandiosity. The bay window was choked with a white boudoir piano, there only to hold the framed photographs; there were huge soiled white plastic divans, Bakelite slabs for coffee tables, a dining-suite of imitation Chinese Chippendale, a large bar made of bamboo and bubbly green glass. He dialled the agency.

Gratifyingly the receptionist knew his name and promised to put him through promptly to Felix. He waited to hear that gravelly reassuring voice with its mere hint of continental accent. Years ago, when the parts had flowed in and the money with them, he had sometimes resented Felix's commission; he had even referred to him spitefully as 'that bloody yid'. But in later years some of the money had trickled back in the form of loans generously given and rarely repaid, and with always the same grave, urbane, unfailing cordiality which he now heard again. He decided to come straight to the point, it was more dignified. Decently, Felix didn't hedge. 'I'm keeping my eyes open for you, Julian, but I'm afraid there simply isn't anything at the moment.'

'I thought maybe a series . . .'

Felix sighed. 'These are parlous times. I can't hold out any false promises. It's a pity you couldn't see your way to taking on that tour.'

He felt a spasm of anger but tried to keep his tone light. 'I just couldn't face it, Felix. Not that abysmal script and especially not those abysmal yobs out front.' There was a silence then, during which he suddenly remembered his one and only serious quarrel with Felix during their long years of association. 'Why do you always hold the audience in such contempt, Julian?' Felix had asked levelly. 'They're just people, you know. Maybe if you were a little more of a mensch

you'd also be a little bit more of an actor.' Jewish sentimentality, he thought. But now Felix's voice came through briskly,
not at all sentimentally. 'Well, that's your prerogative, of
course. Just believe, please, that I'll do my best. How's Ella?'

'Ella's fine,' Julian said. 'Look, Felix, it doesn't have to be
a series. Obviously I'll settle for a one-spot if the script's halfway decent . . .' He winced at the begging note in his own
voice.

'I'll do my best for you,' Felix repeated patiently. 'I won't
let them forget you're around.'

Julian forced a laugh. 'Oh, I'm not wholly forgotten. I got
a letter from Wifey today. You remember my wifey?'

'*Donnervetter!*' Felix exclaimed. 'Did you really? No, who
could ever forget your wifey?' There was a pause and then
he said thoughtfully, 'Look, Julian, a thought just struck.
Perhaps I could interest one of the Sunday tabloids in inter-
viewing her. It would put you back in the public eye . . .'

'No,' Julian said.

'I admit the idea lacks delicacy,' Felix said dryly. 'But with
respect, I think just now you could use any publicity you can
get. It wouldn't hurt her – we could vet the copy to make sure
it didn't embarrass her. I think she might even enjoy it after
so many years of obscurity. How many years anyway – it must
be more than twenty-five. It's quite phenomenal . . .'

Embarrass *her*! Julian thought, outraged. 'No,' he repeated
coldly. 'It's out of the question. Sorry.'

'Well, you must suit yourself,' Felix said without rancour.
'I'll be in touch.'

His hands were sweating as he put down the phone. The
once-famous faces on the piano looked at him in bland
reproach. It would put him back in the public eye, Felix had
said. Certainly it would – in the instant between a bite of egg
and a sip of coffee; the sheer freakishness of it would hold the
attention that long, perhaps even long enough to flap the paper
in someone else's face and exclaim, 'You remember this fellow?
He used to be in films. Well, it seems there's this woman in
Wolverhampton . . .' And there would be a picture of the
council flat which she had described to him so painstakingly,
its walls covered from ceiling to floor with his own face in

stills, snaps, posters and glossy studio hand-outs, his likeness sketched, cartooned, silhouetted, embroidered and even picked out on a typewriter. They would show the piles of bulging scrapbooks, movie magazines, fan-club circulars, letters supposedly signed by him, a handkerchief purportedly owned by him, his head modelled in Plasticine, a record of his voice. Perhaps they would photograph the flat's most insignificant occupant: the poor bewildered working-class clod who was her real husband and who had patiently humoured her obsession for nearly thirty years. And then, of course, Julian Jr whom Julian assumed to be the only child – she had mentioned no others – whose wan acne-spotted visage was already known to him from the snapshots she regularly sent. He had sometimes wondered whether even in the pangs of childbirth she had sustained her lunatic delusion that he, not the clod, was Julian Jr's father. ('You can bet she sustained it when they were making him!' Ella had said coarsely.) And most centrally, inescapably, there would be a picture of her whose face he had never seen and didn't need to because it was the collective face of the popular audience from Blackpool to Peoria, that pale broad fatuous greasy-about-the-lips face with its perpetual look of inane adenoidal gullibility.

Behind that face, though, she had changed over the years. The letters had begun to arrive with the release of his first Ealing film. She could hardly have been more than a girl then. To begin with they had been very long and almost illegible, written with the glottal passion of youth; but even then the hunger, the endearments had been couched in euphemisms so atrociously genteel as to be worse than outright obscenity. Later, of course, they had been engulfed in the hundreds and thousands of letters passing through the hands of his secretaries and press agent, but there was something about their persistence, frequency and bizarre content that made them surface again and 'Wifey' had become a byword in his circle of friends, the fan to end all fans. But with the birth of Julian Jr she had settled down somewhat, and as the years went on her letters had become positively sedate. Yes, they had settled down together, Julian thought with mordant humour; he and Wifey had aged and mellowed to autumnal serenity, intimate reminiscences and cosy domestic gossip.

But now his real and only wifey stuck her head in the door with a look of arch expectancy. 'He said he'd call if anything turned up,' Julian said.

Ella's face sagged. 'Yeah, well, that's that, I guess,' she said tonelessly. She brought in a tray and started to clear the table, clashing the plates together. 'Whaddya want me to do with this thing?' she asked, holding up Wifey's letter. The jeering note was back in her voice. 'Maybe you should keep it. Let's face it – you don't get all that much fan mail these days.'

He made a bored dismissive gesture. But she was right, he thought. Wifey had been the first and she would undoubtedly be the last. What would happen if her letters suddenly and inexplicably stopped? Nothing, of course – he would merely be relieved of a joke gone very stale. Nevertheless he felt a strange uneasy chill as he watched Ella tear it across, toss it on to the slops of toast crusts, smeared jam, spills of milk, and march off to relegate to the Tidybin those meek pink scraps of mad, vulgar, hopeless, helpless, indestructible devotion.

# The Apparition

Rupert, being only fourteen and still subject to fits of coarse schoolboy humour, instantly nicknamed Mr Hinde 'The Monster'. His sister Clara, with a two-year advantage as to the niceties of language, alluded to him as 'The Apparition'. This was, in fact, a neater description of their first encounter with him; he was more of a happening than a person. They had just come home from their respective boarding schools and their mother told them, 'There's a Mr Hinde here giving me some financial advice.' They came into her small, pretty, countrified sitting-room and there he was. The fine china tea-cup clattered dangerously as he rose to greet them. He rose and rose, he loomed at them in the half dusk and both children suppressed a startled giggle. Mummy *might* have warned them, they agreed later. He smiled at them, and that crepuscular hinging of the jaws into a grimace that was clearly meant to be friendly and conciliatory merely made matters worse. They were relieved when he sat down again – seated, he seemed less grotesquely out of scale.

He did not stay long. He left while they were still unpacking and for the moment they thought no more about him. But that evening, while enjoying the holiday indulgence of television, they happened to watch one of the old Baron Frankenstein films and there, strapped down beneath the writhing bolts of electricity, was the poor monster with its unnaturally high overhanging brow naked but for the village-idiot wisps of hair, its glued baffled eyes, its gigantesque ungainly hulk, and Clara sat up and poked Rupert and asked slyly, 'Who does that remind you of?' Rupert shrieked with delighted recognition. They looked at their mother; surely she would see the

humour of it, she was not above occasional mild malice. But
her lips tightened and she looked away from them. They were
astonished to realize that she was somehow offended. In a low
voice she informed them that Mr Hinde was a very kind man,
he had been exceptionally kind in giving her all manner of
good advice on investments and taxes and it was silly of them
to go on appearances.

The children were embarrassed by her solemnity, and perplexed. Nothing in their experience had led them to believe
that appearances were *not* important. Their mother had always
been justly proud of her pretty little house and garden sustained on a barely adequate widow's pension. They, in turn,
had been proud of her presentability; she was a small, fragrant,
comely woman at once practical and decorative like a pomander
ball. And they themselves were handsome, looking almost like
twins with their short shiny dark hair and merry intelligent
faces. They had assimilated at an early age the incalculable
advantage of attractiveness; they knew without conceit that it
exerted a mild but irresistible magnetism, it gave one an edge
at first encounters.

Some days later they had cause to remember her words. She
was going to the theatre and Hinde was taking her. The
children looked at each other. There was nothing startling in
the fact that she was going out. Over the years there had been
a decorous parade of gentlemanly escorts all curiously similar
like linked paper dolls. They found it quite acceptable that
their pretty mother should have male friends. There was even
a cosy excitement in speculating as to whether this or that chap
might 'be serious', and Clara had sanguinely entertained the
possibility that her mother, in a discreetly disembodied sort
of way, might have a lover. But Hinde – *Hinde!* Perhaps she
was only repaying him for his kindness.

It seemed not. There were other dates with Hinde and
even family outings. The children came to know his tall ungainly figure filling their front doorway. His long face with its
lantern jaw and deep-socketed eyes and abject improbable
smile came to have the familiarity of a repeated joke. He wore
suits of a dreadful tan or olive colour that rode and strained
and creased as if the fabric were furious at having to accom-

modate itself to the impossible. He drove them out to the
country in his long bumpy old Humber. He had a dog too, a
liverish bull terrier bitch called Cherry. With its flat obsidian
eyes and trowel-shaped muzzle it had the prehistoric ugliness
of the breed – a pig-dog. There was perhaps a certain rationale
in his choice of such homely accoutrements. They gave him a
kind of protective coloration, so that often when the children
were alone with him and their mother they could almost forget
his unsightliness. In fact, they had to admit grudgingly that
Hinde was a nice man, a kind man. Bereft of vanity, he seemed
similarly devoid of all its companion qualities; of cupidity,
malice, pomposity and combativeness. His kindness nourished
one – it was as simple and trustworthy and uninteresting as
milk.

Apart from his appearance he was in no way remarkable.
His opinions were moderate, his sense of humour hesitant and
a little clumsy, and he played a passable game of chess. He
was not athletic, which was just as well because once he raced
with the children in Richmond Park and they were grateful
that their red faces could be put down to exertion rather than
the mirth they felt at seeing him lumber grotesquely after
them, when they were again put irresistibly in mind of those
scenes where the Transylvanian villagers hunted the creature
in packs. Poor Hinde. 'It wouldn't be so bad if he were a
famous statesman or symphony conductor or something,' Clara
told Rupert, who shrugged, not being susceptible to that
curious and perverse feminine attraction to ugliness when it is
coupled with the power of genius or the genius of power.
But Hinde was neither famous nor powerful. He was incontestably good, but even his goodness was ordinary, lacking the
theatrical selflessness of saints or the bloody sparkle of martyrs.

Still, because of it they could tolerate him, but not in company. When other people came to the house or when they all
went out together in public, the children, especially Clara,
shrank from the interest they aroused. When the four of them
walked down the High Street or entered a restaurant or theatre
the reaction was invariably the same. People glanced idly, took
them in as a group, stared arrested at Hinde, stared again
surreptitiously with amusement and amazement at the trim

pretty trio in thrall to the freak. Perhaps, Clara thought wretchedly, people even took Hinde to be the father; certainly he escorted them with a kind of shy proprietary pride. Incredibly, their mother seemed to feel no embarrassment at all. On the whole their mother seemed much changed – she was different with Hinde from the way she was with other men. Her mannered coquettish air was gone, she laughed loudly and unselfconsciously, she was physically demonstrative, she seemed to slacken into a loose, youthful, almost reckless gaiety. Clara watched worriedly and tried to infect Rupert with her concern, but by that time Rupert no longer seemed to care. Old Hinde was a decent enough chap, he said, and was, moreover, teaching him how to drive.

Towards the end of their spring holiday they were all, Hinde included, invited to a fashionable suburban wedding. For Clara it was an unqualified ordeal from the instant of her first appalled glimpse of him when he came to pick them up. She was used to the look of him in his big sloppy tan suits but she had not anticipated the figure he would cut – if that was the word – in morning dress. The top hat cocked insecurely on the crown of his big unshapely head added inches to his vertiginous height, the sleeves of the cutaway and legs of the trousers were ludicrously too short, the whole ensemble, normally so attractive in its grave Edwardian elegance, was a screaming farce. At the garden reception she tried to keep her distance but her eyes were drawn irresistibly back to him, always standing with her pretty mother, unquestionably a pair, seemingly at ease, seemingly impervious to the silent titters for which Clara's ears burned. And at one point her mother, perhaps a little tiddly with champagne, could actually be seen to slip her gloved fingers into Hinde's ham of a hand. Clara shuddered.

She was glad when it was time to pack for her return to school. Her mother helped briskly, she seemed less downhearted than usual at the prospect of their leaving. She came into the bedroom bearing the delicate white lawn dress she had sewn for Clara to wear at Speech Day. 'I do look forward to seeing you in this,' she smiled. 'Jerry said he'd drive me down, so you can expect us quite early.'

Clara stiffened. Always on Speech Day she had felt a soft melancholy on seeing her mother stroll alone among the other parents in couples. But better that, far better that than her mother with the Grand Guignol apparition of Hinde in tow, Hinde who would have to be explained to her friends and subject to the discreetly curious appraisal of her teachers. She felt a small desperate fury begin to build – how could her mother be so obtuse as not to understand? 'It's only supposed to be for parents, you know,' she said, but her mother smiled comfortably and replied, 'Oh well, Jerry's almost one of the family, isn't he?' And then her eyes met Clara's and their gazes locked and after a moment she looked away. She looked past Clara and at the window with a quite pathetically transparent attempt at casualness. 'I've grown to be rather fond of him, you know. He's such a kind man, a very loving man. I feel extraordinarily at ease with him.'

Clara stared at her, outraged. At ease, at ease, how could one feel at ease with a man who, however kind and loving, would cause normal people to shrink with fear if they encountered him on a dark street at night? With the recent memory of the wedding fresh in her mind, with the white dress lying limply across her mother's arms, she had a sudden prevision of her own wedding and herself wafting down the aisle with stepfather Hinde lumbering at her side in an odiously comical tableau of *La Belle et la Bête*. And she remembered too her mother's little hand engulfed in Hinde's. If *they* married there would be more than hand-holding – but that prospect was simply too much for her squeamish virginal imagination. Yet its possible consequences had to be taken into account; her mother was only just forty. What if there should be a child – a monstrous brother or sister Hinde? Clara longed for Rupert's support yet she knew that this was essentially between her mother and herself. Her mother's face was now flushed and tense, she looked like a small child mutely begging an indulgence. But Clara felt her resolve harden. It was that harsh sorrowful moment when the usual roles are reversed and the child must first instruct its parent. 'Mother, he's just hideous,' she said flatly. 'I know he's nice but he's hideous. Rupert says so, too. I mean,' she added lest the point had somehow been missed, 'he's so frightfully *ugly*! Little children grab at their mothers when they see him. People stare at him on the street. And at you too when you're with him. As a couple you're an absolute laughing stock. It's utterly ridiculous.'

For a moment her mother said nothing. Then, unexpectedly, she laughed. It was a strange, sudden, drowned little giggle and it ended in a kind of hiccup. She avoided Clara's clear stern gaze. She laid the white dress on the bed with ceremonious care and left the room.

There was no more talk of Hinde. The next day the children returned to their schools. Weeks later when her mother came to Speech Day, she came alone. Clara saw the appreciative gleam in the eyes of people who talked to her. She watched her flirt discreetly with the Latin master who was a small dapper handsome man with a goatee. When she was home again with Rupert she commanded him on no account to mention Hinde and he submitted indifferently.

But Clara was to see Hinde one more time. It was many years later when she was herself married and mother to two small children. She was walking with them in Hyde Park on a foggy December day. The promenade by the Serpentine was deserted, even the birds huddled in chill immobility on their sanctuary. She recognized him at once, sitting on one of the benches facing the pale water. Of course he was not a man one could easily overlook. Time had not softened his ugliness. He was still huge. He still looked like the chef d'oeuvre of some demented genius in the special-effects department. But he had a new dog, a large golden retriever, a creature of such benign and noble affability that Clara's young children instantly veered towards it. She was bound to follow. 'He won't hurt them,' Hinde said quickly as he looked up at her. Then he recognized her. She had hoped that he might not. 'It's Clara, isn't it?' He lumbered to his feet, still helplessly conveying that air of menace, still with the same kind, dreadful, sepulchral smile. 'You haven't changed,' he said. It seemed tactless to return the compliment. But, looking at him, Clara knew that she had changed. Herself taller, fuller, older, she no longer saw him through the bright distorted prism of youth. Looking at him as a woman she saw that he was ugly but not hideous, a man not a monster. 'How is Rupert?' he asked. 'And your mother?' 'Very well, thank you,' she said. She thought of her mother gamely making do in a residential hotel in Bournemouth. They chatted for a minute or two. There was not the slightest shadow of reproach in his eyes. Probably he had never known that she had been instrumental in effecting her mother's renunciation of him or at least in weighing the balance of her mother's own social cowardice. In any case, it was long since over and done with. Their conversation puttered awkwardly to a close. Hinde asked to be remembered to Rupert and her mother.

Her son and daughter stared over their shoulders at him as she led them away. It is a popular belief that small children in their innocence can see through outward appearances and turn like flowers towards the lambent warmth of essential goodness. But Clara's daughter giggled and asked, 'Who was that horrid-looking old man, Mummy?'

Clara bit back the standard reproof. 'Just a friend of Grannie's,' she answered. In a way her child's reaction offered her some small sad comfort; it was conventional, as she herself had been conventional, just that. Those many years ago she had acted on no worse than the cruel shallow stupidity of inexperience; no worse and certainly no better.

# Gentle Joy

'The first time it happens might be amusing,' Joy's husband said. 'The second time ludicrous. The third *utterly incomprehensible!*' He often barked out pontifical triads like that when he was hectoring her. She avoided his eye and tapped at the shell of her boiled egg. 'I can't think how it happened,' she said, which was lame but true. For the third time she had got the order to the wine merchant wrong. Or perhaps the elderly hard-of-hearing sales assistant had got it wrong. 'I want you to ring the manager this morning,' Donald said. 'Do you hear me, Joy? Tell him the service we've been getting is absolutely inexcusable. Tell him to take his South African rubbish back and get the hock here by evening. I can't serve that swill to the Sandersens.'

Just then the girl entered with his breakfast and he said nothing more. Joy watched him cut into the eggs and bacon. Slash, slash, slash, three times across. A clever man with a knife, they had said of him, even during his days as a young resident. She had a vision of pale shaved abdomens and, suddenly nauseated, pushed her own breakfast away. But this wouldn't do, she told herself. In almost every novel she read these days, the silent suffering wives began like this, with stray images, and by page 200 were writhing between the electrodes. She sat up straight and said matter-of-factly, 'I'll ring this morning. But this is a busy time of year – they do tend to get muddled.'

Donald frowned at her over his laden forkful. 'It's a busy time of year for me too. Every bloody fool in London wants his duodenal ulcer removed so he can build himself a new one over Christmas. Otherwise I'd deal with this myself. It's a mistake to let women have anything to do with wines. Wines and cheeses. They haven't the palate – it's to do with their menses.' He chuckled then; this kind of reductionism always amused him, especially as applied to her. 'Anyway, do something. You're too damned soft with underlings. Try to develop a bit of spine.'

She imagined the pale embryonic nub of a spine worming its way up from her coccyx. There she was, at it again, and in spades this time, Freudian symbol and all. 'What's the matter with you?' Donald demanded. 'You look positively seedy. See you take a nap this afternoon. I don't like you appearing like a corpse when the Sandersens come to dine. Mona always looks the picture of radiant health. Have you anything to wear, by the way, that they haven't seen at least a thousand times before?'

'I have that kaftan thing I just bought,' she said hesitantly. 'Mona often wears kaftans . . .'

He wiped his mouth, tossed the napkin down and rolled his eyes. 'For God's sake!' he said disgustedly. 'Mona can carry that sort of thing off – you can't. She's a tall stately girl; what my father would have called a fine figger of a woman.'

His father, she reflected, would have used a somewhat more pungent term, but over the years Donald had somehow mutated that lickerish old bore into a quaint Edwardian clubman. In fact he himself had begun to affect a rather Edwardian turn of phrase, as now, while he mused further and with some relish on the subject of Mona. 'She's quite a mettlesome filly, you know – I'm not sure Sandersen knows quite how to handle her. If she were mine I'd keep a very taut rein . . .' His hirsute, stubby but allegedly talented hand tightened a moment on his spoon. She wondered detachedly for a moment whether he had slept with Mona. But no, he wouldn't risk it with his own partner's wife, although he had nothing against intrigues with married women in general, in fact preferred them. They were safely transient. Not for Donald the inconvenience, let alone the expense of divorce, alimony, double housekeeping. She remembered that once ten years ago she herself had been on the point of leaving him. Nothing dramatic, just a quiet cowardly sneak back to the little cottage she owned in Dorset;

her only independent possession. But then she had discovered she was pregnant with Dougie. It had seemed almost like a bargain set by the gods. She was to have the child she had so passionately desired for so many years, and Donald was to have and keep her.

He was talking about Dougie now. 'Keep him at home when he comes back from school. I'll pick him up and he can come and watch me play squash.' Her detachment deserted her. Dougie hated those sessions at the squash courts: the shouts, the hellish racket of slamming balls, the curiously contained violence of the game. Then thankfully she remembered. 'He's having tea after school with a friend.' Seeing Donald frown, she added casually, 'At one of those mansions on Eaton Place.' The frown cleared as she had known it would. 'It's Parents' Evening tomorrow, isn't it?' he enquired. 'I shall want to have a word with his form mistress. I think they're being too slack by half with the boy.' The Edwardian rake was giving way to the Victorian paterfamilias. 'Oh, Donald,' she said sadly. 'He's only nine years old.' Donald stirred his tea vigorously. 'As you well know, Joy, he'll be going away to school in quite a short time. And I can assure you, it isn't any place for namby-pambies.'

She squeezed her hands into fists, forced back panic. It had been a bone of contention between them for years. The school was in the dour, distant north of England. It was clearly third-rate but they made much of Donald whenever he visited – he was perhaps their most distinguished alumnus. It was still run, as he so often said, on the good stern old-fashioned traditional principles. 'Like sado-masochism with a sound dash of pederasty,' Paul Sandersen had once chuckled. Donald had been furious and she terrified. Of course she knew that they could no longer flog or roast or perpetrate unspeakable acts on small boys, but what might they otherwise not do to timid, bookish Dougie? Turn him into what? *'Please,* Donald,' she burst out, 'please, at least consider the alternative of a day school. Or somewhere closer to London, Lancing or Charter-house . . .' She stared at him in passionate appeal. He was losing his looks. His small once-handsome features were becoming obscured in podge. The little moustache he had grown last year detracted sadly from his well-modelled fore-head and dark level brows. It was years since she had felt even a flicker of desire for him. But she believed that she could love him again, or at least like him, if he granted her this one grace. 'They're fine schools, convenient, nearby, up-to-date,' she went on persuasively. 'They even take girls in the sixth form.' She had thought that might get an appreciative snigger out of him, but his mouth tightened primly under its little moustache. 'Girls! That's exactly the sort of progressive non-sense I want to keep him away from. Girls have nothing to do with a public school. It's a man's world, designed to shape men. Oh, you needn't worry about that aspect of it.' *Then* came the snigger. 'When the time comes I'll teach Dougie what he needs to know about handling women.' He actually looked down with a self-satisfied smirk at his own hands, as if the material were there writhing voluptuously between them. She felt a shock of cold hatred, terrifying in its violence. If she read her novels right it was another step towards the electrodes.

The girl returned to clear the table and Donald rose. He patted Joy's shoulder condescendingly. 'Remember your little chore with the wine merchant. And do pull yourself together before this evening. Try to sparkle a bit, like Mona. I mean, don't just sit there and mope. It's downright embarrassing.' Her hands tightened on the edge of the table. Please, *not* in front of Ingrid, she silently screamed. The women in the novels also often silently screamed. Donald looked down and delivered a parting shot. 'And for God's sake do something about your nails.'

When he was gone she hid her hands in her lap – the hands of a woman of thirty-eight with the tiny bitten-to-the-quick nails of a child of five. Ingrid softly cleared the breakfast things. She was an au pair really, but Donald always referred to her as 'the maid' and even insisted that she wear a quasi-uniform. She was young, Norwegian, very beautiful and quite untrained in the art of servile discretion; on her face was writ clear her loathing of Donald and passionate sympathy for Joy. 'It is very cold today,' she said. 'I would be glad to pick up Dougie from his tea party if you like.'

'I'll do it myself – you take your afternoon off,' Joy said. I haven't always been like this, she would have liked to tell Ingrid. Not always this snivelling, quivering, nail-biting wet worm. She had been a shy but happy child and later a quiet but competent and popular nurse. It was thus that Donald, himself slim and lithe then, with thrilling dark eyebrows, had found her. 'My gentle Joy,' he had called her, and then sighed. 'My sweet gentle Joy. It's so restful to find a woman one doesn't always have to do battle with – tame.' Even then she had wondered who those Amazons with whom he otherwise contended might be. But she had been infatuated, flattered by his attention. He had been much sought-after and, incredibly, still was. There were still women who thought him sexy, although most of them were of the type who thought all doctors sexy. She looked at Ingrid's pure Nordic profile. Ingrid at least was not one of them, although Joy sometimes wondered why Donald had never once tried it on with any of the pretty girls who had strayed in and out of their employ ever since Dougie was born. Perhaps he considered it beneath his dignity to dally with menials. Perhaps he foresaw complications – mainly financial – which was also probably why he didn't keep a little bit on the side. Besides, his vanity would have been affronted by the notion that he had to pay. Paying was not Donald's strong suit except as it enhanced his position: a good cellar, a Jermyn Street tailor. *Ergo* a divorce was unthinkable to him, she knew. Two households to maintain or, if he remarried, two women to support? She could leave him herself, of course, forswearing all support. She could get a job at the local hospital in the Dorset village and put Dougie in the village school. But Donald would never forgive her. If she initiated a divorce herself he would move heaven and earth to take Dougie from her, even try to have her declared incompetent. And as things were now developing, he might well soon have a case. Take Dougie's tea, for instance. He hadn't really wanted to go but she hadn't discovered that until after accepting the invitation. 'I *told* you I didn't like going to Scott-Reith's house,' he said almost tearfully. 'I told you that after I went the last time.' She did remember then, but somehow Mrs Scott-Reith's loud insistent self-assured voice on the phone had driven it straight out of her mind. 'Oh, darling, I'm so sorry . . .' she stammered. 'It doesn't matter,' Dougie said. He put an anxious hand on her cheek. 'Don't get upset, Mummy, it's all right.' He, at nine, was reassuring her. 'I can go just this once. But please be on time to fetch me.'

She was there on the dot in front of the imposing Belgravia mansion. A maid – a real one – let her in. In the front hall Dougie, looking rather wan, ran up to greet her. Scott-Reith, who was a stout pale boy of the same age, followed after and then, streaming majestically down the beautiful staircase, came his mother. She wore a hostess gown of apricot velvet trimmed with fur, a trifle flamboyant perhaps for that time of day but undeniably flattering to her high colouring and regal figure. Her eyebrows, which were very dark and assertive like Donald's, swept together in a half-scowling smile. 'How nice to meet you! Do come in for a sherry.' Joy protested that she was really a bit pushed, she had guests coming to dinner . . . 'But you must!' Mrs Scott-Reith insisted. 'Really, it's too tiresome the way we all whisk about collecting our children and never meet one another . . .'

Joy somehow found herself seated in the long elegant drawing-room with a glass in her hand. 'That's better,' her hostess beamed at her in fierce approval. 'I've been hoping to have a word with you. I do so like Dougie. I'm glad he and Richard are friends. I mean, he's a beautifully brought-up little boy.' Joy mumbled a thank-you through which Mrs Scott-Reith broke. 'Not like some at the school. Not like most, I'm sorry to say. They're letting in all sorts of rubbish, aren't they? Greeks, Jews, Americans, God knows what.' Joy looked down at her glass. She wished that the anger she felt at such pronouncements was not so invariably overwhelmed by her deep embarrassment for the person who made them. 'Do you contemplate letting Dougie stay there through Common Entrance?' Mrs Scott-Reith demanded. 'Yes? Oh well . . .' She sighed. 'Where's he going next? Eton?' Most unwillingly Joy forced out the name of the school. Mrs Scott-Reith looked blank. 'His father went there,' Joy added. 'He's *the* Donald

Latham, isn't he?' Mrs Scott-Reith asked. For a moment she looked at Joy through narrowed eyes as though trying to put her together with so distinguished a name. 'You two must dine with me soon. I'm sure we have many friends in common.' She gestured casually with her sherry glass. 'My ex was a doctor too. But very small beer compared to your husband. Anyway, about Douglas. I'd like to make this a regular thing. Shall we say every Thursday afternoon?'

Joy saw Dougie stiffen with apprehension. 'I really couldn't say . . .' she stammered. 'Wednesday, then?' Mrs Scott-Reith suggested. 'Or Monday, Tuesday, Friday?' Joy hastily gathered her gloves and bag, and rose. 'I'm afraid we just couldn't make any fixed arrangement . . .' The eyebrows drew together like angry wings. 'Oh?' 'Dougie may need extra tutoring,' Joy lied. 'It's still up in the air.' 'When will you know?' Mrs Scott-Reith demanded. Joy had to suppress the impulse to grab Dougie's hand and run. 'I – uh – really can't say,' she babbled. 'I could ring you on Monday,' Mrs Scott-Reith said. 'Monday at four.' Although standing quite still, she gave the impression of being about to lunge. Was she quite mad? Joy wondered. Then she remembered from her time as a nurse one or two patients with this same ferociously obsessive will. The issue never really mattered, only that they got their own way, and one had been an outright pathological case.

Mrs Scott-Reith followed her and Dougie to the door. She padded in their trail like a great hungry lioness. 'Why not Saturday?' she called after them. 'He wouldn't be tutored then, would he? He could come and play every Saturday.' The taxi sped away like a rescue vehicle in Safari Park.

Joy leaned back in the seat and laughed weakly. 'I can see why you don't like going there,' she told Dougie. 'Is she always like that?' 'She shouts at Scott-Reith,' Dougie said sombrely. 'I mean, right in front of me. It's awfully embarrassing. And the other time when Myers was there she shouted at him as well. I feel awfully sorry for Scott-Reith. I don't have to go there again, do I?' 'Never,' she promised, and took his hand. It was strange, she thought, how much he looked like Donald, his very image. Yet those even, small-scaled features conveyed none of Donald's mean sparkle, only the glow of a gentle worried spirit, just now very worried by what he must have sensed of Mrs Scott-Reith's barely suppressed violence and rage. 'You know what Scott-Reith told me?' he said. 'That when she doesn't like the dinner she sometimes throws her plate on the floor. And once when she thought the record-player was too loud, she tore its arm off.' 'Goodness!' Joy said. He was becoming over-excited, but perhaps it was best to let him get it out of his system. 'And when she was still married to Scott-Reith's father she used to lock him outside,' Dougie went on. 'She'd bolt the door even when it was raining and things. Scott-Reith used to have to sneak down in the middle of the night and let his father in out of the rain.' 'My word!' Joy said, genuinely awed. 'You mean she locked the poor man out of his own house?' 'It's her house actually,' Dougie replied. 'She has pots of money.' He shivered. 'She's a horrid lady.'

Joy fully agreed. Yet, remembering Donald's brutal out-of-hand condemnations, she felt bound to offer a mitigating circumstance; let Dougie's natural compassion at all costs be nurtured. 'She may not be well, you know,' she suggested gently. 'She looked a bit as though she might have high blood pressure, hypertension. Chronic conditions like that do alter people's personalities.'

'She seemed awfully strong to me,' Dougie said glumly. 'I think she's just a very angry woman.'

She laughed. The phrase brought to mind an article she had read once on just that subject: a newly established psychological category of Angry Women. At another time they'd have been called viragos. They were not Women's Libbers, it seemed, but conventional wives who, within the conventional domestic framework, manifested quite extraordinary aggression and wrath, who were capable of outright violence when thwarted and who had, in turn, created a new class of victim – the pitiable, ridiculous, abused, sometimes even battered, husband. Poor Dr Scott-Reith must have belonged to that humiliated minority. He could have lived off his wife's wealth and in that luxurious house (when allowed into it), but indisputably he would in one or another way have been battered.

'I promise you never have to go there again,' she repeated.

'Now put it all out of your mind.' But Dougie was already
distracted by the fascinating apparition of a maniac capering
in the middle of Brompton Road. He was quite young, not a
derelict, not drunk but unmistakably mad, dancing and bawl-
ing loudly in the stream of traffic. 'He's not dangerous,' Joy
said. She had seen the type many times in the psychiatric
wards. Their lunatic world was contained; one only caught
glimpses of it in their harmlessly aberrant behaviour and the
bright mad windows of their eyes. 'They ought to lock him
up,' Dougie said. 'It's disgusting. I mean, it's not nice for
people to see, is it?'

Joy froze. For a moment he had looked not like some Fine
Arts edition of Donald but exactly like Donald himself, the
same priggish intolerant set to the mouth, the same pitiless
lack of imagination in the eyes. 'What a dreadful thing to say!'
she cried. Dougie gave her a quick sulky look. 'Daddy says it.
And about euthanasia and things for handicapped babies.'
Yes, Daddy did, she recalled. Daddy, physician and healer,
delivered himself quite freely of such opinions when in the
bosom of his family. She was often thankful he was not an
obstetrician – he would have been all too ready with the God-
like prerogative and the gloved hand over the mouth. 'Never
mind what Daddy says,' she said sharply. 'Listen, Dougie, our
only grace as a species is in the responsibility we feel for the
sick and helpless. Otherwise we're just talented apes. Promise
you'll never, never . . .' But it was too heavy for poor Dougie
and her voice too shrill. His face was rigid with embarrassment as he gazed at the taxi driver's neck. For how long, she
wondered, could he retain his equilibrium before he toppled
over on Donald's side? Because he loved Donald too, in a
small boy's worshipful way – Donald took care to be very
charming towards him. And although his deepest attachment
was to her, his love was already tinged with anxiety and
distrust of her weakness, her proven inability to cope.

It was proved again during the dinner that night when
everything fell ludicrously apart right from the very start.
The wine had not been delivered. The duck smelled very high
as she cooked it. And, desperate over her nails, she had
borrowed a set of false ones from Ingrid, but the glue wouldn't

stick and during cocktails Paul Sandersen found one of the ghastly little carmined objects on the floor. He held it aloft with a reflective smile. 'Poor Joy! Has Donald been up to his Gestapo tricks again?' Donald had not been amused. But during the dinner he got his own back, what with the duck and the wine, elaborating long and humorously on her short-comings, her quite comical ineffectualness, on and on, anecdote after anecdote, until she could tell that even cold and witty Paul was embarrassed on her behalf and Mona downright disgusted. She was a silly woman but not a heartless one. 'Oh, leave off, Donald,' she said. 'You're not so perfect yourself, you know.' 'No?' Donald enquired with a coquettish smile. 'Not by a damn sight,' Mona replied levelly.

'Contentious bitch!' Donald said of her after the Sandersens had taken a rather early departure. 'She's spoiling for a fight – did you notice, Joy? Throwing challenges at me right and left.' He sounded excited rather than angry. 'Of course it's Paul's doing. He hasn't a clue as to how to handle a spirited thoroughbred like Mona. He gives her her head entirely. Whereas what she's longing for is a sharp twitch at the bit, a good firm seat in the saddle . . .' Joy sighed. Donald's sexual imagery had become overwhelmingly equestrian ever since he had started bobbing around Rotten Row three mornings a week. And a little while later, while he huffed and puffed over her in the dark, she knew full well that he was imagining him-self riding Mona at a full gallop to the finish. Not that there was much of a finish, there never was. There was very little to show for all the bluff and bluster, very little in the way of either tenacity, vigour or style. It was just as well he only rode fat ponies in the park; a real horse would have unseated him in a trice.

She woke the next morning with a blinding headache. They were more and more frequent of late but she hadn't told Donald about them, fearing he would force tablets on her that would make her even more of a cabbage than she already was. By the time they went to the Parents' Evening she was sick with pain. She barely recognized the other mothers she knew, although she could hardly fail to register Mrs Scott-Reith's spectacular apparition, booted, swathed in sable and with a slubbed silk turban on her head.

Donald rushed her through the displays of student work: 'This isn't really what we've come for.' Then for ten minutes, quite impervious to the queue of parents waiting behind, he bullied and patronized the pleasant young woman who was Dougie's form mistress. Joy hoped he might be willing to skip the social thing afterwards, but of course he loved preening and strutting in that mill of wealth and privilege. He took issue with the sherry, though. 'You'd have thought with the fees we pay they'd have offered something better than Cyprus,' he grumbled. 'Do open your eyes, Joy – what's the matter with you? One is expected to make some effort at these things. Who's that handsome woman in the turban over there – she looks as though she knows you.'

Joy painfully prised open her lids. Mrs Scott-Reith was indeed looking at them, or rather at Donald, and by then Donald was staring fixedly back at her. Her dark shapely brows drew together like the wings of the famished untamed falcon. Donald scowled masterfully in return. Joy blinked – what was it all about? Donald raised his sherry glass and squinted over it meaningfully at Mrs Scott-Reith, who dropped her gaze in tolerable imitation of one blinded by such glory. 'Who *is* she?' he asked again of Joy. 'Why, it's Scott-Reith's mother,' she stammered. 'She's divorced, frightfully rich . . .'

All at once her head miraculously cleared. Had Donald looked down at her then he would have been greatly astonished by what he saw, but his gaze was still locked with that which beamed back from beneath the turban; one could almost hear their little gulps and yips of excitement. It was a genuine coup de foudre, Joy saw. Carefully coaxed along on the momentum of their monstrous vanity, patiently and skilfully nursed to fruition it might just . . . she shut her eyes again. For the first time in years she felt the emotion for which she was named, though it was not the mild joy of her youth but something quite new, terrible and cruel. But she opened her eyes and managed to smooth her face. She slid her hand into the crook of her husband's arm. 'Come along then, dearest,' she said gently. 'I'll be happy to introduce you.'

# A Birthday

❦

Miss Belsop woke with an obscure sense of obligation: something was due to be celebrated. Something *was* being celebrated; she heard bells, horns, angelic choirs singing hosannas, Beethoven's Ninth by the sound of it. Music, she thought – one of her problems that day had to do with music – and then she remembered Loretta Moon. The radio downstairs was suddenly switched off. She could imagine her father clucking at himself exasperatedly for having wakened her earlier than necessary. She looked down at the long chaste bump of her body under the bedclothes. Technically there was cause for celebration. It was the morning of her fiftieth birthday.

She looked with the same somewhat ironic detachment at the room to which she had wakened most of her life except for the time at university, the four years spent teaching in the north and a few trips abroad. Like her body it was long and narrow but serviceable. It could have done with a bit of redecoration but it was pleasant enough in a faded, girlish sort of way. On that window-seat she had sat more than thirty years ago, read Ronsard and Mallarmé, crammed for exams and sometimes looked around with the tender reflective nostalgia reserved for the venues of childhood. It had never occurred to her that she might return to live in it permanently, let alone that she would become that walking cliché, an old-maid schoolteacher living with an elderly parent. Her professional pride stirred in protest. Well, headmistress then, she amended impatiently.

Her father entered with a prettily laid tray. The tea steamed fragrantly in a thin china cup and there was a rose in a vase.

She looked at him affectionately. Infirm and elderly parent he might be, but he failed utterly to conform to the usual stereotype, he was not whining or dictatorial or cantankerous, nor was he given to maundering reminiscence or bursts of ghastly whimsy. With his pointed face and the backward fling of healthy white hair he looked rather like a benign Bertrand Russell, the asceticism without the ferocity. He sat gingerly down on her window-seat because he was still recovering from a recent prostate operation. She kept her sympathy to herself because she knew he hated to talk about it; his fastidious sensibility had been revolted by the mess, the intimacy, the ransacking of his delicate old-man's sexuality.

'Shall we do something to celebrate tonight?' he asked. 'Perhaps I could get tickets for the Old Vic. They're doing Pirandello.'

'I'm afraid I have a Parents' Evening on,' she reminded him.

He grimaced at his own lapse of memory. 'Yes, I forgot. Well, perhaps this weekend then, if you haven't anything else laid on.' Part of the civility with which they treated each other was this fiction that her weekends were a riotous whirl of social activity on which he would on no account intrude. He had never intruded, never interfered, not even during the course of her long, indecisive and rather shabby affair with Howard.

He stood up and moved restively about the room. 'In my experience, Parents' Evenings were always rather a waste of time. Much bandying back and forth of tactful pleasantries and very little said.' His own career, like hers, had been almost entirely with grammar schools, but in an era when parental participation was not warmly invited.

'Sometimes they offer the only access we have to a child's problem,' she pointed out mildly. She was amused to see scepticism battle with professional curiosity on his face. 'I have a girl called Loretta Moon, for instance. Going on for fifteen, very nondescript record academically although she has shown some interest in nursing. But now her parents want to take her out and educate her privately.'

Her father shrugged. 'It happens. Misguided social ambition, probably. Perhaps they've come into some money.'

'They haven't a bean,' she said. 'They're from Jamaica, the father's a bus conductor. But someone's put the idea into their heads that the child has singing talent.'

Her father's interest was suddenly engaged. 'Really? Well, you shouldn't dismiss it as a possibility, Verity. The Negro voice can be quite extraordinary – sublime, when it's trained.'

'Black, Father, not Negro.' Miss Belsop smiled.

'Rubbish!' her father said testily. 'Why substitute an inaccurate euphemism for a dignified ethnic term? But if this child should have a voice . . .'

'We haven't had the slightest indication of it,' Miss Belsop said. 'She's never studied music in any form. She hasn't joined any of the singing groups, not even the choir. And I've checked out the school they want to send her to. It's some fly-by-night so-called Dramatic Arts Academy in Camden Town. Unaccredited, charging astronomic fees and promising instant success.'

'Yes, I see.' Her father sighed. 'The usual swindle. Well, in that case . . .' But the doorbell rang then and he left to answer it.

Miss Belsop put Loretta out of her mind as she dressed. Bearing Parents' Evening in mind, she took more care than usual. Also it was her birthday, although no one knew it apart from her father and herself. That evening there would be a gift of jewellery from her father. Records and Royal Copenhagen at Christmas, books and jewellery on birthdays. She had quite a little collection by now of amber, coral, garnet, jade and some fine Victorian silver. She wore some of it each day as a modest concession to vanity, like the shoes she had custom-made for her long, slender, high-arched feet. Modest and very discreet, as befitted her age and position. Yes, indeed, she thought wryly, looking at herself in the glass: prominent collar-bones and a long neck, a grave, sallow, affable face, pale-framed glasses, short, indeterminately waved brown hair; in brief, a bit of an old stick. But old-stickishness she knew was held to be a rather reassuring quality by conservative school boards, which otherwise reeled under the onslaught of militant Maoists and giggling dolly-birds from the Teacher Training Colleges.

She joined her father for breakfast, which was their usual healthful but chilly meal of grapefruit and muesli and melba toast. 'I've been thinking about your problem,' he said. 'Be firm with the parents. Tell them you'll arrange to have the child audition for your singing mistress. If there's real promise perhaps she could get an ILEA grant. In the meantime she should get her A levels. The nursing thing sounds rather more realistic. Don't hesitate to bully them a bit if you have to. For their own sakes, poor devils, and, of course, the child's. A grammar school head can bring quite some influence to bear.'

She didn't resent his advice which she knew to be sensible and well-founded on his own experience, but she felt bound to point out, 'It's not strictly speaking a grammar school any more, you know.'

Her father sighed glumly. 'More's the pity.' He leaned back and lit the first of the five Woodbines he allowed himself each day. 'I'll never come to terms with comprehensivization. Even the word is absurd – a semantic mongrel. Still, I think you acted very sensibly in not putting your back to the wall, Verity. You achieved much more by reasonable compromise.'

'There really wasn't much choice,' she said. She had sniffed the wind of change, as it were, long ago, unlike the then-headmistress who had charged head-on into the ILEA ultimatum. Poor Miss Noble, she remembered sadly, and poor bewildered anxious parents with their petitions and letters of protest and placards: 'Preserve the best, improve the rest'; 'Save Noble's noble school'. But in the end they had all had to back down, the parents, the governors, the diocese, all but the headmistress. 'I'll resign!' she told Miss Belsop bitterly. 'Rather that than see the school *violated*!' Appalled, Miss Belsop had realized that to Miss Noble she was the school, the school was her. It was as if her own flesh were to be ravaged by the first non-selective intake of eleven-year-old girls. Don't let me ever become like that, she prayed. When Miss Noble did resign the forces she had rallied fell into confusion. Amalgamation was threatened, with two huge neighbouring secondary moderns. Miss Belsop, appointed in her place, had found in herself a cool-headed energy, a capacity for manipulation and manoeuvring she hadn't known she possessed. Almost single-handedly she had regrouped the disheartened opposition but along more moderate lines. The ILEA was appreciative, a compromise was struck. The school must become non-selective but could remain small and where it was in its pretty ramble of Georgian buildings facing a park. It had been an exciting time, the most exciting time of her whole career apart from one or two teaching experiences. Her father had been sympathetic and supportive and mildly amused. 'Wheeling and dealing like someone in a C. P. Snow novel – who'd have thought it of you, Verity!' he chuckled. It was not quite the corridors of power, she had demurred; still, she had saved the school, or at least saved its gentle, disciplined, small-scale character. Except that just now, in the transition period when it was neither fully grammar nor comprehensive, things were a little difficult, morale was low. Some of the older teachers spoke peevishly of resigning, the best of the younger ones were being lured to the independent schools.

Like Jennifer, she thought as she eased her smart little Rover – that much ostentation she allowed herself – out of the garage. Jennifer had not been above trying a spot of luring on her own. They had been friends since university and their careers had run a close parallel. Jennifer was also now headmistress of a girls' school, although of a somewhat different type. Miss Belsop had visited it once and been awed by what she saw: the cloistered silences of the place, the fluted ceilings, the lavishly equipped labs and libraries, the sophisticated standard of the girls' work and the girls themselves, serious, purposeful, articulate and formidably self-assured.

After her tour she had lunched with Jennifer who had commiserated about the comprehensivization. 'But of course it works out nicely for my sort of place. What with grammar schools getting the chop and boarding school fees going out of sight, everyone's converging on us.' 'Those that can afford to might,' Miss Belsop said dryly. 'Yes, of course, it's tragic for the others,' Jennifer agreed with a brisk wave. 'But that's all the more reason for us to soldier on, isn't it? I mean, who else is left to maintain decent educational standards? And I can assure you it's no longer a question of anyone wafting into our portals just because Mummy happened to go there or Daddy can afford the fees. We set our own exam and we're getting a quite outstanding type of student.' She had sat back in her chair twiddling her strand of pearls – real ones; her husband was very rich – and her tough, amused, tomboyish face wore a look of cautious speculation. 'What I'm leading up to, Verity, is that if you should feel like crossing over to our side of the fence I'd make a good place for you. As a matter of fact, I'll need a new deputy head next year and the job is yours for the asking. Of course you'll have to apply and all that rot, but that's just a formality. I have the Board of Governors in my pocket.'

And so she had, Miss Belsop had thought. The Board, the students, the parents, the whole school were snugly there in Jennifer's well-cut Jaeger pocket and there they would remain for many many years. If she herself came in as deputy head, that was as far as she would ever go. She had declined with thanks and a muttered reference to better-Caesar-in-a-village. Jennifer smiled regretfully but her cool gaze made it quite clear what she thought of villages . . .

It was not a choice she regretted, she thought as she entered the school. Today on her fiftieth birthday she might look back on other decisions with a certain sorrow, but not that one. A clutch of little first-formers giggled at her approach and dispersed. The first form was always in awe of her, the third jeering and rebellious, and the fifth- and sixth-formers, tall swaggering busty girls who were allowed to wear jeans and make-up, were generally friendly. Their nickname for her was Belsie, hardly the most engaging diminutive in the world but better than the alternatives which sprang immediately to mind, and there was something endearing in their wistful attempt at mateyness. She knew she was not – well – *loved*, not in the Mr Chips category. She did not inspire the fanatical loyalty Miss Noble had or even enjoy the rapport Jennifer sometimes struck with one of her brilliant and ambitious head-girls. The children sensed her cool ironic detachment rather than the deep fondness underlying it. Perhaps it was just as well, as her father said. 'They come, they go, they forget you,' he told her. 'It's heartbreaking to become too attached.'

She set to work in her pleasant study. She dealt with two cases of chronic truancy, a re-scheduling of A-level classes, an order for lab equipment, a teaching replacement, a questionnaire on sex education, a dozen letters, a pathetic application for re-entry from a student who had left last year to have a baby. And there were staff problems; the staff were always nervy and irritable before Parents' Evening. She had an uncomfortable interview with young John Boles who taught Romance Languages and who was having his usual problems with discipline; he was fresh from Teachers' College and the tough teasing coquettes of the fifth form made mincemeat of him. She gave some counsel and made a mental note to have a word with the ringleaders, but it was really a question of time; he was hardly more than a child himself and a rather scruffy one at that. She liked having her staff peppered with a few men. The girls generally responded well to male authority; male presence lent balance and stability to the high flimmering pitch of adolescent femininity. But it did sometimes pose certain problems. She could not, for instance, bring herself to tell John that his disciplinary situation might be greatly improved if he trimmed his beard, brushed the dandruff off his shoulders and occasionally remembered to finish zipping up his flies.

She could have had lunch sent in on a tray but this was a privilege she generally forswore, disliking its air of exclusivity. Besides, today on her birthday she had a small wistful yearning for company, although the company she got at her table in the staff dining-room was not quite what she would have chosen. Dr Sokolow was a dour, silent, elderly émigré whose talents were clearly wasted in teaching chemistry to small girls. Mrs Bridgewater was young, chic, superior and married to an up-and-coming surgeon. Her conversation abounded with references to the glittering life she led outside school hours. The more worldly girls at Jennifer's school would quickly have cut her down to size but here her smart West End clothes and laconic manner conferred on her considerable éclat. Miss Chase had taught classics at the school for decades and been one of

Miss Noble's Praetorian Guard. Her gaze was set firmly and grimly back to the Good Old Days when refractory students could be smacked across the palm with a ruler. She was discussing student behaviour now. 'It's just what you'd expect, given the class of girls and parents we're getting now. Miss Noble knew it would happen. Discipline's gone completely to pot.' Mrs Bridgewater giggled. '*Le mot juste*, I should say.' Miss Chase looked at her coldly. 'I don't find that amusing. Although I don't think the drug problem's really endemic here yet, do you, Head?' Miss Belsop, who intensely disliked that form of address, murmured something non-committal. If there was a drug problem it was far more endemic among the younger teachers than the students. 'Just the same,' Miss Chase went on sombrely, 'it's only a matter of time. Only this morning I heard one of the new girls shout an obscenity in the halls. Full and frank as you please. I've sent her name to your office, Head.' Miss Belsop ate steadily of her rissole but began to wish she had had a tray sent in after all. 'Which obscenity?' Mrs Bridgewater enquired interestedly. Miss Chase's heavy jowls flushed. 'You can hardly expect me to repeat it,' she said stiffly. 'It was the usual one suggesting sexual congress. Once that sort of thing creeps in one can say goodbye to all decent standards. Academically as well. Not one girl, not one,' she added bitterly, 'is taking A-level Latin next year. Not to mention Greek.'

Miss Belsop glanced at her with a certain pity. It would be hard, yes, to see one's well-beloved old disciplines kicked negligently aside. But she wished Miss Chase would not let her bereavement push her over the top as she was now doing. 'One need only see what's happening at other schools. Students running amok, vandalism, theft, teachers assaulted, mugged . . .' 'Raped,' Mrs Bridgewater put in, straight-faced. 'Precisely,' Miss Chase snapped. 'Not, I think,' said Dr Sokolow in her rusty torpid voice, 'by little eleven-year-old girls.' Miss Belsop glanced at her appreciatively. 'You can joke if you like,' Miss Chase said. 'But things have deteriorated badly in just two years. The school's not what it was.'

'It's not a delinquent zoo in Harlem either,' Miss Belsop said. She was surprised at the sharpness in her own voice.

She saw Miss Chase's hand shake with humiliation as she lifted her glass of water. Quickly she said to Mrs Bridgewater, 'I've been meaning to ask you about a girl called Loretta Moon. How is she doing in biology?' Mrs Bridgewater shrugged. 'Rather dimly. She might have scraped through her O level but recently she seems to have lost interest. Some nonsense about a singing career.'

'She told the careers counsellor she wanted to be a nurse,' Miss Belsop said. Mrs Bridgewater snorted derisively. 'Maybe. The kind that spends all her time in the sluice washing up. I certainly shouldn't want her hand on my fevered brow if I were ill. I mean, she really is rather thick. But Tony says they have to take almost anyone these days. Anyway the question's academic now that she fancies herself as a diva or whatever. I'm afraid I've had to write her off.'

Miss Belsop felt a surge of anger. One did not write off a child not yet sixteen. It was one of the most deeply held of her convictions. For a moment she studied Mrs Bridgewater's pert pretty face. She was popular, casually competent at her job, but she would never make a real teacher. Even Miss Chase, despite her maniacal views, had more of what it took. She was glad when they both excused themselves, although that left her with Dr Sokolow who always made her faintly nervous, unaccountably apologetic. 'This transition period is hard on people,' she said. 'Particularly people like Miss Chase.' 'One must move with the times,' Dr Sokolow replied stolidly. Miss Belsop looked down. Indeed Anya had moved through two world wars and five years in internment camp. The shift from grammar to comprehensive status would hardly strike her as earth-shattering. But because of the older woman's almost unimaginable experiences, and because she herself was getting older, she would greatly have liked a moment of real communication. 'Are you happy teaching here, Anya?' she asked. She was much disconcerted by the response. Dr Sokolow stiffened, her eyes narrowed, her voice was tense with fear and hostility. 'Is there some dissatisfaction with my work? If so, I would like to know because I have still two years before I can take my full pension.' 'No . . . no, nothing like that!' Miss Belsop stammered. 'I was merely interested . . .' Dr Sokolow appeared to relax. 'I have my daily bread, I have independence, I have peace. I need no more than that.'

Miss Belsop nodded respectfully. Just the same the tiny suspicion drifted into her mind that there was something almost histrionic in such bald understatement. Dr Sokolow spoke almost too exactly as one would have expected her to speak had she played her part on a stage. But now she was waxing positively loquacious. 'Miss Chase considers herself a victim of circumstance. It is not so. We are what we make of ourselves, we are what we choose. That applies equally to her, to you, to me, even to the children we teach.'

'Are you saying there are no victims?' Miss Belsop asked incredulously.

'I say it is irrelevant,' Dr Sokolow said. Her square bull-doggish face gleamed pallidly with contempt between the wisps of white hair. 'We are each responsible for our own survival. It is useless to blame circumstances. If you have the consciousness to blame you have the consciousness also to manoeuvre them in however small a way. You should read Mandlestam *veuve*: "The realm of inevitability is confined to our historical co-ordinates – beyond them everything depends on us." '

'Yes, but . . .' Miss Belsop began, and then tailed off perplexed. Besides, Dr Sokolow was already rising to leave. 'What was the name of that book?' she asked.

Dr Sokolow looked down at her with an almost wolfish grin. 'It is called *Hope Abandoned*,' she replied.

*Hope Abandoned*, Miss Belsop thought a few moments later. She was back in her office. Her desk was piled with work but she stood at the french window leaning her forehead against the pane. She felt deeply depressed. The voices she had heard at lunch resounded in her ears, Miss Chase's defeatism clanking against Mrs Bridgewater's bright heartlessness, and where she had expected wisdom from Dr Sokolow she had perceived a bitter chilling arrogance. She heard a sound and looked through the glass. Two sixth-formers were exercising their privileged use of the little rose garden outside her office. She wondered that they weren't freezing to death in their grotesque costumes of tattered jeans and bulging tee-shirts, but of course

their skin was warm and firm with youth. They were as
beautiful as Renoirs. Howard had said that at one of the rare
moments when he wasn't talking about himself. They looked
up and saw her then. They giggled and waved a bit uncertainly. She could imagine them telling their friends, 'Old
Belsie was just standing there! With the weirdest look on her
face!' She waved back briskly and turned to her desk.

The parents began to trail into the auditorium at seven o'clock.
Miss Belsop had not bothered to go home in the interim but
had settled for biscuits and tea in her office. Her father would
have prepared an elaborate birthday dinner for later anyway.
The teachers were already in their places, seated at little tables
facing the rows of chairs. Some of the younger ones must
have whiled away the time at a nearby pub – their breath was
redolent of peppermint. She could have used a drink herself.
But some of her depression eased as the auditorium began to
fill. She was almost as fond of the parents as of the children:
these shy, sober, devoted parents queuing up to discuss
seriously and with such hope – misplaced sometimes but never
abandoned – the futures of their daughters. Not for a moment
would she have exchanged them for Jennifer's self-assured
mink-coated swillers of sherry. Of course even among these
were the chisellers and snobs – those who took pains to assure
her that their *sons* went to public school. And the overbearing,
the flash, the obtuse. But by and large she knew that they
justified her faith in them. Their enthusiasm was sincere, their
sacrifice sometimes very great. She owed it to them to do her
best for their children, she owed them also this evening. She
had tried to convey this same imperative to her staff but it
didn't always take. She saw John Boles writhing with embarrassment in his chair – he was even more terrified of the
parents than of their offspring. Mrs Bridgewater was being
friendly – too friendly. Her accent, her smile, conveyed just
enough patronage to be subtly intimidating. Dr Sokolow was
talking to the Fortuines whose daughter Wendy had absent-
mindedly set the chem lab on fire two months ago. Miss Belsop
hoped she wasn't hectoring the poor apprehensive Fortuines
about historical co-ordinates. But no – her face was intelligent,

attentive, concerned. She might despise them all but she was reliable, a professional.

A queue was forming in front of her own table. The parents who sought her out were either the bold and chatty or the very worried. She had a manner appropriate to either category. For more than an hour she was very busy conveying reassurances and sometimes gentle warnings. It was mostly, of course, as her father said, an exchange of euphemisms. Still, it was useful to come face to face with them, even informative. Amy Howell's paralysing stutter, for example, might be accounted for by that bad-tempered curl in her handsome father's lip. And Zandra Inch's rampant sexuality was somehow connected with her very plain, thin, hot-eyed mother who wriggled constantly as if impaled on her chair.

Someone from the Parents' Entertainment Committee put a cup of ectoplasmic tea in front of her. She looked up to assess the size of the remaining crowd and saw two black couples. The Tellifers she recognized at once; their daughter was doing very well and they came proudly and faithfully to each one of these functions. The others would be the Moons whom she had met only once before during Loretta's first year. The recent fuss about the child had been conveyed via one short scrawled note from Mrs Moon and a very unsatisfactory phone call. She noticed that they weren't queuing up for any of the teachers. They were waiting for her alone. They were waiting to get her alone after all the others had left.

When it came to that point she felt a twinge of tired resentment. More than anything she longed to go home, put her feet up by the fire and sip a long drink. On this, her fiftieth birthday, it seemed little enough to ask. But the Moons rose and slowly approached. The Moons were on the ascendant, she thought with a weary giggle. They sat down before her. He seemed much the younger but perhaps that was because she was large and stout and he slender and small, a little black wasp of a man with secretive sullen eyes. But between them they had begot Loretta; Loretta was the case in point. She quickly outlined much the same arguments as her father had suggested that morning. When she was done, she looked at them. It seemed they hadn't heard a word. Their faces were silent, black, obdurate. Finally Mrs Moon said, 'There's this man, see. That said Loretta had a great voice. That she might go on the TV.'

'He was at one of Loretta's mama's church socials,' Mr Moon put in. 'They put on this kind of talent show. That's where he heard Loretta.'

'Is this man,' Miss Belsop asked carefully, 'in any way connected with the school you have in mind?'

Mr Moon looked wary of the trap but his wife fell happily right into it. 'It's him as runs the school. They got lessons in make-up, elocution, everything. He says in six months' time he could get Loretta ready for *You're a Star*.'

'Ah,' said Miss Belsop, unwilling to reveal her ignorance. 'You do realize, though, that this sort of – training – can be very expensive?'

'We got some money saved up,' Mr Moon said. 'What we don't got we can borrow. Loretta's our only kid.'

'I was only suggesting,' Miss Belsop said, 'that it might not be too wise to put all your eggs in one basket. Loretta has also shown some interest in nursing.'

Mr Moon's eyes narrowed. 'I don't want her wiping up after other people's shit. That's all she'd get a chance to do in your whitey hospitals.'

So it was like that, was it? Miss Belsop mused. She also felt a small tremor of alarm at the flash of hatred in his eyes. It occurred to her that, save for the three of them, the large, brightly-lit, untidy auditorium was quite empty, the whole school was empty. Everyone had gone home except for the night-watchman whose cubicle was far away. It was silly to be afraid, but she was tired and nervous after the long day. Mrs Moon put a mollifying hand on her husband's wrist. 'Miss Belsop don't mean no harm, Eddie. I know what you're thinking, Miss Belsop. That we're going to get ourselves took by this fella. But it's not like that. Loretta's got this voice in her. I heard it myself. It's in the blood. Her grandma back in Jamaica, she sang so good they came down from the States and taped her to put on the radio. It's big, Loretta's voice. Like most people got to use a mike to get. You got to hear it to believe it.'

Miss Belsop felt a tiny quiver, a minuscule assault on her very great scepticism. 'By all means let's have her try out for Miss Tewell . . .'

'She don't like Miss Tewell,' Mr Moon said sullenly. 'She says she don't know nothing about real music.'

Miss Belsop remembered that the singing teacher was an etiolated spinster with a great preference for Franz Lehar. '*You* listen to her,' Mr Moon said commandingly.

'Of course I'd be glad to be there when she sings for Miss Tewell,' Miss Belsop said. 'Now,' Mr Moon said. She gaped at him. 'She come along with us tonight,' Mrs Moon said eagerly. 'She's waiting upstairs in the library.' 'This is absurd!' Miss Belsop laughed. 'It's late at night. She wouldn't even have an accompanist.' Mr Moon pointed to the baby grand in the far end of the room. 'Her mama can thump along on that.' 'You don't understand,' Miss Belsop said. 'I'm not a musician. I'm not qualified to judge a voice, let alone an untrained one. I'm almost tone-deaf,' she lied, to make her point stronger.

'It don't matter,' Mr Moon said. 'You're an educated woman. What her mama and me can hear, you can hear. We been waiting all evening. We don't want no trouble with transferring Loretta to this other school. The man says Loretta's got a chance. Maybe she can be a star. Maybe she can do that instead of carrying slops all her life for some smart-ass white sister. You say eggs all in one basket. We only got the one egg. Maybe like her mama says you mean right by Loretta. Then you got to let her show what she can do. You owe us.'

His eloquence strangely moved her. And although it was preposterously unorthodox, although her father would strongly disapprove, she thought, well, what the hell. It would only take a few minutes. Why not improvise for once? 'All right,' she said.

Mr Moon shot his wife a triumphant look as if to confirm some theory that it paid to go right to the top. She rose with alacrity despite her bulk. 'I'll go fetch her,' she said.

When they were alone he didn't seem disposed to converse. Almost light-headed with fatigue, Miss Belsop let her mind wander. If – *if* by some remarkable chance the child did have talent, her troubles would be only just beginning. She would

have to persuade these two that bad training could ruin a
voice. She would have to chivvy Miss Tewell into a co-opera-
tive attitude. She would somehow have to contrive to cram
into the child a belated O-level course in music. She would
very probably have to take her home for some intensive
sessions of record-listening. It would not be the first time – it
had happened twice before. Once early in her teaching career
she had found in a most unlikely girl a quite phenomenal
linguistic ability. She had coached and coaxed her patiently
right through the Oxbridge exam. The second instance, during
her first year as deputy head, had been even more interesting.
Her attention had been drawn to an eleven-year-old behaviour
problem, sullen and obstructive. Studying her primary school
record and eleven-plus results, Miss Belsop had discovered
certain mystifying anomalies. But the maths teacher whom she
consulted had been frankly fed up. 'It gives me a migraine just
to look at her scowling and doodling in the back of the class.'
'Why do you doodle in class, Theresa?' Miss Belsop asked the
child in her office. 'It's boring and stupid,' she replied flatly.
'See if this bores you,' Miss Belsop said, and casually slid
over the test her father had devised. She turned to other
things, keeping an eye on her watch. At the end of the allotted
time, Theresa was staring vacantly into space. Miss Belsop
took the paper and checked the answers. 'Give her forty
minutes,' her father had said. 'If she has a really prodigious
aptitude for logic and numeracy, she might get through about
half of it.' Miss Belsop checked the answers again and then
sat for a moment quite still. She experienced a curious dis-
orientation of the senses, like music without sound, light
without heat. Perhaps, she thought, it was the kind of mad
exultation it was generally only given to truly creative people
to know.

Of course she had quickly composed herself and it was
quickly taken out of her hands. A few consultations and tests,
and Theresa was whisked away to a boarding school maintained
by the state for exceptionally gifted children. It was the last
she had ever seen of her. Naturally there had been con-
gratulations. Jennifer, she remembered, had been particularly
fascinated. 'What a rotten shame you had to lose her, though,'

she had commiserated. At Jennifer's place Theresa could have stayed. Special tutors and classes would have been laid on at great expense until at fifteen or thereabouts she would have moved on to Cambridge or MIT: another jewel in the school's glittering diadem of successes. But it didn't matter. She, Miss Belsop, had been instrumental, even vital. Her father had expressed great pride but with a gentle warning. 'Of course, it's the educator's dream, Verity, the sublime achievement. But don't expect it too often, don't yearn for it.' He smiled. 'We have our form of hubris too, you know. Remind yourself that real brilliance usually surfaces one way or another anyway. Your important work is with the normal children, even the mediocre and dull, perhaps especially them.'

True, she mused now. Just the same, she suddenly, passionately yearned. If this was hubris, she was committing it. Let it happen again, she prayed. Just this third, this one more and final time on this, my fiftieth birthday.

When Loretta entered with her mother she sat up quivering with alertness. She saw a large plump girl very neatly dressed with an Afro hair-style round as a dandelion. A good big chest, Miss Belsop thought hopefully, a sound pair of lungs. Mrs Moon sat beaming down at the piano and Loretta stood in its curve. She opened her mouth.

A few minutes later Miss Belsop unclenched her hands. She realized that all three Moons were staring at her expectantly. She simply didn't know what to say. Her own sense of the ridiculous threatened to overwhelm her. 'Well,' she finally managed. 'I agree that Loretta certainly has volume . . .' The din of it was still in her ears. She didn't know what it was the child had sung – rock, reggae, punk or whatever. She hadn't understood a single word. The toneless blast had been accompanied by an extraordinary display of gymnastics: kicks, wriggles, eye-rollings, twitches of hips. Now Loretta stood again in absolute repose like a clockwork toy wound down. They were all awaiting her verdict. Her mirth vanished and she felt a sudden savage depression compared to which her mood of the afternoon was the song of a lark. Why not let them go ahead? she thought. Let them put the poor child in the gyp school. Even if they were swindled out of every penny, even if they went into debt, even if their hope was pathetically deluded, at least for a few weeks or months hope would be there and excitement and glamour. For the first and last time in their lives. She remembered Dr Sokolow and the sentence she had quoted. It was all very well for case-hardened Russian intellectuals whose moral fibre had the temper of purest platinum. They could speak with impunity of the free choice beyond the historical co-ordinates. But for the Moons there was no beyond, the co-ordinates were all there was. And she was one of them. Even the man was susceptible to her authority – she saw it in his eyes. She could take from them their one chance of doomed, irresponsible joy. It was too much to ask. But naturally all her training, all her sober honourable dedication as an educator did ask it of her, as it would have of her father and Jennifer.

She caught and held Mr Moon's eyes – his was the more subtle mind. 'I shall want to think this over very seriously,' she said. 'But I can tell you already I think it would be most unwise for Loretta to drop her other options. I have to keep her welfare uppermost in mind. Legally she's too young to leave school. I'm fairly certain the one you have in mind for her wouldn't be acceptable to the authorities. But I hope it won't come to a confrontation between us. I'm sure we can work out some way for Loretta to develop all her abilities.' She deliberately kept her voice cool and aloof to intimidate them. The man was silent. Mrs Moon started to protest excitedly but Loretta whined, 'Aw, come on, Momma.' As Mr Moon turned to leave she heard him mutter what Miss Chase would have called an invitation to sexual congress.

When they were gone she resisted the impulse to sit back down. If she did she would simply fold up like an old broken umbrella. As she left the building she saw a thin figure lurking in the shadows. She had a moment of panic. Moon coming back to strangle her in a fit of pique? But it was young Boles who stepped into the light. 'I saw you alone with those two,' he said. 'I thought they looked pretty belligerent. I thought I'd better hang around.'

She was greatly astonished and touched. And he wasn't trying to curry favour – the solicitude in his eyes was quite genuine, brave and masculine. She had an impulse to hug him, dandruff, beery-smelling sports coat and all. He was young enough to be her son but for just a moment he had made her feel like a woman to be protected and cherished. Which was more, she reflected dryly, than Howard had ever managed. They walked together to his bus stop as she was going a little farther to the late-night delicatessen. As they parted, she thanked him again. 'Oh, that's all right,' he said. 'You can't be too careful. They can turn pretty nasty on you.'

'Who can?' she asked.

'Niggers,' he cheerfully replied. She opened her mouth and shut it again. She was simply too tired to take on his re-education just now. A mental note would have to suffice.

She bought the cheesecake she had promised her father to get. As she left the shop she ran into Howard. This was not unusual as the bookshop he owned, and where indeed she had first met him, was just around the corner. From time to time they encountered each other just here. Whenever it happened she looked at him dispassionately and wondered why she had stayed with him so long. Perhaps because her two previous affairs had been too brief and inconclusive to give her any sense of satiety. Perhaps because she was afraid of turning out like poor half-mad Miss Noble. Perhaps because she envied Jennifer her charming sons and the bluff indulgent sensualist she had married. Perhaps simply because sometimes, when lying under Howard on the whining camp-bed at the back of his shop, she could, by a heroic effort of the imagination, squeeze from the experience a twinge of carnal pleasure which she felt to be her due.

Howard eyed her cake box. He was fond of sweet things. Everywhere in his shop were half-eaten sticky buns, nubs of Mars bars. It was while watching him eat during one of their rare furtive excursions to a restaurant that she had decided to pack it in. Seeing Howard gobble his food with tired, absent-minded greed, it had occurred to her that that was exactly the way he made love. It seemed hardly worth the trouble, hardly worth listening to him complain endlessly about his shrewish ignorant wife with whom he had nothing in common except possibly the itch to produce children – there were five of them.

They exchanged a few words. She heard a church bell ring the hour. It had rung at the moment she was born, her father once told her. Her parents had taken it as a good omen. Exactly half a century ago they had celebrated her arrival with joy and boundless hope. Into the dangerous world I leapt. 'It's my birthday,' she blurted out to Howard. 'My fiftieth.' It seemed unbearable suddenly that only she and her father should know. He had, after all, been her lover, he was someone to tell.

'Ah,' Howard said. Then, perhaps feeling something else was called for, 'How time flies! *Ou sont les neiges d'antan* and all that.'

*Ou* indeed, Miss Belsop thought. How banal he was. And how banal of it to rain, which it was just then starting to do. 'I'd better get home,' she said.

'Happy birthday,' Howard called after her a bit wistfully. He wouldn't have minded having a go at that cheesecake.

She didn't immediately start her car. She rested her arms on the wheel and cradled her head on them. She hoped that some parent or teacher, having nipped into the pub, would not come out and see her there. But she didn't hope it or anything else enough to make a move. Only when hope was dead, she had once heard, utterly lost, did thoughts of death set in. And it was true that for the first time in her life she could think equably about death. If one chose it freely, it could surely not be much worse than the cool dark silky rain pattering on the roof. If one chose freely to abandon hope, if that was possible. So now she was back with old Sokolow and her damned co-ordinates. But Sokolow had been right after all, like the woman she quoted. They all had their choices beyond the realm of inevitability. Even the Moons in their limited way did. She could choose just now to live or die. Hope didn't enter into it.

She chose, of course, to live. These maunderings had been mere affectation, fiftieth-birthday blues. It had been a bitch of a day, she realized; one blow after another straight into the solar plexus. Yet her despair was already gently diminishing like the rain on the roof. She chose to turn the key in the ignition. It seemed to her that if she could keep that fact of choice pure, abstract, inviolable, severe, her right and responsibility, she might just make it through the rest of her natural life. It seemed a strange but appropriate present to give herself on this, her fiftieth birthday.

# After The Funeral

Leonard looked sadly at his young wife and wished she would use a proper handkerchief instead of a small soggy clutch of toilet paper, shreds and pellets of which were scattered all over her skirt. He wished she would stop crying. She had cried almost continuously for the past three days all the way from Scarsdale to Kennedy Airport, from Kennedy to Heathrow. 'She's just lost her mother,' he had been obliged to explain to the stewardess when for the third time she had leaned over them with her smile of shellacked concern. She had cried nearly all the time here in London. Even last night when he had taken her to Simpson's in the hope that a bit of rare beef might restore her, she had turned from him, huddling her shoulders in that furtive way, and he heard her sad catarrhal sniffling. The waiter, unlike the stewardess, had mercifully ignored it.

Oddly enough, the one time she had not cried was this morning at the funeral, although her loathing of her mother's husband might have accounted for that. Leonard had squeezed her hand anxiously as the coffin was lowered. The woman inside it meant nothing to him personally although he felt revolted pity at the manner of her death, but taking into account the depth and tenacity of Shirley's grief, he had greatly feared that this terminal vision of her mother's body rendered to foreign soil might push her right over the edge. But composedly, almost coldly, she had dropped a single rosebud on to the coffin when it was at rest and it had been left to Tarquin, the bereaved widower, still sweating profusely from his exertions as pallbearer, to sprinkle the token handful of earth.

But now that they were alone in their hotel room she was at it again, sitting curled up forlornly in the armchair she had dragged over to the window with its dull, tranquil and wintry view of Hyde Park. 'Hon, take my handkerchief,' he offered. 'Cloth hurts my nose,' she said. She dabbed again at her sore and reddened nostrils with the little wad of paper. How could anyone, he wondered, have that much salt water in them; where did the glands take it from? Perhaps Lot's wife had been no more than a calcified teardrop, a warning against unseemly excesses. 'You'll make yourself sick . . .' he said helplessly. 'That cheap bastard!' she exclaimed bitterly. 'He couldn't even get her a private room! She had to die in a public hospital.' 'It's not like that here, honey,' he said. 'I mean they've got socialized medicine. Practically all the hospitals are public.' 'That's not so!' she said angrily. 'That time Chuck Maynard had his cardiac here, they put him in a place called the London Clinic. Private room, menus, TV, everything.' Leonard forbore to point out that to her mother, dying in the last stages of alcoholic asphyxiation, such comforts would have meant little. 'Oh God!' Shirley yearned through another freshet of tears, 'I wish I could talk to Paul.'

Leonard rubbed his jaw. This allusion to her therapist back in Scarsdale made him feel all the more inadequate. He wondered what Paul actually did in such situations. Just listened, he supposed, which at fifty dollars an hour he damned well might. A thought suddenly struck him. 'You could call him up if you like, Shirl. If you think it'd help.'

For the first time in these many days Shirley smiled at him. It was hardly more than the colicky grimace of a small infant, but it was something. 'Oh, could I, Lee? Honestly, if I just could . . . ! I know he could straighten me out. Aren't you smart to think of it! I could dial direct – I got his number here . . .'

Now how, he wondered, had she acquired that? Perhaps Paul gave his patients a card with all the international codes, just as diabetics and epileptics are equipped with a little dossier for moments of high emergency. He watched as she rummaged excitedly through her bag. 'Oh, Jesus, I can't find it!' she said, once more on the point of tears. 'Take it easy,' he said. He took the bag from her and upended it on the bed and helped her paw through the mess of make-up, small change, traveller's cheques, credit cards, a compact, a tampon, a pearl ear-ring, a glove, a broken Cartier's watch, a bottle of veronal, a bill from Bergdof's, a vial of Magie, a capless gold pen, the careless debris (hers) of affluence (his) and he felt a flash of irritation, he felt his age which was many years older than hers. 'Maybe you ought to get it tattooed on your arm,' he said dryly, but just then with a whoop of relief she found it in a side-pocket. She sat on the edge of the bed and dialled the many numbers, her face tense with concentration like a small child's. That smallness and slimness of hers had captivated him at first glance, and even after six years of marriage it still had the power to move him. Now in her disordered grief she resembled less the chic young Westchester matron she had become than the hippy actress she had been when he first saw her in some avant-garde play he had been invited to back. At that time he hadn't supposed himself to have much chance with her – how could he compete with the lithe young men who prowled potently around her on the bare and dirty stage? 'Oh, they're all banging each other,' Shirley had giggled to him afterwards. He hadn't backed the play but he had excised Shirley from it. Knowing she would never make it as an actress, knowing she was one of those loose disoriented half-educated waifs that drift around Washington Square, he had extracted her from that environment with a neat quick-wristed brutality, putting the heft of his money and position and sexual sophistication behind it. And it had worked out pretty well, he reflected. Sometimes she yammered about her lost career and how her family situation was a mess, necessitating those visits to the shrink, but her booze-hound of a mother had fortunately kept herself out of the picture until now, living here in London with her third or was it fourth husband, and by and large she had made the transition smoothly enough.

'He isn't answering,' Shirley said tearfully. 'Even his Ansa-Phone isn't answering.' Leonard looked at his watch. 'It'd be about noon there. Maybe he's out to lunch . . .' But then Shirley shrieked, '*Paul?* Oh God, Paul, it's so good to hear your voice! Did you get my message? About my mother?

Yeah, here in London, England. Oh, Paul, honestly, it's all coming apart on me . . .' Here followed a long fit of sobbing during which she settled herself back against the pillows. It had the look of a lengthy session and Leonard wondered whether Paul was talking through the sobs or just listening at God knew how many dollars per transatlantic minute. It seemed he was saying something because after a while Shirley hiccuped meekly. 'Yes, I am. I am, Paul. I remember what you told me.' Another pause and then she said dully, 'Jesus, I don't know. Not really. She had this coloured doctor. You know what that cheapskate husband of hers did? Put her in a public hospital. What? Sure, I know that's a significant reaction. Pardon? Oh . . . liver failure . . .'

Leonard blinked. The young Indian doctor had been compassionate but blunt. Liver, heart and kidneys had all failed, yes, but what had actually killed Shirley's mother was the sixty-proof vomit filling her lungs. That Shirley should genteelly gloss over this fact when talking to her guru faintly shocked him. He didn't know much about psychiatric treatment; he had been too poor as a young man and too busy since to avail himself of what he secretly considered to be a fashionable affectation unless you had something really wrong with you, like suicidal cravings or a yen for small kids. But he would have thought one of its prime requisites was a state of unvarnished truth between doctor and patient.

Shirley was listening again with a look of strained and passionate concentration. Leonard walked softly to the chest-of-drawers and poured himself a small scotch. He had only met her doctor once and then quite by accident at a theatre in New York. As a rule, physician and patient's spouse were not supposed to meet. But Paul had taken this mischance with aplomb. His blue eyes had twinkled during Shirley's flustered introduction, he had given Leonard a boyish smile and shaken his hand with a crushing tennis-player's grip. 'Don't worry, you can handle this,' he had said reassuringly to Shirley. Leonard had torn his fascinated gaze away from the pendant Paul wore in lieu of a tie: a gold miniature of the Willendorf Venus. What did one say to one's wife's shrink? I've heard so much about you? He cringed at the thought of how much

more truthfully Paul could say that to *him*, the truth including
details of the most devastatingly intimate nature. In the end
he had mumbled something vaguely appreciative of Paul's
help. 'Oh, she's coming along fine,' Paul said with a fond wink
at Shirley. 'But it'll take time. What we're aiming for is a
totally integrated personality. We're only just beginning to
ventilate the whole bag of bananas.'

The following day Leonard had initiated certain discreet
enquiries respecting Paul. But the man's professional qualifi-
cations turned out to be impeccable, also he was much older
than he looked. Anyway, he seemed to be on the level. If his
speech and social manner were – to say the least – breezy, what
could one expect of an age where a president of the United
States invited his cohorts to let everything hang out?

Shirley was talking again. 'Tarquin,' she said. 'No, *Tarquin*.
It's some goofy English name. No, I haven't, Paul. I mean
there isn't any *basis* for communication. He's a bum. He's
supposed to be an actor but take it from me – ' her voice
firmed unexpectedly – the ex-thespian speaking – 'he's just a
no-good free-loading sonuvabitch and years younger than Mom
was and I just know he . . .' She broke off for quite some time
and when she spoke again her voice was once more tearful and
very humble. 'Yeah, I know, Paul. I'm trying to. The thing is
we've got to meet him again tonight. He's coming here for a
drink. Some stuff about Mom's estate. And I just can't . . .
hang on a sec . . .' She covered the receiver with her hand and
looked at Leonard. 'Honey, do you mind? I guess this is turning into a real session after all. I feel kind of up-tight with you
in the room . . .'

Leonard went into the bathroom with his drink. As the
session was going to cost him at least two hundred dollars he
might as well not sabotage it with his up-tight-making presence. He looked at his image in the mirror: a blue-black sheen
of stubble, squinty eyes, a surly drag to the mouth. Come to
think of it, he looked very like ex-President Nixon – remarkable that no one had ever said so. You're an ugly bastard, he
told himself glumly. He wondered, not for the first time,
whether Shirley had married him only for his wealth or even
indirectly for the presence and assurance wealth gave him. His

first early marriage had broken up over money, the money his wife wanted to put into house and furniture and which he needed to nurse his various enterprises through their infancy. Now in the next room Shirley was sighing and sobbing and once even giggling the dollars away by the minute. Not that it mattered. He finished his drink and then whiled away a little more time by using his electric razor. The door opened. 'All finished,' Shirley said. 'What – uh . . . ?' Leonard enquired hesitantly. He was never quite sure whether he might ask for the gist of the session. Sometimes yes, sometimes no. Shirley sank down on the toilet seat. 'We agreed we're going to have to kick around this hang-up I've got on Tarquin,' she said. 'Paul says I attach a lot of significance to him being in acting like me. But what we've got to figure out is whether I identify him with my real father or you or myself. I think I can handle my hostility now. Paul pointed out I was kind of over-reacting to the whole thing.'

He could, Leonard reflected, have pointed that out to her himself at a considerable saving of time and expense. He would also have thought it rather more germane for Shirley to forget Tarquin and kick around whatever hang-ups she had on her mother. He himself had met the woman only once at the Connecticut sanatorium where she was drying out after one of her binges. She had been rather cool and ladylike towards him – the rich parvenu – and there were references to her father who had been a state senator in Rhode Island. But in the rheumy corners of her eyes, the tremor of her hands, he had seen the recidivist, the eternal back-slider, also the sexual tramp – although she was then well past fifty. He had been secretly relieved when she went to Europe soon after and met and married her Englishman. He had sometimes suggested to Shirley that she hop a plane and go over there for a visit but this was always met with a grimace, a shrug. Shirley hadn't wanted to see her embarrassing mother, and perhaps all the weeping and wailing now was the price paid for that disavowal. But of course, an explanation so simple couldn't possibly be right. He had best leave the psychoanalysing to Paul, whom in all fairness he had to credit with the first peaceful look he had seen on Shirley's face in days, a look almost

of exhausted bliss. It happened when you had an insight, she
had told him once: everything got tighter and tighter and then
POW, BANG, it all busted open and the feeling was indescrib-
able, you felt like crying, laughing, rolling about with the sheer
ecstasy of relief. To Leonard the process had sounded strangely
laxative although Shirley had another analogy to offer. 'It's
kind of like,' she said shyly, 'the feeling you have after you've
made it in the sack.' He didn't much care for the thought that
another man could manipulate his wife to mental orgasm even
by the sheer power of his voice from three thousand miles
away, but at least Shirley's post-insight serenity would ease
their meeting with Tarquin which was now almost due. He
himself suspected that his mother-in-law's finances would be
in a muddle far exceeding their actual worth, and would have
much preferred to hand the whole mess over to his own lawyers
and accountants to deal with, but it had been Tarquin and
Shirley who pressed for the conference during their one and
only moment of unanimity.

Tarquin was already waiting for them in the crowded bar
downstairs, he had even secured a table. He jumped nervously
to his feet as they approached. He was a short bluff man and
must once have been very good-looking in the way of society-
comedy juveniles, and even now appeared much younger than
his age. From the start, from that first horribly awkward meeting at the airport, Leonard had found him inoffensive and
rather pitiable. He was no better than a gigolo but the chances
were that he had worked hard for his bread and butter. The
question now, of course, was how much he would keep of it.
Leonard thought the discussion both indelicate and pointless
until they sorted out the tangle of English and American
inheritance laws. Sitting next to Tarquin he caught a rich and
fruity breath, and perceived that his – what? – stepfather-in-
law? – had steeled himself with a few quick ones for the
encounter. Shirley ordered a plain tomato juice. 'I guess we'd
better get down to cases,' she said curtly. 'I've had a word
with my solicitor,' Tarquin said. 'Of course it's a bit of a bother
that Bettina died intestate. I was always after her to put her
affairs in order and make a will . . .' 'I'll bet,' Shirley said

caustically. Tarquin flushed. 'I hope we can avoid any un-
pleasantness. I can assure you this is quite as painful for me
as it must be for you.' He spoke in a tony high-class accent
which Leonard, who had a good ear for such things, suspected
was a stagey imitation rather than the real thing. 'Personally,
I think we ought to let our lawyers handle the whole thing,'
he said. 'I quite agree,' Tarquin said quickly. 'It's just that
there're a few little things that require immediate attention.
Bettina's bank account, for instance, and our house in Chelsea.
It was in her name, of course, for tax reasons but . . .'

'I wouldn't say a hundred-thousand-dollar house was a little
thing,' Shirley broke in coldly. 'As soon as I can get hold of
a lawyer I'm putting it on the market. And I'm freezing the
account. You'd better find someplace else to live.'

Leonard looked at her in astonishment. Was this the girl
who had been snivelling interminably upstairs? Was this how
she had been counselled to handle her hostility towards Tarquin: cut the poor guy's balls off? He had, after all, wet-
nursed, tended and laid the old lady for quite some years, and
most of all kept her out of the way. 'Now wait a minute,
honey . . .' he said. 'Could you please just let me handle this,
Leonard,' said Shirley in her new hard-bitten Joan Crawford
manner. He started to protest but all at once felt a small
warning flutter. He touched the digitalis in his breast pocket.
It wasn't bad enough for that yet but he knew what he had to
do: breathe deeply and shrink his concentration to a pinpoint
that focused on anything but the stress area right around him.
It wasn't easy as both Tarquin and Shirley were talking now
in voices approaching the shrill. He concentrated on the group
at the next table. There was a woman among them of about
his own age, a shade plump but attractively dressed with
beautifully cut, short dark hair, good jewellery and a shrewd,
comely, humorous face. He suddenly coveted that woman, not
pruriently, but as an exhausted man longs for a comfortable,
crisply-made bed. He envied the people who were listening to
her talk in some language he didn't recognize, he envied
passionately the man who touched her wrist with fond posses-
siveness, and for a moment he imagined himself as that man
who would later share a meal and a bottle of wine with her

and then sleep next to her body, which would feel large and firm and smell of good soap. It was just then all he would have desired in the world. He wondered wryly what Paul would make of it, how many fifty-dollar sessions it would take before Paul worked his way around to the astounding insight that tired old men want peace.

The woman, sensing his regard, caught his eye. Her gaze quickly took in Tarquin and Shirley who were quarrelling across him in furiously subdued growls and hisses. She looked back at him and smiled sympathetically. With mixed amusement and sorrow he read her thought: she was sharing with him a parent's commiseration and in her own language, Greek, Portuguese or whatever, she was thinking The Children, always The Children.

His flutter had quieted but The Children were getting out of hand. Most reluctantly he turned his attention back to them. Shirley had, by then, completely lost her cool. 'Yeah, well, what I'd like to know,' she demanded of Tarquin, 'is just how come you dumped my mother in a lousy public ward to die with some coloured doctor, which is not to say I've got any racial hang-ups but it seems kind of funny that my mother, who always had the best medical treatment money could buy, should wind up like some bum . . .'

'For Christ's sake, she was falling-down drunk!' Tarquin all but screamed back at her. His aristocratic accent had gone the same way as her cool. 'We were at a pub called The Pig and Whistle, you can ask anyone there. Then she suddenly started to choke to death. The landlord rang for an ambulance and I nipped out to find a copper with a car. Anyway we got her to the nearest hospital and who was going to start cruising around frigging Harley Street with her turning blue in the face? And you might like to know she'd been boozing non-stop for a month before that, the worst toot I've ever seen her go on and I was getting damn-all fed to the teeth with mopping up after her . . .'

'Could we just take it easy?' Leonard said quietly. He was stiff with revulsion; the woman was not yet cold in her grave. But Shirley broke in hysterically, 'Yeah, I'll bet! I'll bet I know who was getting fed up with who! And if you were getting tossed out of a soft pad, God knows what you might have poured into her . . .' 'Just watch it!' Tarquin said menacingly. 'That's libellous, that is!' And then yawing back rather pathetically to his upper-class voice: 'I intend to report all this back to my solicitor.' 'Report, report,' Shirley jeered. 'Maybe I'll do a little reporting too, like to the cops, and how come she was buried so fast anyway? I always wondered how you got hold of her in the first place, because if there was one thing my mother had it was taste . . .' Tarquin laughed sardonically. Shirley's eyes narrowed. 'My mother was a lady!' she snapped. 'Your mother was a bloody whore,' Tarquin replied.

Shirley gasped, stood up, slowly and deliberately raised her glass of tomato juice. Perceiving her intention just in time, Leonard grasped her wrist and tightened his fingers hard. 'Sit down and shut up,' he said, and to Tarquin, 'You too, buster. Now. Not another word.' The menace in his voice was, unlike Tarquin's, perfectly genuine and drawn from an ancient source, because there had been times in his past when he had been unscrupulous, even cruel without compunction. Anyway, it convinced them, it worked, they were silent. Glancing at Shirley he was depressed to see her eyes once more fill with tears. Tarquin was staring sullenly down at his glass. It was a funny thing about the English, Leonard thought; they talked round and round the point but when they finally got down to it it was in a big way. A bloody whore – what American would have said that? – so strangely orotund and biblical an epitaph for the poor old soak. He sighed. 'I think we'd better break this up,' he said.

Shirley remained silent until they were back in their room. Then in a small quavering voice she said, 'I guess I sort of goofed, huh?' 'It doesn't matter,' Leonard said. But he hoped she would some day stop talking like a teenager. She disappeared into the bathroom and returned with a fresh wad of toilet paper. 'See, the thing is, Paul told me I really ought to stand on my own two feet on this. Not fall back on you.' Leonard started to undress. He was desperately tired, he really couldn't bear to discuss just then the latest communiqué from the oracle. 'You'd better go down to the dining-room if you want some dinner,' he said. 'I'm not hungry.' 'Me neither,'

Shirley said. 'The thing is, Lee, Paul suggested I call him back tonight. I mean he said to try it on for size and if it didn't work and I was feeling any hassle to call him back before it seized up on me.' Leonard felt a certain seizing up in his own chest, the same dull quiet warning as before. 'No,' he said. 'When we get back you can have a round-the-clock session if you want. But not tonight. Take a pill or a shot of scotch instead. I've got to get some rest.' He had his back turned to her as he put on his pyjamas and she was silent. When he turned again he saw her eyes shine, but not with tears. 'You sort of get to me when you're like this,' she said. 'Like what?' he asked, perplexed. She blushed very faintly. 'Oh, you know. Sort of . . . mean.'

He stared at her. She had caught all right, in her rudimentary fashion, the note in his voice downstairs and its quietly controlled viciousness had turned her on. It was the bastard she wanted, Tricky Dicky, the Mafia Chieftain, despite all those months and years of soul-searching with Paul to become a Totally Integrated Personality. All it would take was a quick, not too hurtful smack across the chops – no, not even that, just a churlish tone of voice and she'd be spread out like a palpitating blanket of down. And all he wanted still was the big warm lady downstairs to rest his tired body and faltering heart against. 'I've got an idea, honey,' he said. 'You go use one of the lobby phones and tell them to charge the call to our bill. You talk to Paul as long as you like.' He went quickly to the bathroom to escape her look of childish disappointment.

When he returned, she was gone. He took a tablet and got into bed. He imagined her talking earnestly on the lobby phone. He wondered if she would tell Paul of her masochistic yen – assuming she even knew the word – or glide over it as she had with the cause of her mother's death. Yes, she would tell, he decided. The other lie had been rooted in her vestigial social embarrassment but she had no embarrassment at all in showing the inner seams of her poor shabby unfinished little psyche. Besides, she would relish the shock value: Honestly, Paul, for a minute I actually wanted him to slug me! And he could imagine Paul, whom he suspected of being basically none too bright, worriedly fingering his Willendorf Venus as he pondered this relapse back into the Stone Ages of Shirley's evolution as a TIP. But he would rally, of course, with some snappy line about guilt or what-have-you. Guilt, Leonard thought scornfully, thinking back on the things he had done, the wife he had driven away, the girls he had laid and left, the babies he had caused to be curetted, the taxes he had evaded and the debts ruthlessly collected, the shady deals he had swung, the several politicians he had corrupted, the two men he had outright ruined, all this under that narrow over-hang of the law where the law cannot touch – guilt was some-thing you swallowed like a cold hard stone and there it lodged in your breast for ever, your portion in life. Only the naïve like Shirley and the fatuous like Paul thought you could jargonize it away, because what they took for guilt was actually its humble and manageable little brother, shame.

When Shirley returned her face had a woebegone look: no insight this time, no come. 'You okay?' he asked. 'He said we've got a lot of work to do when I get back – maybe some double sessions,' she mumbled. The shrink had blasted her, he surmised, perhaps taken on the role of disciplinarian before he, Leonard, could pre-empt it himself. 'Never mind, baby, you take all the time you need,' he consoled her, adding silently, 'and I've got all the cash it will take.' It was perhaps as fitting a use as any for his tinged wealth that it should allow this child and her playmate to gambol artlessly in the Elysian fields of infantile self-fascination. 'You're awfully good to me, Lee,' Shirley said tearfully, and went to tear off another yard or two of toilet paper; but he turned on his side to sleep while the chance was there.

# In Passing

'Here comes your fan,' Charlotte's mother said. 'The pest. What's she called again – Hedgerow, Heathrow? What extraordinary names Americans give their children!'

'Jedrow,' Charlotte replied. 'Apparently it's a family name. Anyway, she's not coming over. She's going to the baby ski classes.' She watched as Jedrow, short and stout, laboured up the slope after the other children.

'Thank God for that!' her mother said. 'That *voice*! It goes right through you like a buzzsaw.' She settled back on the bench, offering her oiled face up to the sun. She and Charlotte's father had had a quarrel that morning which would account for her bitchiness now, Charlotte reflected. Her father had been irked because, save for himself, they barely touched the gargantuan Norwegian breakfast served buffet-style in the hotel dining-room. 'We're paying for it, you know,' he said. 'We *are* paying for it.' Her mother had looked at his demonstratively laden plate with distaste. 'Paying or not, I simply cannot stuff myself with cheese and salami and cold fish at eight in the morning.' She tapped fastidiously at her boiled egg. 'We could have taken a chalet,' her father said. 'Self-catering is what people do when they travel with children.' 'Self-catering is what *I* do eleven months out of the year!' her mother had snapped back. 'Shopping and cooking and washing-up. I know it sounds utterly bizarre but I did fancy a change from that.' 'Hotel-keeping is what I do eleven months out of the year,' her father replied. 'Hotels don't hold any particular charm for me, especially when we don't use half of what we pay for.'

Charlotte and her brother Jamie had sat with eyes downcast

during the whole of this debate, which was conducted furiously *sotto voce*. It ended when the handsome solemn Norwegian family with whom they shared their table sat down. After breakfast her father announced that he was taking Jamie up to the intermediate slopes. 'I don't suppose you ladies will favour us with your company?' he enquired sarcastically. 'I suppose this morning will be energetically employed with the varnishing of nails and the writing of love-letters.'

'We'll take care of ourselves, thank you,' her mother replied with hauteur. Charlotte hadn't liked that 'we'. Once it had been much simpler. She and Jamie, even with six years' difference in age between them, had been The Children. Their parents had been The Parents. But now that she was nearly seventeen, new lines had been drawn, subtle shifts of alliance. Jamie wasn't any too happy about going up to the intermediate slopes. She could tell that by the slump of his shoulders. But he was going just the same, just as she had somehow been drawn into a sort of collusive entente cordiale with her mother. It had its advantages, of course. Her mother didn't mind, for instance, about the thick letter she wrote each day to Ben, whereas her father rolled his eyes when he was in a good mood and made cutting remarks when he was not.

She picked up her writing-case and pen. Page Four. 'Mother and Daddy had one of their delightful little tiffs this morning. The joys of a family holiday! I'm sitting on one of the benches against the wall of the hotel. The sun is bliss. I wish you were here with me now – it really is beautiful . . .' She paused and looked about, wondering how to convey its beauty. The snow glittered – well, Ben would know that. He would consider the description banal. But glitter was what it did in huge voluptuous dollops on the eaves of the roof, on the dark sturdy firs which dotted the slopes, it crunched and sparkled thickly underfoot between the complex of small timber buildings that belonged to the hotel, the distant peaks were confectionery with it against a sharp Nordic blueness that made her eyes ache. She had never thought cold could create a beauty so opulent. The compound where she and her mother sat was brisk with activity like a market square, people stamped back and forth in the bright functional chic of their ski clothes. 'It's like a

Breughel painting,' she wrote – but then the urge to write further suddenly left her. As sometimes happened now in the middle of any given activity, she felt seized by a curious listlessness, a torpor as absolute as death; at such times she could sleep twelve hours at a stretch.

Through half-closed eyes she saw the young American couple, Jedrow's parents, swing by. No torpor there. With their dark hair, agate eyes, impossibly beautiful smiles, they seemed about to burst into song together like the Osmond brother and sister whom they greatly resembled. 'You know, I don't think those two are really human,' her mother observed with lazy amusement. 'I think they're androids. Something produced at some underground factory in California.'

She was annoyed to hear herself giggle. She detested her mother's malice and never more so than when it exactly hit the mark and made her laugh. 'It's funny they should have had a child like Hedgerow,' her mother went on. 'I mean, a kind of unfinished blancmange.' Charlotte stopped smiling. Her mother never knew when to leave well enough alone. She picked up her pen again. 'There's a little girl here who's attached herself to me. I baby-sat her once when her parents went down to town. Now she follows me around all the time. I tried to foist her off on Jamie but naturally he regards her with the Olympian disdain of the ten-year-old male for the six-year-old female.' She read that sentence over again and was pleased with it. Then a new and altogether fascinating thought struck her. 'It just occurred to me: when you were ten, *I* was six. If we'd met then you'd have felt . . .' 'Ahem!' her mother said meaningfully. Charlotte looked up frowning, met her mirthful gaze and followed it to the entrance of the hotel. The young Norwegian standing there smiled. He had stared at her before on other occasions with quite straightforward admiration. He was wonderfully good-looking. 'What a dish!' her mother murmured. 'He really fancies you, you know.'

Charlotte flushed. She wished her mother wouldn't inflict on her her middle-aged slang, her salacious middle-aged whimsy and above all the awful girl-to-girl mateyness she had affected recently. She moreover suspected an ulterior motive because although her mother was oh-so-charming, hospitable and kind whenever Ben came around, she also, on other occasions, got her subtle little digs in, and once or twice not so subtle like the time when she'd had a few drinks and leered across the kitchen table at her: 'He's not the man for you, Charlie. He's a nice kind lad but he's not the one. You're going to want someone with a bit of dash, brio, machismo. You're my daughter, after all.' Her voice had slurred with self-satisfaction and gin. Charlotte grew cold with embarrassment at the mere recollection. And who was supposed to be the model for all that dashing macho brio: *Daddy*? It was ludicrous. Admittedly, the Norwegian, who was now loping off towards the piste carrying his heavy cross-country skis as if they were toothpicks, might have it, whatever it was. And it was true that once or twice when she had caught him looking at her she had felt a treacherous little flutter of excitement. There, she thought disgustedly, there, she *was* her mother's daughter. Betrayal, two-facedness, was in the blood. Or the sex. Her father at least was bluntly, consistently disapproving of her thing with Ben. There was none of this butter-wouldn't-melt-in-your-mouth sympathy one minute and sly suggestive pandering the next. Well, she thought, her mother had just very satisfactorily hoisted herself on her own petard. With all her winks, nudges and chuckles she had killed any interest in the Norwegian stone dead. She felt a surge of love for Ben, dear, skinny, bookish Ben, who would have crumpled to his knees under the weight of those bloody skis.

She started writing again with great zeal. But she hadn't been at it for more than five minutes before she heard the small callow voice she was coming to know so well. ''Lo, Charlotte.' 'Ho-hum,' her mother said with an elaborate mock-yawn. Interrupted in mid-sentence, Charlotte felt a twinge of exasperation but she forced a smile. 'Hello, Jedrow. How was your class? Are you learning anything?'

'*I* don't know,' Jedrow chanted. 'Don't ask *me*!' It was her standard reply and always accompanied by a palms-up gesture of her plump hands, a heavenward roll of her china-blue eyes, in short, an act clearly patterned on the tediously winsome performance of juveniles in American TV series. 'But we are asking you, sweetheart,' Charlotte's mother said with a nasty-nice smile. Jedrow tossed her sparse curls cutely like Shirley Temple. 'All right, I s'pose. I s'pose I'm learning something. I'm learning how to snow-plough. But I fall down on my bottom lots and lots and *lots* of times!' She looked over her shoulder and with comic exaggeration slapped the snow from the back of her ski pants. Charlotte laughed because it seemed expected of her but her mother did not. Her mother enquired, 'Voulez-vous que cette enfant ennuyeuse restera avec nous tous le matin?' Charlotte turned red. She knew as well as her mother that Jedrow was a pathetic little bore but there was no reason for her mother to act like such a pig. 'It's nearly lunch-time,' she pointed out. 'Lunchtime, munchtime,' Jedrow said with heavy gaiety. 'My daddy always says munchtime.' 'Our daddy calls it stuff-as-much-as-you-possibly-can-into-your-mouth-time,' Charlotte's mother said dryly. 'I hope you're prepared to make an effort, Charlotte. And finish whatever you take. I've noticed those Norwegians at the table practically scrape the glaze off their plates.' 'I like the meals,' Charlotte said. 'Except when you and Daddy bitch all the way through them.' 'Ooh la!' her mother said with raised eyebrows. 'Aren't we being testy?' 'It's always like this,' Charlotte muttered. 'I didn't want to come on this damned holiday anyway. I'd rather have gone on the school trip. Or just stayed in London.' 'With Ben,' her mother said smoothly. 'With Ben,' Charlotte snapped back.

Jedrow had been standing patiently throughout this exchange, her round eyes moving back and forth as if at a ping-pong game. Into the silence her voice fell like a small flat stone just perceptibly edged with wistfulness. 'Can you play with me, Charlotte?' Charlotte hesitated. She felt wretched and fed up. 'Charlotte has a letter to finish, Jedrow,' her mother said. 'Okay,' Jedrow said. She toddled off, resigned to rejection as a bothersome puppy becomes used to the foot edging it out of the way. 'Poor little beast,' Charlotte's mother said dis-passionately. 'I know the type. I've seen them hundreds of times at your father's hotel. Allowed to inflict themselves inter-minably on other guests. Encouraged to show off. Given an exaggerated idea of their own lovability to make up for the fact that their parents don't give a rap about them.'

Charlotte had to nod. It was a sad but just assessment. At such times, when her mother spoke not patronizingly or in that ghastly we-chums manner, but sensibly adult to adult, she was quite bearable. But then she exclaimed in her alarmed Sister-Anne-Sister-Anne voice, 'Oh God, here comes your father!' Charlotte hastily shut her writing-case.

'How was it?' she murmured to Jamie, meaning How Is His Mood? and Jamie who was a brat but not stupid made a so-so gesture with his hand. Her parents were reserved, each waiting for the other to make the first move, either hostile or conciliatory. She had seen such wary circling hundreds of times before and it had to be admitted she and Ben sometimes did the same. But Ben was usually the first to give in, as her father did now. Perhaps women were better equipped to be Keepers of the Grudge as they had once been assigned to be Keepers of the Flame. 'I got a bit chilly up there,' her father said, rubbing his hands together. 'Shall we have a drink before lunch?' Her mother instantly thawed. And at lunch they ordered wine and struck up a conversation with the Norwegians at their table who, as it turned out, had relatives in the hotel business, so the talk turned quickly to shop. Of course her mother's casual allusions to union troubles, Arabs and take-over consortiums gave the impression that their own establishment was something along the lines of the Savoy. But on the whole it was fairly jolly. It still mattered, she mused. One still felt anxious when The Parents quarrelled and relieved when they made it up. Silly, but there it was. 'Nice people,' her father said of the Norwegians after lunch. 'I thought we'd meet someone amusing if we stayed at a hotel instead of a dreary old chalet,' her mother said. He yawned and gave her a meaningful look. 'I could do with a little kip.' Her mother, smiling enigmatically, said, 'Charlotte, you and James can take care of yourselves for an hour or so, can't you?' What a performance they made of it, Charlotte thought. As if anyone really cared that they were going to sleep together.

James ran off to the nursery slopes so she was left to herself. The compound was almost deserted, pooled in sunlight, deliciously both hot and cold like a Baked Alaska. She had plenty of time to sit here and finish her letter in peace. She

shut her eyes. The rough pine logs at her back emitted a tang
of resin. The sun's heat on her face was as sensuous, as
imperative as a lover's hand. ' 'Lo, Charlotte,' she heard.

Oh, piss off! she thought wearily. Really it was a bit much!
'Hello, Jedrow,' she sighed. 'Don't you take a nap after lunch?'

'My mommy and daddy are taking a nap so I got to go
play,' Jedrow replied. 'They didn't want me around.'

Norwegian lunches seemed to have an unusually lubricious
effect, Charlotte surmised with a coarse giggle. Anyway, those
two looked as though they were at it morning, noon and night.
But it was odd, as her mother said, that they should have
produced a child as plain as Jedrow. Her little outfit was almost
egregiously trendy and must have cost a bomb, yet she might
as well have been tied wobbling in a sack. Her features were
all right in themselves but it was as if something had failed to
ferment – the yeast of personality perhaps. At six she looked
like the woman of forty she would one day be: podgy, childish,
meekly petulant, baby-talking her small dogs. Charlotte felt a
reluctant twinge of gratitude towards her own parents. Whatever their faults they had at least not turned her into something
like this. Gratitude made her kind. 'Listen, Jedrow,' she said.
'Why don't you and I take a little walk to those woods over
there? Although afterwards you'd have to run along and let
me finish my letter.'

Jedrow plodded at her side as they made for the stand of
trees a few minutes away. 'My mommy and daddy were talking
about you at lunch,' she said. 'They said you were one of the
prettiest girls they'd ever seen. They said you ought to come
to the States and get a job in the movies.'

'Really?' Charlotte said sceptically. Looking down she saw
that Jedrow's eyes had the ingenuous glaze they always wore
when she lied, which was often. 'You know, sweetheart, you
don't have to tell fibs to get people to like you,' she said. One
part of her approved of the mature considered tone of her
voice. But another told her dryly it was rubbish. Jedrow lied
because she had to lie, as she would always have to lie to get
at least a modicum of attention. Still, she thought, it could be
said that she had a way with children – look at the devotion
she had inspired here. As Jedrow began on some long-drawn-

out anecdote, she permitted her mind to wander. Suppose the parents asked her to come to America as an au pair on terms so favourable that her own parents would let her leave school for a year? Then perhaps Ben could scratch together the cash and leave his meaningless dead-end job and join her. They could hitch-hike together to California and New Orleans. Her native vigour and enterprise – that which her father said she had got from him – responded energetically to the idea. The au pair thing was pure pie-in-the-sky of course, but something like it ought to be possible one day. If only Ben could bring himself to it. But Ben sometimes reminded her of some lines he himself had read to her by an American poet he admired: '. . . the cleanliness of indigence, the brilliance of despair.' Of course he was neither actually indigent nor despairing, but there was about him the finely pared-down quality of defeat when it is styled by intelligence. Her father put it another way. 'The lad lacks gumption,' he said. 'Not an ounce of get-up-and-go. Why, at his age . . .'

'It's spooky in here,' Jedrow said in an affectedly quavering voice as they entered the dark wood. 'It's like Disneyland.'

'It's not a bit like Disneyland,' Charlotte said rather sharply. Her recent line of thought had made her cross and unhappy. But then she registered her surroundings. 'It's beautiful,' she said. 'Listen, Jedrow.' 'What to?' Jedrow enquired. 'The silence,' Charlotte said. But it was not true silence; a twig occasionally crackled with frost. Between the snow-sculpted banks of a small stream a thread of water sparkled darkly. The firs stood fastidiously, aristocratically straight with no litter of roots or leaves about their feet, their arms ermined with snow. Above the nocturnal shadow the sun flashed and struggled in the net of high branches and beyond that was the shocking hard blue of the sky. 'I'm sort of cold, Charlotte,' Jedrow grizzled. Charlotte sighed. She could have wished for a more sensitive companion. Or, better still, no companion at all. Then she heard something else, a mere scuffle of sound, yet dense and rushing. Beyond the trees she saw the young Norwegian returning from his cross-country run. Even at some distance away she recognized him by his brilliant scarlet jersey. Watching him from within the dark and magical silence, and despite

Jedrow sniffling plaintively beside her, she felt like one of those
enthralled tree spirits of Greek mythology. He coasted easily
down the gentle grade, his poles tucked casually under his
arms, and as he approached he pulled off his knitted cap and
the sun struck spectacularly on his hair. Charlotte caught her
breath; she felt a moment of pure joy. He didn't see her as
he went by, nor did she want him to. Her feeling for him was
not sexual or even personal but one of twinship, total identifi-
cation as if he had, in passing, torn her from vines and leaves
and deified her like himself, made her superb in the consciousness of the affluence and infinite promise of their shared youth
and beauty; not like her parents who were past it, not like
Jedrow who would never have it, not like – she felt a small
wrench of sorrow – poor lovely lost Ben who had somehow
missed it altogether. 'Charlotte,' Jedrow whined sadly, 'can we
go home now?'

'Of course we can, my poppet!' Charlotte exclaimed. She
bent down and hugged the little girl, having no better object
on which to expend her almost uncontainable exhilaration. 'I'm
starving, aren't you? I'll buy us some marzipan when we get
back.' Jedrow rolled her eyes and dutifully jumped up and
down to express joy. She took her windfalls as they came. As
she did with her handsome parents, she accepted light for
warmth, basked in the cast-off radiance, the great beams of
goodwill that flash and refract from the diamond heart of the
consummated ego.

But Charlotte had vitality yet to spare. 'I'll race you back!'
she said. The snow crisped satisfactorily underfoot. She ran,
not with the knock-kneed wobble of recent years, but hard and
straight as she had as a child. She was nearly back at the hotel
before she remembered the little girl huffing and panting far
behind. With the easy generosity of the natural winner she
slowed down so as to let Jedrow catch up and totter past her
on short fat legs.

# Do Not Forsake Me,
# Oh My Darling

'I don't mind,' said Ben, and slid the wine list back across the table. No, he didn't mind, David thought sourly. Liebfraumilch, Erbacher Marfobrunn or plain plonk, it was all the same to him. He tried to be fair, to remind himself that a young fellow of Ben's age couldn't be expected to know wines let alone know what an experienced hotelier would. In fact, had Ben bounced back with some polysyllabic German name he would have been irritated to an extreme. What really annoyed him was his daughter Charlotte's rich adolescent giggle. Charlotte seemed convulsed with mirth by his act of simple courtesy in letting her friend see the list. Charlotte seemed to think Ben's response the quintessence of wit. Now Charlotte said, 'I don't want wine anyway. I think jasmine tea goes better with Chinese food.' 'I want wine, please,' her younger brother said. David looked at his son fondly. 'Half a glass,' he said. James was just ten, but there was no harm in starting to educate his palate. 'Remember the time Jamie invented a new wine?' his wife said. 'A roselle,' she told Ben. 'He thought that's what would happen if you mixed a rosé with a moselle.' 'It sounds quite logical,' Ben said gravely. Jamie shot him an appreciative glance.

David placed the order, to which Charlotte added a few favourite items of her own. 'And the seaweed,' she concluded, 'I want Ben to try the seaweed.' David realized that she was playing for Ben's benefit the part of the indulged adored daughter – her whim was their law. She was also letting Ben see the range of her expectations. For a moment he felt a detached twinge of sympathy for the boy. Women could be bitches, he thought. Of course Charlotte at sixteen was not strictly speaking yet a woman, not emotionally anyway, although physically she was all there. Once recently he had come upon her stepping out of the bathtub – she had forgotten to lock the door. She had shrieked like a banshee and doubled over as though fending off imminent rape. But for one startled instant he had taken in the nubile breadth of hip, the gentle indentation of the waist, the full and creamy breasts. Had *he* produced that? The thought almost unmanned him. The other thought, the one which these days had degenerated from the Ultimate Taboo to practically a cocktail party cliché, also struck him. Did he carnally desire his own daughter? His mind and elsewhere shrivelled with horror at the idea. It simply wasn't true, whatever Freud and his kind might say. Her flirtatious little friends, that was something else again. There were those among them who were not above giving him a half-conscious invitation, although it was given, he knew, in the certain knowledge that it would never be taken up. In their first nervous essays at sexual guile, their first tentative reconnoitrings, middle-aged fathers would be deemed something like safe houses in espionage. They were merely practising on him. Even knowing that, he enjoyed it. 'Whatever has happened to her chums?' he asked his wife recently. 'Moira and that lot. They never seem to come around any more.' 'When a boy-friend comes into the picture, girl-friends fly out of the window,' she had smugly replied.

He looked at her now. She was the only one among them adroit with chopsticks and he thought she was making rather a lot of this minor accomplishment, especially as the prawns she was putting with such connoisseur relish into her mouth were not prawns at all but something moulded out of inferior whitefish. He would have expected someone who had married into the catering trade to know that. But no, she continued to wield her chopsticks with great panache, her gold bracelets tinkling busily. She was dressed to the nines for this occasion. Ben and Charlotte, on the other hand, wore frayed jeans and shapeless, none-too-clean sweatshirts. Quite possibly each other's jeans and sweatshirts. 'They do that now,' his wife had chuckled. 'Switch clothes. They go shopping together to make sure that what suits one will suit the other. All the youngsters do it. It's the custom.' David had thought the custom ridiculous and repellent, really almost perverted. His wife's insouciance astonished him. But of late she seemed to have become a self-styled expert on teenagers. She delivered her finds with the confidence, the amused detachment of an anthropologist au fait with all the secrets of some recondite minor tribe. Nor was she shy of value judgements. 'You have no idea,' she had said, 'how lucky we are that Charlotte chose Ben for her first serious relationship. He's mature, he's intelligent, he doesn't drink, he doesn't smoke, not even cigarettes let alone pot. And he likes her as a person. He doesn't have his mind solely on tearing her clothes off. You should see the punk rocker Moira's running about with.'

So that was it, David thought. The oracle had spoken. They were supposed to sit back and accept all, meekly grateful that Charlotte was not being regularly assaulted by some acid-head delinquent with a cheekful of safety-pins. As to the assault or whatever, who could know? They were young, after all, and in full vigour. God, how young they were, he thought, watching them eat with quiet and busy greed. Did they or didn't they? 'Do they or don't they?' he had asked his wife only that evening as they were dressing to go out. She had frowned consideringly. 'I don't *think* so. I can't really be sure. I can't just come out and ask her.' Well, why couldn't she? he had thought, outraged. It was, dammit, what mothers were supposed to do. If not actually to interrogate, then at least to winnow out the clues with mysterious maternal guile and in wise and subtle ways give guidance and direction. Mothers to daughters, fathers to sons. He would certainly not shirk his duty when it came to James. It would not be a question of giving James The Facts; these days they seemed to be in full possession of the facts from the age of three onwards. But the finesses, the fruits of experience, a child had a right to expect that of its parent. And what was Charlotte's parent doing now? Giggling over her glass of wine as if she herself were sixteen. 'Honestly, that was her name,' she was saying. 'Lula Ramsbottom. I mean, can you imagine?' Charlotte, momentarily replete, was sitting back with her fingers entwined with Ben's. 'Names are frightfully important,' she said thoughtfully. 'I'm going to pick lovely ones for my daughters. Angharad. Leonie. Caitlin.' 'Actressy,' her mother scoffed. 'Whoever heard of anyone in real life called Caitlin?' 'Dylan Thomas's widow is called Caitlin,' Ben put in. His mind seemed stuffed with bits of information like that, David thought. Very nice, but it wasn't going to put clothes on Charlotte's back or a roof over her head. Let alone the sort of clothes and roof she was used to. He knew he was thinking in clichés, acting in them as well. And he was not even the awesome Heavy Father of drama – Barrett père of Wimpole Street – but the comic Heavy Father of farce. He had the feeling they were all greatly amused by him, apart from James whom he could perhaps still trust. It had even inhibited him from sending back the wine which was corked and over-chilled and wouldn't have passed muster for a minute with his own wine-steward. Then Charlotte caught his eye and over a forkful of chicken almond gave him a smile of such radiant sweetness that his heart turned over. He remembered the time when she was six years old, and very ill with measles while her mother was in hospital having James. He had sat up with her all night, clamping down his anguished fears of encephalitis, brain damage, death. She had kept her fever-bright eyes on him all the time for reassurance while he bantered and joked and sponged her with tepid water as the doctor advised. When the fever finally broke he had fallen asleep, exhausted, next to her. Let Freud make what he would of that. It was desire he had felt, certainly, then as now; a passionate desire to keep her and James from harm, a rage against whatever might conceivably, even inadvertently, hurt them.

Like aloof and quiet Ben. Not that he was a bad fellow. In fact, had he come as a stranger to ask for a job at the hotel, he, David, would have chosen him above any twenty others for his look of gentle reliable probity. But that was an entirely different matter from Charlotte's fatuous simper whenever his name was mentioned, from daily hour-long telephone calls, from in-and-out of each other's clothes, from whatever went on behind the closed door of her bed-sitting-room, and above all from their most worrying air of settled conjugal permanence. It was the done thing these days to go steady, his wife assured him from her new mysterious fund of knowledge. Young girls didn't flit around any more like something from a Viennese operetta, peeking over their fans and breaking hearts all over the place. Well, why didn't they? David thought mutinously. At sixteen it was what they bloody well should be doing. No one single boy should be allowed so confident, so complete a monopoly. Anyway, for the life of him he couldn't see the attraction. Judging by the film stars and pop singers Charlotte had been mooning over only a year ago, he would have expected her to go for someone with considerably more sophistication and aplomb. He quietly slid on his spectacles for a closer scrutiny. It wasn't often he had the chance. Usually Ben was no more than a soft-footed shadow gliding past, or one half of a hand-holding silhouette at the kitchen table. Then Ben looked up and caught his eye. Something that could have been described as the ghost of a smile creased his cheek. And from somewhere within the folds of his sweatshirt, he took his own spectacles and put them on.

David sat back, though not dropping his gaze. So it was going to be like that, was it? he thought sardonically. A duel. At least he had been allowed the choice of weapons. His big, imposing, fifty-quid Christian Dior genuine tortoiseshells against Ben's little gold-washed metal-framed National Health Service granny-glasses. He would have thought it clear who had the advantage. But then Charlotte warbled, 'Oh look, Mummy! Aren't Ben's new glasses dear?' 'Adorable!' said his wife without a trace of irony.

David sighed and took his spectacles off and folded them away. It was no use. They were all in a conspiracy against him, bemused and besotted with Young Love, including his wife, she who had refused to marry him till she was twenty-four on the grounds that they were too immature, she whom he had had to wrestle with grim patience for months on end for each tiny erotic concession before marriage. Well, *autre temps, autre moeurs*, and by and large they had been a happy couple. But how could she now so completely reverse herself and, leering like Juliet's nurse, positively thrust those two into each other's arms? It was not suitable, it was not even fair. *She* should have been severe and he the one allowed to be indulgent.

The bill came. What with two bottles of expensive wine and all Charlotte's capricious little extras, the total was high. For some reason this gave him a glum satisfaction. No one else expressed interest or even glanced at the money he handed the waiter. Of course he paid inconspicuously; there are some weapons which it is not honourable to use, particularly when they are bound to be totally ineffective. It would not even have registered on Ben that the amount was about equal to his entire week's wages. The young these days didn't make that sort of connection; they neither coveted nor resented the affluence of their elders, at least the more passive ones didn't. Modest luxury of the sort he was able to provide for his family, they seemed to view as an inevitable consequence of age. It somehow happened, they thought, whether you wanted it or not, like wrinkles or flab. They were Peter Pans, preferring the mythic horrors of pirates and crocodiles to the dull sober responsibility of growing up. He looked at James, whose tenth birthday they were celebrating. James, his son, at least seemed to have some sense of it. That morning, while pondering the wonder of having reached an age that could be expressed in two digits, he had looked at David solemnly. 'You know,' he said, 'I'm getting to be pretty middle-aged for a boy.' He smiled, but the smile faded when James, drowsy with food and six sips of wine, leaned his head against Ben's arm. On the other side Charlotte was leaning her head against Ben's shoulder. Well, Goddammit, he thought, who's the bloody pillar of this family anyway? 'We'd better go,' he said curtly.

After the fug of the restaurant the icy air outside woke them all up. James shivered in the thin leather jacket he had insisted on wearing. 'It's just a little walk home,' David reminded him. 'Even less if we go by way of the hill.' At that both his wife and Charlotte started grizzling. The hill, like many in Hampstead, was short but very steep. But David found the cold exhilarating. 'You're a bunch of namby-pambies!' he scoffed. 'We'll take the hill.' Charlotte and Ben, arms twined around each other's waists, started to lead the way, and James ran to catch up with them. 'Give me a piggy-back ride up, Ben?' he pleaded flirtatiously. Ben's dry, pleasant voice drifted back. 'You must be joking! You're six stone if you're an ounce. I'd as lief carry Charlotte.' There was some horseplay then as Charlotte pretended to jump on his back. Any excuse to touch, David thought. 'Come back here, James,' he called sharply. 'I'll carry you.'

They all stopped and looked at him. 'Don't be absurd, David,' his wife said. 'Tom Besser had a heart attack climbing up this hill last year.' 'Tom Besser was seventy-nine years old,' David said. He bent down. 'Hop up, Jamie.' 'Don't you dare, James!' his wife commanded. 'Do you want to kill your father? You're much too heavy. And with all that food and wine and being chilled after the heat . . .' 'I'd really rather walk, Daddy,' James said unhappily. 'Up,' David said. He heard Charlotte's uncertain laugh while Ben regarded him gravely. 'I can take him,' Ben offered. 'I can *walk*!' Jamie insisted. He seemed almost on the point of tears. 'Oh, this is ridiculous!' his mother exclaimed angrily. 'Really, David, what's got into you?' *Now* she was being maternal, David thought grimly, towards him, a grown man, her husband. 'Hop up, Jamie,' he repeated in a matter-of-fact tone so as not to frighten the boy, who was confused enough already. 'On your head be it, James,' his wife said darkly. James hesitated an instant longer but he had his priorities right. He hopped up.

Jesus, he *was* heavy! David thought, startled, as he rose. He really feared for a moment that his knees would buckle humiliatingly under him. Once he had carried a sixty-pound rucksack all over the Pennines, but that had been years ago. He could feel that Jamie, wriggling wretchedly, was trying to lighten his own weight. He tightened his knees around David's waist and his hands elsewhere. For one horrifying instant David felt all go black. 'Not round my windpipe, son,' he managed in a strangled croak. He took the first dozen lurching steps up the sharp incline. The others began to walk slowly, his wife casting him frequent anxious glances. The cold air was no longer exhilarating but burned unpleasantly in his labouring lungs. He knew full well the folly of what he was doing in his out-of-condition state, also its banality. The old ram, the old gunfighter rallying after having been forced to a showdown by the young contender. Not that the young contender seemed particularly aware of it. He and Charlotte, though entwined like Laocoön, were swinging up easily and well ahead. They would neither know nor care if he let Jamie get down. He passed the bakery halfway up. His wife was ineffectually trying to prop Jamie's bottom up with her hand and giggling. She seemed reassured that he was not going to collapse dead at her feet. He himself was not so sure. Hillary and Tensing, he reminded himself, Scott and Amundsen. But they hadn't been a stone overweight and spent the last twenty years at a desk. He wished he'd had less to drink that evening. Or more. He heard Charlotte's laughter drift back. At the crest of the hill she and Ben stopped and looked down. 'Come on, Daddy – vroom, vroom!' she called enthusiastically. Ben appeared to make some sort of remonstrative gesture at her. David bared his teeth in what he hoped would be taken for a carefree smile. He felt a warning pain in his groin. But he hitched his arms more securely under Jamie's legs and made it almost at a bound to the top.

Jamie slid down and shook himself, immensely relieved to be rid of the awful burden of patricide. David straightened up. He would have liked to say something nonchalant but couldn't trust himself yet not to gasp. 'Now what was that all about?' his wife asked curiously. The others were walking ahead. After a moment he smiled. 'Do not forsake me, oh my darling,' he said. 'You mean me?' his wife enquired. 'No, not you,' he replied. She glanced ahead and then asked a bit guardedly, 'Charlotte?' 'Not Charlotte either,' he said. He looked down at her. It was her own cry too, although she didn't recognize it; the same appeal she made with her too-blue eyeshadow and slightly too youthful dress and her wistful havering in the wake of Charlotte's little romance. It was pure sad envy. Not all the pricey Chinese meals in the world would make up for the loss of that insouciance, that boundless expectation of the future and at the same time that innocent and sybaritic bliss of living only for the moment. It could not be competitively regained because those ones walking ahead wouldn't compete, didn't need to, the prize was theirs. The old gunfighter shot into empty air. Now Ben, Charlotte and James waited shivering because he had the key to the house. Yes he did, he thought wryly, at least have that.

# The American
# Ambassador

❧❧

The American Ambassador was not *en poste* in London, nor
could he ever expect to be, as he was a career officer and the
Court of St James was one of the plums reserved for political
appointees. Being a man of mild and equable disposition, he
accepted this without the rancour of many of his colleagues.
It was enough to visit here where he had spent some happy
years as Third Secretary a long time ago. He would be well
enough content to return to his own much more modest field
of operations which was the capital of a small surly Balkan
state.

It was not that he lacked ambition. When the news of his
appointment came through he had stood for some time before
his shaving mirror and whispered over and over again:
'Ambassador Extraordinary and Minister Plenipotentiary.'
That was he. The words rolled deliciously on his tongue like
brandied chocolates. And some day he might get a post of
more importance. Meanwhile he did his best and knew himself
to be held in good esteem at the State Department. He was
conscientious, popular, and a man of such unimpeachable moral
rectitude that the secret police of the country where he now
served had long since scratched certain schemes involving the
use of whores of both sexes. Those who remembered the
halcyon days of imported American films had given up on him
at first sight anyway. No one who looked so uncannily like the
late Gary Cooper could possibly be corruptible.

Here in London he was staying with his old friend and
colleague Harvey Mandlebaum. In his heart of hearts, the
ambassador had mixed feelings about Harve. They had known
each other for years, studied at Georgetown together, served

together abroad and on the Selection Board at State. And in the friendly rivalry that can exist between even the best of pals, he definitely had the upper hand, being already an ambassador while Harve was still a counsellor. But for how long? Because Harve was incontestably a go-getter; Harve, to use his own word, had chutzpah. And in the next round of appointments when Harve would most certainly get his ambassadorship, it was not inconceivable that he might nab one of the top posts that were left after the ex-film stars, exiled politicians and steel magnates had taken their pick. There were times in his most secret heart when the ambassador thought back with secret longing to the early days of the Foreign Service when Jews hadn't even got a look-in. It was not that he was prejudiced or thought Jews inferior. On the contrary, they were distinctly superior. They were too damned clever by half. He sometimes wondered at Harve's avuncular hints that he take it easy, retire early, rest on his laurels. 'You could write a book, Andy,' Harve suggested. The ambassador smiled and shook his head. A book was fine if you were Galbraith or Chester Bowles. Otherwise it would be just another dull volume of memoirs gathering dust on the DACOR library shelves. 'Or teach,' Harve went on. 'Like Bud Nutleigh, remember him? I just read in the Newsletter where he got himself appointed as Ambassador-in-Residence at the College of Lena, Kansas.'

The ambassador was not famed for the quickness of his humour but now he laughed long and loud. 'What's funny?' Harve frowned. The ambassador wiped tears of mirth from his eyes. 'Well, I mean,' he replied, '*Ambassador-in-Residence?* At some mid-west cow college? What's next? Minister-Counsellor at Sweet Briar? Vice-Consul *in situ* at Brown?'

Harvey gazed at him disapprovingly. 'I'd say there was a lot to be said, And, for implementing the theoretical element of polisci teaching with a pragmatic angle accrued from experience to reduce the life-situation differential.' The ambassador stared back at him, saddened and awed. Something very strange was happening to Harvey. He was beginning to talk like his own dispatches.

While Harve was at the embassy, his wife Daisy took the

ambassador around to see the sights. He himself had never married. This was a trifling blot, he knew, on his own career-situation differential, but only once had it become serious during the height of the McCarthy red-baiting era. A superior had taken him aside. Did Andrew, he enquired casually, have any plans in the foreseeable future for getting hitched? Andrew allowed that he had not. The other man at that point became strangely embarrassed. His eyes fixed themselves on the standard office presidential photo as though contemplating the Holy Grail. It was none of his business, of course, he said. He had just thought that if there *was* some nice girl some-place . . . because the fact was that in these perilous times a single man of certain age and rank was – well – open to certain suspicions . . . Andrew very rarely became angry but he had become angry then. In a voice edged with steel he declared it would be a snowy day in hell before he chivvied some poor girl into marrying him just to allay suspicion that he might be a blackmail- and espionage-prone queer.

It was the last he heard of it but he had in fact, some years ago, come quite close to marriage during his time in Vienna. He met Lottie while searching for more of the Limoges and Dresden porcelain of which he had a modest collection. Lottie, who was a widow five or six years younger than he, owned one of the shops he visited. Within a month he was seeing her regularly. It was the happiest three years of his life. They strolled together through the Vienna Woods and the Prater. They slept together under billowing eiderdowns in tiny, obscure, clean Alpine hotels. In the warm fussy sitting-room above her shop they together consumed sachertorte and hot chocolate and whipped cream. To his embarrassed delight she licked the cream from the corners of his mouth. He would never have suspected so matronly a little woman to be capable of such sensuality. At the end of his time in Vienna, he asked her to marry him. He was greatly distressed to see her eyes fill with tears. 'No, I cannot, Liebchen,' she said sadly. 'With the best will in the world, I cannot. I have been thinking about it – I knew you would ask me. But I cannot do like the clever efficient wives at your embassy: move from place to place, pack and unpack, organize bazaars, make myself useful to the ambassador's wife, entertain VIPs, give big glittering parties. I don't even understand protocol. Don't say it doesn't matter; we both know it matters. Soon you will be ambassador yourself and then it will matter very much. I would ruin your prospects as much as if you resigned at once and came to live with me here and helped me run the shop . . .'

He had caught the hopeful tremor in those last words and soberly thought it over. But his career was approaching its peak. Opposed to that was a life of puttering about in a cardigan selling shepherdesses to tourists. It was no go. And just as soberly did he respect Lottie's decision. It was honourable of her to decline a way of life to which she could not make a full commitment. He thought of that sometimes while contemplating the young Foreign Service wives of today. Marry they did, and then instantly rebelled. They clamoured for dialogues on their status as spouses, a Spouses Talent Bank, family liaison counselling, child care centres, language training, job training and overseas job opportunities where none existed. His own present secretary was a spouse who could barely type ten clear words in a row. While abroad they sulked, while back in Washington they eschewed entertaining as work befitting only menials. Many a time he had had to counsel some haggard young officer who was having problems with his emancipated wife. 'Well, we'll have to see what we can do to meet Amy's needs,' he would soothe, while privately reflecting that what Amy most needed was a swift kick in the pants. He was all for Women's Lib, he told himself. If *he* were a woman, he would certainly not want to be just a spouse. But if they felt like that, then let them for God's sake not marry diplomats. Let them make a clear sad choice as he and Lottie had each had to do. Or if they did marry into the Service let them get down to the job like Daisy Mandlebaum. Daisy was definitely of the old school. She ran her huge elegant flat like a dream, gave superb parties and was not above going into the kitchen herself to make one of the specialities for which she was justly famous. Many a prince and minister had munched in happy mystification on Daisy's sour-dough biscuits and spoon bread and Indian pudding. In some ways she reminded him of Lottie; she was small and cosy despite her awesome efficiency. And she liked him as well. 'You're such a sweet guy, Andy,' she told him once. 'I think you're just about the sweetest, most restful man I know.' There was a rather wistful note in her voice. It struck him that perhaps it might not be the easiest of lives to be married to Harve.

The fortnight passed quickly. On the last night of his visit he was invited with the Mandlebaums to a large catch-all reception at the Embassy Residence. He had been there once before to lunch with the London ambassador, a small non-descript gentleman most notable for the fact that he did not own a world-famous private art collection. By way of compensation, he was married to an immensely wealthy tobacco heiress. The ambassador had thought his London counterpart pleasant, uninformed and dull, and his wife an overbearing bitch. But he looked forward to the party. He had to admit that the scale and style of entertainment here was rather different from that at his own post where once a year he invited the relevant government officials to a buffet supper and once a year was invited back to a grim government function where the locals glowered dangerously at the foreigners until, high on hard-boiled eggs and vitriolic native schnapps, they would become even more dangerously friendly. But tonight he knew would be a party in the grand old style. The tobacco heiress's millions would see to that.

He and Harve and Daisy met in their drawing-room for a cocktail before departure. 'You do look gorgeous, And!' Daisy exclaimed. He smiled sheepishly. But it was quite true: at six-foot-three and very lean he cut a splendid figure in evening clothes. Harve frowned as he poured out the martinis. 'We've got a problem with one of the guests tonight, And,' he said. 'Maybe you can help out. In fact I sort of suggested it to the Chief. It's his lady wife's grandad they've got staying with them. I mean he's the problem.'

Calculating the heiress's age, the ambassador said, 'He must be pretty old.'

'Pushing ninety,' Harve said. 'But still full of ginger. He's one of the last real old-time Southern colonels. In his time he put in some years as state senator, also as head of the local

Klan. I mean he was big with the necktie parties and burning cross and all that.' Daisy made a clicking sound of disgust. 'Yeah, it's a drag.' Harvey sighed. 'It also totals to a potentially explosive situation. Because the old gentleman's still pretty outspoken when it comes to race. Especially when he's had a snootful. And at this shindig tonight there'll be a lot of African top brass and you know what they're like.'

No, he did not, the ambassador reflected thankfully. Throughout his career he had kept well away from the African Desks at State and all their extensions. Better even the dreary little Balkans than that. It was a huge dark trouble spot with which he wanted nothing to do. Not before and not now. Besides, the whole thing struck him as faintly ridiculous. 'Why don't they lock the old fellow up with a bottle of Jack Daniels till the party's over?' he asked.

'Me, I'd opt for a bottle of chloroform,' Harve said gloomily. 'But the Chief's wife won't hear of it. Just between thee and me I think she shares a lot of her grandaddy's opinions. Besides which, he's still sitting on about fifteen million bucks. And that's a lot of Dior dresses. So she wants to keep him happy. And parties make him happy.'

'How do I fit in all this?' the ambassador asked.

'Well, I figured you might sort of liaise,' Harve said. 'During the supper there won't be any problem. He'll be sitting close to where the Chief can keep an eye on him. Besides, it'll take him a while to get tanked up. But later when he starts strolling around he might go on what he calls a coon hunt.' 'Merciful God!' Daisy exclaimed. 'So that's where you come in,' Harvey went on quickly. 'If you could just sort of keep close to his heels. I'd do it myself but I've got people I've got to talk to. Steer him away if he looks like getting into trouble. Get him to talk about mint juleps, bird dogs, anything like that. But for Christ's sake, keep him off the subject of niggers, coons, poon-tang and spades. You can see how it could easily work up to a diplomatic incident.'

The ambassador reflected in silence. A diplomatic incident seemed unlikely – Harve had a tendency to dramatize. But an embarrassing situation, yes, and smelling of the most hair-raisingly inept mismanagement and quite egregious bad taste. It was not unprecedented, of course; it happened all the time when amateurs blundered about in jobs meant for professionals. He remembered the political ambassador who had thrown Havana into an uproar by slapping his valet's face for lacing his stays too tightly. And then it was left to the pros like Harve and himself to soothe ruffled feelings and clean up the mess while their substantive work piled up. Not that he cared much for this ad hoc solution whereby he was to act as a watchdog. A vice-consul or the officer responsible for protocol should have been detailed to it. It was not a mission suitable to his rank. He was surprised that Harvey should not know that. Or perhaps Harvey had enjoyed impressing the inexperienced London ambassador with the implication that he had an ambassador of his own who would come running at a snap of the fingers. It would not be the first time Harve had indirectly belittled him. Besides, it would ruin the party for him. He was on the point of refusing when he caught sight of Daisy's face. It was very white with a pinched look about the mouth; she was clearly in the grip of one of her agonizing migraines. If he now thwarted Harve, Harve would take it out later on Daisy. He suddenly knew that. And he knew Daisy knew it too. 'All right,' he grumpily agreed.

For the first part of the evening he was able to forget the whole silly business. The champagne flowed. The hostess wore a gown that was exactly colour-keyed to the paintwork of the drawing-room in which she received. He wondered curiously whether she would change for the dining-room. But no – there it was her sapphires that matched. The seating was at round tables for eight. At his own the men outnumbered the women. He found himself sitting next to an elderly black, the Minister of Culture from a small Central African republic. It seemed to be a night for race relations all around, he reflected wryly. Conversation between them was halting to begin with but then it began to pick up. By unspoken agreement they avoided politics but otherwise managed well enough, in fact very creditably. They discovered a shared affinity for the German Romantic poets. A devotion to dry-fly fishing. A passion for collecting small beautiful *objets d'art*; the ambassador had his porcelain, the minister his Benin sculpture. Better and better. It was the kind of conversation of which the ambassador often dreamed but seldom encountered these days: a gentle civilized discourse between two gentle civilized elderly cosmopolites. Their rapport bloomed shyly like a flower. He was actually distressed when the meal came to an end and it was time to circulate again. He knew his regret was shared by the minister who would return tomorrow to his little African republic as he himself would return to his small Balkan police state. They would never meet again but it had been a most charming encounter.

A few minutes later he saw Harve across the room. Harve was giving him that discreet wriggle of the eyebrows which in The Diplomatic signals wild alarm. A moment later they met. 'Where the hell you been?' Harve whispered hoarsely. 'The old toot's had a skinful. He's raring to go . . .' And then in a quite different voice as a tiny figure trotted up to join them: 'Colonel, sir, I'd like you to meet my good friend Andy Macyntyre. Andy's ambassador down in . . .' The little colonel interrupted with a shrill cackle of laughter. He squinted waggishly upwards. 'It don't make no matter mind to me, son, where he's ambassador. I mean what Goddamn little pip-squeak country. But he's a big sonuvabitch, in't he?'

The ambassador had a decent respect for great age. But within five minutes he decided that the colonel, aged or not, was a vulgar, ignorant, foul-mouthed, vicious old soak. He was extremely drunk but not so drunk that he couldn't shrewdly use the threat of the mischief he might wreak to cow and intimidate like a nasty child. Although his voice was high and squeaky, it carried his rustic obscenities within a range of twelve feet. He plucked frequently at his groin and spat into a large red bandanna. He commanded the ambassador to fetch him a drink. 'None of this lady-piss likkyure though. Get me a sour-mash bourbon. Something that'll put lead in my pencil.'

The ambassador signalled a passing waiter. Harve was gone and he didn't dare leave the little horror unattended. Then there was a slow surge of movement – people were ambling to one of the further reception rooms where a recital had been arranged. The colonel paused in the act of slurping up a large pinch of snuff. 'What's going on?' he demanded. 'Music,' the ambassador grimly replied. He had an almost ungovernable impulse to pick the tiny man up and stuff him head first into one of the huge Chinese vases at the side of the room. 'Well, let's get cracking then, son,' the colonel cheerfully said. 'Nothing I like better'n an old-time hoedown.'

In the music room the ambassador found a row of gilt chairs at the back still almost empty. He placed the colonel at an end chair and himself next to him. 'Cain't see nuthin' from here,' the colonel grumbled. 'Whyn't we sit up front? You reckon there'll be some gals? I ain't seen a passable piece of woman-flesh since I come into this mausoleum.'

The ambassador ignored him. He was distractedly noting that the row was filling up although the seat next to him remained empty. It was with a despairing sense of fatalism that he saw at last his new friend the Minister of Culture enter, survey the crowd, recognize him and approach with a delighted smile. 'I was so hoping we might sit together, Your Excellency,' he said. But by some extraordinary act of grace, the colonel didn't notice. He was sound asleep. Relieved, almost over-joyed, the ambassador smiled gravely back. 'I hope you will enjoy the concert, Mr Minister.'

The colonel snored and bubbled gently through the Bach Passacaglia and Fugue, the Mozart Quintet and the Weber Concertino. At one round of applause he nearly woke but then tilted slowly sideways with his head touchingly at rest on the ambassador's shoulder. The minister saw and smiled. 'Your poor old friend is tired,' he whispered. 'Like a small child.' 'Yes, indeed,' the ambassador replied.

The last performer was a black contralto who sang lieder by Schumann and Wolfe. The ambassador was not much for vocal music but he had to admit that the voice was glorious. She was also, in the fulsome way of lady singers, a very beautiful woman. He was pleased for the friend at his side that the recital should end with so virtuoso a performance by one of his race. At the end he applauded vigorously like the rest – too vigorously. The colonel was sitting bolt upright next to him. But he must have been awake for some minutes. His small eyes, evil and bright as an adder's, flickered past him to the minister, gleamed with malicious mirth. 'Well, dawg my cats!' he drawled. 'Who'd have thought to hear all them high-falutin' noises from a little ole piece of black ass like that? They sure don't sing that way down in the old watermelon patch back home. I reckon we'd've figgered out a better use for a nice bit of poon-tang, but like they say –' he nudged the ambassador roguishly – 'there ain't no stopping them coons once they get shoes on their feet.'

The ambassador shrank back, speechless with horror. But surely, he thought, the intelligent and sophisticated man at his side would not take this ghastly little gnome seriously? Surely he would not imagine them to be in any way connected? Sadly, he was wrong. The minister looked from him to the colonel and back again. His face had altered entirely. His eyes gleamed with a red primordial wrath and the ambassador realized how confident, how authoritative in rage the indigenous African was as compared to the shrilly despairing American black. But when the minister spoke it was with cold brief formality. 'I greatly regret, Mr Ambassador, your choice of companion.' He rose, jostled roughly past them and left. 'Back home we'd have sliced his dingus off for doing that,' the colonel observed detachedly.

Harve was passing by in a great hurry. The ambassador called his name in a voice that brooked no argument. 'Hassle?' Harve enquired *sotto voce*, looking from him to the colonel. The ambassador picked the little man up from his seat. He handed him like a doll into Harve's very surprised arms. 'Now you take him,' he said. 'He's all yours. You follow him around and wipe up his puddles. I've had it.'

He ignored the indignant squall that followed him. He looked in the next room and the ones after that for the minister but saw him nowhere. He had probably left at once in his glow of bitter and righteous anger. It was time for him to leave also rather than wait for Harve and Daisy. There would be repercussions from this, he knew. The colonel would report to his granddaughter who would report to her husband. It might even get back to State. Or maybe not. He really didn't care.

He had lost a friend and gained several enemies. He had lost an enchanting woman and gained a title. He caught sight of his tall distinguished reflection in a looking-glass and sighed. Indisputably he was an Ambassador Extraordinary and Minister Plenipotentiary. Perhaps some of those extraordinary many-splendoured powers would help get a taxi to take him home.